Peter & Max

A Fables novel

Peter
&
Max

A Fables novel

By Bill Willingham

with illustrations by Steve Leialoha

VERTIGO/DC COMICS NEW YORK, NY

PETER & MAX: A FABLES NOVEL
Published by DC Comics, 1700 Broadway, New York, NY 10019.

Copyright © 2009 Bill Willingham and DC Comics.
All rights reserved. VERTIGO is a trademark of DC Comics.
The stories, characters and incidents mentioned in this book are entirely fictional. All characters featured in this book, the distinctive likenesses thereof and related elements are trademarks of Bill Willingham.

Printed in Canada.
DC Comics, a Warner Bros. Entertainment Company.
HC ISBN: 978-1-4012-1573-6
SC ISBN: 978-1-4012-2537-7

Cover by Steve Leialoha
Publication design by Amelia Grohman

Karen Berger, *SVP-Executive Editor*
Shelly Bond, *Editor*
Angela Rufino, *Associate Editor*
Robbin Brosterman, *Design Director-Books*
Louis Prandi, *Art Director*

DC COMICS
Paul Levitz, *President & Publisher*
Richard Bruning, *SVP-Creative Director*
Patrick Caldon, *EVP-Finance & Operations*
Amy Genkins, *SVP-Business & Legal Affairs*
Jim Lee, *Editorial Director-WildStorm*
Gregory Noveck, *SVP-Creative Affairs*
Steve Rotterdam, *SVP-Sales & Marketing*
Cheryl Rubin, *SVP-Brand Management*

This novel is dedicated to Mike,

respected, admired and reliable friend,

who first explored these dark and

wonderful lands with me long ago,

before pen was ever put to paper.

TABLE OF CONTENTS

Chapter One   Fables   17

Chapter Two   Going to the Fair   37

Chapter Three   Wolf Valley   65

Chapter Four   What Max Saw   85

Chapter Five   Fabletown   109

Chapter Six   The Black Forest   121

Chapter Seven   Peter & the Wolf   137

Chapter Eight   In Flight   159

Chapter Nine   A Little Touch of Max in the Night   161

Chapter Ten   Hamelin   173

Chapter Eleven   In Transit   199

Chapter Twelve   The Trial   203

Chapter Thirteen Fire Time 213

Chapter Fourteen The Piper at the Gates of Dawn 243

Chapter Fifteen The Pied Piper 249

Chapter Sixteen Cloak and Dagger 275

Chapter Seventeen A Festival of Vermin and Lost Children 299

Chapter Eighteen Frost and Fire 307

Chapter Nineteen Coming to America 333

Chapter Twenty Celebration 355

Epilogue 365

The Price of a Happy Ending *a sequential bonus story* 373

Acknowledgments 385

Illustrations

26 She drove slowly, northeast out of the village's main square...

31 Peter Piper appeared in the doorway, pushing his wife Bo in front of him in her wheelchair.

53 Little Bo Peep was standing in the greenest field of grass Peter had ever seen.

59 Now we can never know if Jorg defeated the giant solely by his own strength...

68 Then, with a soft rustle of leaves, a huge shape detached itself from the concealment of rock and root, and padded forward through intervening trees, resolving into the form of a wolf as it did so.

102 He flailed at Peter wildly, hitting, scratching and clawing at him, screaming "Give it back"...

112 She looked small and frail, but Peter knew she wasn't...

135 So he turned, with the blade still in his hand, and walked back towards the firelight, which was partially obscured by the trees of the great and terrible Black Forest – his home.

142 *They began sliding downwards, going faster and faster.*

152 *Bo turned all of a sudden and ran. The giant wolf immediately sprang after her...*

169 *Both girls crawled out from under the fallen tree and clutched at him...*

184 *Almost without pausing, he grabbed a crust from out of the big half-barrel...*

211 *Peter raised the flute to his lips and began to play.*

219 *It was a coat like no other, and Max loved it.*

230 *"Blood of the gods!" the second knight said. "I can't abide animals that pretend to a man's speech."*

241 *"I can play that," he said.*

263 *The sound of music drifted like a fine mist through Hamelin's countless alleyways and thoroughfares.*

270 *They were never seen again, unto the end of days.*

292 *"We need you to marry us," Peter said, with a broad grin splitting his face.*

316   *Any traveler would have to pass by the tower, through the barred gate, or turn back. There was no other option.*

326   *Almost as soon as Max had begun playing, a burning sensation began in Peter's feet and started working its slow but steady way up his legs.*

344   *"He's lying," a voice said from behind him, once Max had concluded his story.*

358   *"Isn't this lovely?" Max said.*

368   *Peter played with the band...*

A Short Note Before We Begin

This novel is based upon my long-running comic book series called FABLES, but it is its own tale, autonomous and self-reliant. No one needs to be familiar with the comics to fully enjoy and understand this book. For those who do follow the comics and wish to know where this falls in the more or less official FABLES chronology, the modern day portions of the story begin about two years before the Fables go to war to overthrow the Adversary and conclude a few months before that same war.

Chapter One

FABLES

*In which Rose Red
takes an early morning drive
and finds our story's hero
at the end of it.*

FOR MOST OF HIS LONG YEARS, PETER PIPER wanted nothing more than to live a life of peace and safety in some remote cozy cottage, married to his childhood sweetheart, who grew into the only woman he could ever love. Which is pretty much what happened. But there were complications along the way, as there often are, because few love stories are allowed to be just that and nothing else.

Somewhere in New York City there's a tiny, secretive neighborhood no one knows about except those who live there and a few scattered others in our wide world. It's a private enclave taking up only one modest block along a small side street named Bullfinch, and a few other buildings close by. It's called Fabletown by its residents and called nothing at all by anyone else, because, as we've said, they don't know of it. Fabletown has been there longer than its general location has been named the Upper West Side, and was in fact the very first settlement in that area, when all of the other dwellings were huddled together down at the southern tip of Manhattan Island. Unspoiled fields and forests were Fabletown's only neighbors at first, way back when New York was still called New Amsterdam. But the city grew up around it over the centuries, as cities tend to do, so that now Fabletown is just a small, quaint and largely ignored little side street in a much bigger enterprise, which suits them just fine.

If you were to accidentally stroll down Bullfinch Street — and it would be by accident, because strong spells of misdirection, obfuscation and "there's nothing important here" have been laid over the place, to keep outsiders out — its residents would look much like us, just normal folks in a normal place. But these people are far from normal. For one thing they've been around for awhile, some of them for millennia. The very first founders of the settlement still live there and look no older now than they did then. It's impossible to say just yet if they're immortal, because the only true test of that is to see if they're still alive at the end of time. But so far they seem to be on pace to finish that race in good position.

The Fables, which is what they call themselves collectively, are a magical people who weren't originally from this world. They arrived here long ago, over a span of years, alone or in small groups, as refugees from their own equally magical Homelands, hundreds of scattered worlds which had been overrun by the invading armies of an ambitious and merciless conqueror, who seemed determined to build himself an empire, killing all who resisted and enslaving those who didn't.

Once here they discovered their new home to be a small and humble world so excruciatingly mundane, so bereft of natural magic that the Adversary — their name for the conqueror — expressed no interest in it. All available evidence promised that they'd found a place of long-term safety. And so they settled in.

Pretty quickly they discerned a few odd things about their adopted home. Our world seemed to contain miniature

versions of every Homeland world they'd originally come from. Here was a small island nation called England that mirrored the entire world they once knew as Albion. And over there was a country called Russia that was a rough sixteenth-scale sketch of the vast old world of The Rus. Ireland resembled the world of Erin, infant America slowly grew into an approximation of Americana, and so on. For some as yet undiscovered reason, or perhaps for no reason at all since some truly remarkable things do seem to be the result of mere (or possibly mighty) chance, our unimportant out-of-the-way little world turned out to be a map of sorts for all of the much grander ones they'd left behind.

Now Fables seems an odd name for any sort of people to choose to call themselves, and especially odd for this group, since the word implies that they're folks with stories to tell. They aren't. They were and continue to be adamantly secretive. But this brings us to another weird phenomenon they discovered after arriving here. It may be that when you introduce a number of very magical creatures into a decidedly unmagical environment, some of that magic seeps out, spreading by osmosis into the mundane natives (us) whom they, often pejoratively, call mundys. Perhaps the spilled magic grants the mundys some rudimentary, but unconscious, awareness of their new neighbors. Whatever the explanation, shortly after Fables arrived, mundys all over the world began telling stories about them; stories no one knew were based on actual people and everyone assumed were simply creative and occasionally clever works of fiction. These stories sometimes became distorted, as they were passed from person to person, and those that were finally written down often contained many errors of fact. But for the most part they were accurate enough that our mysterious Fable immigrants eventually realized they were being talked about. They were the subjects of many popular fairy tales — and some did indeed arrive here from the land of faeries. Their private histories were inscribed and revealed in the form of folktales, nursery rhymes, epic poems and doggerel ditties, haunting ballads, ribald songs and, of course, fables.

A thousand different mundy authors scribbled every variation on the story of Beauty and the Beast, for example; how a wicked witch cursed a nobleman with a dire enchantment, but its power was finally broken by a woman's true love. But no mundy wrote what happened next; how years after they'd married to live happily ever after, all sorts of disturbingly unhappy things befell them, until they arrived here. Now Beauty has an office job as

Fabletown's deputy mayor, and her husband Beast serves as the underground community's sheriff. You've heard many tales of the dashing and heroic Prince Charming, but did you know that he's been thrice divorced and now runs Fabletown as its mayor? Elsewhere in Fabletown Cinderella runs a shoe store, the Sleeping Beauty is living off her investments, while trying not to prick her finger again, a certain famous bridge troll works as a security guard, and many a (formerly) wicked witch now resides on the thirteenth floor of the Woodland Building, which, among other things, is the community's informal city hall.

These strange and wondrous people, leaking raw and enchanted histories wheresoever they went, became known to us through conjured stories of their past adventures in abandoned lands, while their continued lives in this world remained hidden from us.

So, perhaps it was inevitable that the refugees, coming together from so many scattered lands and diverse cultures, wanting to select some collective name under which they could become a unified people, would settle on the one quality they all seemed to share in common — their tendency to become the subjects of so many stories in our mundy world. At first they tried calling themselves The Story People, but when that inevitably got shortened to Stories, it seemed a tad confusing, seeing as how both books and buildings already contained stories, and adding a third definition to so basic a word seemed overly burdensome. They tried The Folklore People for a while, but gave it up too, when it first became Folk, which was already in widespread use among the mundys, and then Lores, which never quite fell trippingly from the tongue. For similar reasons Ballads and Rhymes were also tried and discarded, leaving them ultimately with The Fabled People, which became simply Fables, which turned out to fit just fine, after a reasonable period of getting used to it.

Fables, the personification of story and song, live among us in New York and we for the most part are none the wiser. Except that some Fables don't live in the city, because they can't.

Far to the north of Manhattan and the other boroughs, deep into the wider, wilder reaches of Upstate New York, there is a vast area of largely undeveloped land known as the Farm, because some of it has indeed been cultivated. And some of it is occupied by a quaint, rural village of huts and houses, barns and stables. But most of the Farm's uncounted acreage has been left in its original wild state. The Farm is Fabletown's sister community, its upstate annex for housing all of the Fables who also fled their Homelands for this world, but who can't pass as human. Where the human-looking Fables are largely free to come and go wherever in the world they wish, Farm Fables are confined in this one place for all time — a large and comfortable prison to be sure — but a prison just the same. They're confined to the Farm because the most vital of all Fable laws strictly forbids anything that might reveal their magical nature to the mundys. And nothing is more immediately and unmistakably identifiable as magical than a talking duck, with a penchant for discussing the collected works of Jane Austen, or a moo-cow who can leap over the moon. Granted it was the moon of another land, which was both smaller and nearer than ours, but still an impressive feat, all things considered.

You can't find your way to The Farm, even more so than to Fabletown proper, because many more-powerful concealment and misdirection spells protect the place, deflecting all nosy mundys away or around it. But if you could, if you could bring yourself, by some tremendous act of will and raw, stiff-necked determination, to drive along that narrow old road, by the low, moss-covered stone wall, and turn in on the dirt track, where the tired wooden gate sags against the ancient, brooding chestnut tree, you might possibly discover that the Three Little Pigs live in a piggy-sized house of bricks (they learned their lessons long ago) just down the lane from where the Old Woman dwells in her giant shoe. Being perfectly normal looking, she could leave the Farm any time she wished, but not with her beloved shoe-house, where she'd raised so many children, so she chooses to stay where she is.

Our tale, the one that couldn't quite remain a simple love story, begins then in Fabletown and almost immediately moves up to the Farm. It happens because a witch learned something that she told to a beast, who phoned a wolf, who in turn called his wife's twin sister, who never was a princess but perhaps should have been.

Rose Red, the no less lovely but considerably less famous sister of Snow White, wiped the sleep from her eyes as she climbed into her rust-colored Range Rover; hers at least in the sense that she ran the Farm and this was one of the vehicles owned in common by all who dwelled there. She had glossy red hair the color of fire in the daylight and dark satin at night. She wore old boots and farmer's clothes: denim pants and a flannel shirt, both of which started out in different shades of blue, but which had since been worn to the universal color of fade. Clara the raven, who'd once been a fire-breathing dragon, sat perched on the front porch railing of the main house, where Rose Red lived, and where she'd been sound asleep until just a few minutes before.

"You're out and about early," Clara said. Her breath sent a sharp flicker of fire and an attendant wisp of smoke into the brisk morning air. Having elected years ago to turn from dragon into raven, she nevertheless decided to keep the fire.

"I got a call," Rose mumbled. "Have to deliver a message."

"It can't be good news then," Clara said. "Nobody wakes someone to give out good news. Nobody civilized, anyway. Want me to go with you?" Clara served as Rose Red's personal bodyguard, a job considered necessary due to an attempted revolution against Farm authority some years back. That was why Clara thought it prudent to hold onto her fiery breath. It was a brutal and devastating weapon which served as a no-nonsense deterrent against further uprisings.

"No," Rose said. "I'm just the messenger. This business won't put me in any danger, though I can't promise the same for its recipient." With a few light curses and some pleading, Rose Red coaxed the truck's cold and reluctant engine to life. "Go back to sleep, Clara. All is well, more or less."

She drove slowly out of the village's main square, past the blacksmith's forge attached to one of the stables. She maneuvered carefully around Tom Thumb's miniature castle keep, with its tiny moat and curtain wall, and then past the goat pen, where there was a mailbox out front with the name Three Goats Gruff painted on it. An intrepid squad of mail mice was already out beginning their morning rounds. They looked dignified in their miniature frock coats, puffing important little clouds of white vapor into the cold air. And dignified they were, for it's as true among mice as among men that the swift delivery of the mail is a sacred trust. They had their delivery ladder propped against the box, and one of them was making the ascent with a letter addressed in a bold hand to one Mr. William Gruff, Esquire slung over his back. It was hard to guess which of the goats it might actually be for, since all three of the brothers were named Bill.

Rose left the village behind, driving northeast and then due north along a single-lane dirt and gravel road. After a few hundred yards of undeveloped scrubland, she entered the farmlands proper. There were cultivated fields to either side of her, newly planted winter wheat to her right and endless rows of silage corn to her left, tall yellow-green stalks, as high as an elephant's eye and groaning under the weight of their treasures. The corn harvest would have to begin in a few days, which made her wince a bit, as most of the harvester's engine was still scattered across the tractor shed floor. She'd have to get back to work on that today. To the east, the sun began peeking over the distant high hills that folks in this part of the country insisted on calling mountains. On the other side of the hills was Wolf Valley, which used to be part of the Farm, but had recently been turned over to the family of a legendary monster – her brother-in-law.

Rose came to a fork in the road and turned northwest. As she did so, the rising sun stabbed at her from her rear-view mirror. Grumbling, she angled the mirror away from her line of sight, squinted to banish the spots from her vision and drove on. The road paralleled a small but determined river for a while and then crossed it with a short wooden bridge, when the river abruptly changed direction. She left the cultivated fields behind and entered a wide rolling expanse of grasslands, where the mundy livestock were fed and fattened. Herds of cows were moved into an area to graze, bringing the grasses down to a reasonable height, then flocks of sheep were moved in after them, reducing the same grass to low stubble. A few farmhands were already in the fields, driving scattered clusters of cattle in the distance, towards fresher grass. Most of the farmhands were Fable animals earning their keep; talking horses, who talked seldom, unless they really had something to say, and talking dogs, who chattered constantly, believing that just about anything that was possible to say should be said, just in case it turned out to be important. But there were absolutely no talking cows among them. Fable cows wouldn't normally mix with mundy versions of their own species, finding the thought of their dumb cousins' eventual fate as steaks and burgers more than a little unsettling. Some of the farmhands were human Fables who lived up here because they preferred it to city life, or because they'd been caught breaking one or more Fable laws and were working off the judgments. Fabletown imposed a lot of laws on its citizens.

After crossing another dozen small bridges, as the river settled into an entrenched meander, constantly turning back on itself, Rose crested a rise and looked down into a golden field full of mundy sheep being pushed around by a half dozen Fable sheep dogs, who scolded their charges with heavily accented epithets. At the far end of the field she spotted her destination, a small isolated stone and timber cottage, perched on the top of the next rolling crest and nestled under a stand of cottonwood trees. Rose was pleased to see a trail of smoke coming from the home's chimney. At least I won't be waking anyone up, she thought. Maybe they'll even give me breakfast.

Rose pulled her truck slowly into the barely used driveway and parked it. Closer now, she noticed more details. The cottage was surrounded by a complex multi-terraced wooden porch that had all manner of ramps connecting each level. It spread out from the house in every direction and looked as if it had been added to over a large span of years. There was a green lawn and several small, well-tended flower gardens, which were also surrounded and traversed by a maze of raised wooden pathways venturing out from the porch.

As Rose stepped down from her truck, the cottage's front door opened and Peter Piper appeared in the doorway, pushing his wife Bo in front of him in her wheelchair.

"Good morning, Rose," Peter said, his wife's echo only a half beat behind him.

Then Bo said, all on her own this time, "What brings you out all the way to Casa Piper?"

They seemed cheerful at least, Rose thought. She hadn't run the Farm for very long, and hadn't lived here much longer than that. She didn't know the Pipers very well, except that they preferred to keep to themselves, way out here in their remote home, where they'd lived alone with each other, year after year, century after century, ever since escaping from the Homelands.

"Morning," Rose answered. "I need to talk to Peter."

"Sounds ominous," Peter said. "Can Bo join in, or is this a private matter?" Bo had pale blonde hair that was nearly white in the morning sun. It was long but she wore it pulled back into a loose knot at the nape of her neck. She was lovely, as most Fable women tend to be, but hers was a wistful beauty that threatened to disappear into sadness at any moment. She wore a tan sweater

and a green tartan blanket covered her legs, concealing the ruined limbs beneath. Rose had seen Bo's dead legs only once by rare accident, at one of the Farm dances, when a pair of geese, overspirited by too much dancing and too many beers, tumbled into her chair, causing her blanket to slip for a brief, terrible second. Rose had been embarrassed at how quickly she'd turned away from the sight. Bo laughed off the incident at the time and didn't seem to mind for the rest of the evening, but she never returned to the main village after that.

Peter was of average height and slim, threatening towards skinny, without quite getting there. He had dark brown hair cut short and matching brown eyes. He wore a maroon cotton shirt over a long-sleeved undershirt, khaki pants and old hiking boots.

"I'm not sure," Rose said. "I think we better make it private, until you hear what I have to say. Then you can decide if it's something you want to share. I apologize if that seems rude, Bo."

"Don't be silly," Bo said. An uncommitted smile touched her lips briefly and then vanished. "It's such a lovely morning, we were going to have breakfast out on the patio. You two have your talk while I move everything out to the picnic table. You'll join us of course." Not waiting for an answer, she turned her chair deftly and wheeled herself back inside.

Rose and Peter walked away from the house, along one of Bo's wooden wheelchair pathways. This one led out quite a distance to where a thick wooden target had been securely propped upright. It was roughly carved into the shape of a full-grown man and had hundreds of tiny cuts and gouges in its surface.

They left the wood pathway at its farthest point and stepped down onto the turf, where the green lawn grass ended and the taller yellow livestock grass began, and then continued farther out into the fields. Itinerant gusts of wind bent the tall grass in playful patterns. Fifty yards away a pair of energetic sheepdogs yawped and maneuvered, pushing a portion of the flock their way.

"They're good dogs," Peter said. "Good friends. They always keep a few of the sheep near our house, especially the new lambs when they come. Even after all this time, Bo still likes being near her lambs."

"Even if it means being out here so far away from anyone else?" Rose said.

"We're happy out here. Happy enough, anyway." Peter had a number of old scars on his lips and at the corners of his mouth. They were tiny and nearly invisible, except with a lucky combination of proximity and perfect light. In the distance, through the cottage's open door, they could hear the muted dry tink of porcelain cups being mated with saucers and then one quick scrape of a heavy skillet along the top of a cast iron stove.

Peter was generally a quiet man, never demonstrative, except on those rare occasions when he came into the Farm's village to play his pipe, often accompanied by Boy Blue on his horn, Seamus McGuire on his harp, and Baby Joe Sheppard on drums. And sometimes, when the mood struck, even dour old Puss would join in with his wild, screaming fiddle.

Peter would take his time getting through a sentence, punctuating even the shortest of them with one or more extended pauses. Some Fables got like that. They lived so long that they could no longer work up any sort of hurry. Urgency just faded out of them over time. His facial expressions were even more reserved than his speech, almost to the point of nonexistence. But Rose thought she could detect a contained sadness there, matching that of his wife. "Why don't you tell me what you came to say?" he said, after awhile.

"Bigby phoned me from Wolf Valley," she said. "He isn't allowed on the Farm proper, so he wants you to go see him. Today," she added.

"I guess I could do that. Long walk though."

"You can take my truck most of the way. Just drop me back home first, and return it when you're done. You'll still have to hoof it over the hills."

"That doesn't bother me. Only —"

"Only you want to know why?" Rose interrupted. "What was the part that I didn't know if your wife should hear?"

"Yes. Only that."

"Bigby can tell you more details than I can."

"All conditions, exceptions and dissembling are duly noted and acknowledged, Rose. Now please tell me the bad thing you know but don't want to say."

"Your brother is back in this world," Rose said, almost so quietly that the wind took her words.

A shadow passed over Peter's features and stayed there.

He didn't say anything for a long time. Then he said, "Someone will have to come out here and stay with Bo."

"Why? You should be back from Wolf Valley before nightfall, provided you leave right away. Even with her wheelchair and all — Well, I thought she was pretty independent."

"She is," Peter said. "She'll be fine on her own today. But later, tomorrow probably, when I leave, I'm not sure how long I'll be gone. It could be for some time, and there's always the chance I won't make it back. Someone needs to stay here with her, while I'm hunting Max."

Out in the golden fields the dogs herded sheep and the winds played their early October games, while overhead clouds gathered to spoil the blue skies.

Chapter Two

GOING TO THE FAIR

In which Max finds a mystery and Peter comes into possession of a family heirloom.

LONG AGO IN THE LAND OF HESSE, FAR from the fields that we know, a gray spotted mule named Bonny Lumpen pulled a fat and rickety caravan wagon down a dusty road. No one sat up on the caravan's front bench to steer her. In fact, no reins connected her to any driver, present or absent, because she was one of the talking sort of animals who could simply be told where to go. And besides, she'd traveled this route many times before, once every year in fact, and she knew the way. Bonny Lumpen plodded along at her accustomed sedate pace, pulling the caravan behind her, which swayed precariously, first one way and then the other, in the road's deep ruts, always threatening to turn over, but never quite making up its mind to do so.

The caravan belonged to the Piper family who, as their name implied, were traveling musicians. Just as Millers mill and Fletchers fletch, the Pipers piped. At least three out of the four did. The father, Johannes, and his two sons, Max, the eldest and young Peter, all played the long pipe, which was sometimes called the single pipe, or occasionally even the flute as it was still known back then, before some enterprising soul came along later and decided all true flutes should be turned sideways to play. Mother Piper though never had a knack for playing any sort of wind instrument, but instead found herself gifted at playing just about everything else. While Johannes, Max and Peter would weave intricate melodies with their three flutes, madly sweeping and swooping in and out of one daring harmony after another, Mother, whose name was Beatrice (thank you for asking), would accompany them on a skin drum for one song, or strum along on her lute for another, and then deftly switch to a lovely and resonant wooden xylophone – the pride of all her personal possessions – for yet a third. Or she'd ring bells, or crash cymbals, and generally find some way to coax music out of anything that could be struck, strummed, picked, thumped, whacked or plucked.

The family had no home, except for their wagon. They lived the life of happy vagabonds, traveling here and there, throughout the year, going to festivals and fairs, and every other sort of scheduled celebration, where they'd make their living by letting anyone call the tune, provided they were willing to pay the Pipers.

On this particular day, when the autumn leaves were just beginning to flirt with a change of dress, they were on their way to their favorite venue of the year, the harvest festival which would take place in Old Winsen Town just two days hence. It wasn't the quality of the celebration that attracted them, though it was certainly one of the nicer ones, nor was it any aspect of the town itself, which seemed in every measurable way a pleasant town indeed. No, it was the stop along the road that they would make later this afternoon, provided Bonny Lumpen could keep up her pace and no unforeseen hazards blocked their path.

Every year, on their way to the fair the Pipers would stop the night before at the country estates of Squire Radulf Peep, a gentleman farmer of local renown, husband to Cresentia, and father to Arianne, Agathe, Brigitte, Dorthe, Elfride, and Esmerault, or as young Peter once called them on a previous visit, "An entire flock of daughters!"

On their annual visits, Squire Peep, who was a generous soul by nature, and never more so than to his dear friends, would host the Pipers, welcoming them into his home and treating them to as lavish a banquet as he could supply and anyone could ever hope to receive. Then, after the dishes were cleared away, and the various frosted, berried and custard-filled desserts were merely a happy memory, the Peeps and their seventeen house servants, along with an ever-changing number of farmhands, shepherds, swineherds, cowherds, brew masters, stable masters, stable boys, carpenters, wheelwrights and sundry other hired workers, would crowd into the mansion's great room for a night of entertainment, which they anticipated year round. Someone would stoke a crackling fire in the huge stone fireplace. Someone else would bring in pitchers of mulled wine and giant steins of frosty beer – and because of the special occasion, even the younger children would get to try a sip or two. There'd be laughter and small talk, followed by intermittent cries of "shush" and "settle down," until gradually an eager, anticipatory hush would enfold the room, taking hold in fits and starts over the entire hall as, one by one, they'd realize the Pipers had started to play.

The first notes always came low and stealthy, a murmured promise, a light tickling of the ears. But slowly the melodies grew, and retreated and then grew again, back and forth, sometimes like a lover's tease and sometimes like the unstoppable tide, until finally the music swelled into a grand and glorious thing, taking absolute control over the room and everyone in it. It was always in the Peeps' great hall once every autumn, playing not for money but only for the entertainment of sweet friends, that the Pipers gave their best concert of the year.

Then, the next morning, they'd pack up their caravan again, for the last day's journey into Old Winsen Town. And the Peeps too would load their many wagons with harvest goods and ride behind their friends to the festival, where the Pipers would find a bandstand to play and the Peeps would find their stall in the farmer's market. Along the way, Johannes and Radulf would usually walk together, some distance out ahead of the slow-moving wagon train. They'd fiddle with their pipes – the kind for smoking, not playing – and exchange tobaccos. They'd talk about which giant pumpkin Agathe Peep had selected this year to enter into the judging, and which little lamb young Esmerault believed had the best chance of winning the grand palm. Or they'd talk about how Father Johannes had two sons while Father Radulf had too many daughters, and maybe it isn't entirely too early to start thinking about the future. Every year the particulars of their conversation would change, but unknown to either man the subject was ever the same – how they were good and true friends and would always remain so.

Now, on the country road, bordered on both sides by the dusky trees of the Schwarzwald, the endless Transylvanian Black Forest that blanketed the entire continent of the Hesse, Peter Piper lay silent but awake in his bunk in the back of the caravan and thought about what the coming night might portend. His parents were dozing in their great bed which took up the entire front of the compartment. His father's quiet snoring was rhythmic and comforting, like a metronome. Max wasn't in the caravan's cabin, which was crowded with everything they owned in all the world, but that wasn't unusual these days. He'd grown oddly sullen and ever more insistent on privacy of late. His father told him this was because Max was fourteen now, on the threshold of becoming a man, and it was a time in life when every young man begins to ponder his place in the world. Max was no doubt sleeping outside, up on top, sprawled across the baggage tied up there, or maybe stretched out in the front of the wagon, on the driver's bench. It was their family custom in the cool of the afternoon to take a nap, so that they could stay awake longer into the night. A musician's day typically begins when the workdays of all others have ended.

Peter shifted and squirmed in his bed and couldn't sleep, partly because he'd outgrown the small bunk. He'd turned ten this year and had experienced a surprising spurt of growth. Now he could no longer quite fit into the cozy little space tucked under the polished legs of Mother's xylophone, where he'd always fit so snugly in years past. This was becoming a problem, but it wasn't the real reason sleep eluded him. He was thinking about the amazing dinner to come, and the treats and the gifts that would follow. He thought about the large and roly-poly Mr. Peep, who turned bright colors when he laughed, which was often, and who always treated him kindly, even though the squire was an important man of wealth, while Peter was merely the penniless son of a traveling minstrel. He thought about the gigantic estate, where they would spend the night in lavishly appointed guestrooms, one of which, astonishingly, Peter would get all to himself. And besides the main house, there were all of the other buildings and the endless expanse of land, full of dogs and animals and other people — people who never changed from one day to the next and one town to the next — and a home that never moved, but stayed in one place all of the time. Always there. Always reliable. Always home. But most of all Peter thought about the youngest Peep daughter.

She was eight, or maybe nine years old by now; practically of an age with him. She'd been christened Esmerault at birth, but no one ever called her that, because, from the first day Mr. Peep had lovingly dubbed her Father's Little Rainbow, which had caught on with Mother Peep and the five older sisters and the informal extended family of hired hands. Later they'd shortened it to the more manageable Rainbow, and later again just to Bo. So, though Esmerault might have been her given name, Bo Peep was her real name, earned through the only true tests of such things: time and repetition.

Peter couldn't sleep because he thought about Bo, and also he thought about how odd it was to be thinking about her. She'd been his once-a-year playmate for as many years as he could remember. They'd scaled imaginary castle walls together and vanquished fierce dragons. They'd made mud pies and mud forts and just about anything else that could be formed out of mud. No matter how often the games changed, they'd always played together, because they were friends, and that was that. But then last year something happened that changed everything. On the final day of the harvest festival in Old Winsen Town, when both families were loading up their wagons and saying their reluctant goodbyes, the Peeps to return home and the Pipers to move on, Bo had done a strange and alarming thing. She'd taken Peter around behind the wagons, where they were all alone, and solemnly kissed him on his cheek, saying, "We can marry when we grow up."

Peter was appalled. He vigorously and savagely wiped her kiss off his cheek right in front of her, which brought instant tears to her eyes. She turned and ran from his sight, with an angry huff of breath, which quickly turned into a great wet honk of despair as only a thoroughly miserable, blubbering, runny-nosed child can make. That was the last he'd seen of her.

Over the intervening year he'd often remembered that small chaste kiss, and wondered what it meant. And he wondered if they could become friends again this time, or if she'd somehow grown into too much of a girl, like her sisters, so that their children's adventure games were done forever. He was ten now; if not close to being a man yet, he was not nearly a child any longer. Maybe it was time for him to put away silly children's games as well. But then what would they do instead? If you had a friend and wanted to spend as much time with her as possible, in the very little time you had, what else could you do but go out and play? Once in a while he'd seen how some of Bo's older sisters spent time with the boys who'd call on them. They wouldn't do anything but sit on the front porch and talk all day, or stroll together through the gardens and talk some more. How many things could there possibly be to talk about? And why would anyone want to waste his time doing that, when instead he could do something fun? Peter had seen those boys who came to visit the Peep daughters, and every one of them looked nervous and fidgety, sometimes completely miserable, and always as though they'd prefer to be anywhere else but where they were, talking and talking endlessly throughout the day. Lord of the murky depths! What if that's all Bo wanted to do from now on? Sometime in the last year, while he wasn't even looking, his entire world had transformed into something alien and impossible to understand. And somehow it was all Bo Peep's fault.

 This is what he thought about, as forest gradually gave way to fields and a turn in the road brought the caravan wagon into view of the Peep estates. "Time to wake up," Bonny Lumpen called from outside. "We're here."

"Welcome!" Squire Peep bellowed from the shade of his columned veranda. "Welcome back to our home!" He'd been sitting in a high-backed cane chair as they drove up and needed the help of his walking stick in one hand and a solid tug from one of his daughters on the other hand (it was Dorthe, or possibly Brigitte) to rise to his feet. "We couldn't get a single thing done today, because we were all too excited waiting for you!" In the time it took Mr. Peep to negotiate the three steps down from the porch, the front doors burst open and Mrs. Peep flew by him and rushed into the yard, making happy squealing sounds all the while.

There followed a long bout of hugging and backslapping, as Mother Piper hugged Mother Peep, and then Mr. Piper hugged Mrs. Peep, while Mr. Peep hugged Mrs. Piper. The men happily whacked at each other, as men will do. And then the daughters, more of whom had materialized seemingly out of thin air, joined into the thick of it and the greetings went on and on. Only five of the six Peep daughters were there, which might seem like plenty, unless, like Peter, you were looking for one in particular, who just happened to be the one absent.

Some time passed before anyone noticed that Max was missing too.

Max, it turned out, hadn't been napping up on top of the baggage or in the driver's bench. He was nowhere to be seen. This wasn't immediate cause for alarm. The caravan moved so slowly that many times one or more of the family would step down along the road to stretch his legs, walking beside the wagon, or wander off on some brief side trip, knowing he could easily catch up again. More than once the two brothers, back when they still enjoyed each other's company, spied a nice pond to swim in, or a creek promising fish, and spent entire afternoons letting the caravan get far ahead. But they always managed to catch up again by dinnertime.

"I didn't notice when he'd left us," Bonny Lumpen said.

"Nothing's amiss. He'll turn up soon enough," Johannes said, though Beatrice couldn't help but show a mother's worry.

Her worry was misplaced though, because in little time at all, Max came trotting down the dirt road, excitedly waving his hand, where he carried something the others couldn't see at this distance. Max was tall and lanky and so skinny that concerned farm wives and town wives all along their travels constantly tried to feed him back into good health. Max didn't much mind the attention, possibly because it was his alone and something he didn't have to share with his little brother, who was also slim, but not alarmingly so. And he didn't mind the food. Max could eat like a horse, after having eaten a horse. But no matter how much he put away, he never added an inch of girth. He had a mop of tangled hair on his head, which was brown, like all of the Pipers, but a lighter shade than Peter's very dark brown hair. Max was barefoot. He wore bright red pants and a yellow shirt of good linen. Over that he wore a forest green tunic that was elaborately decorated with gold stitching. These were his performance clothes, which he liked to wear at all times, unlike Peter who couldn't wait to get out of his gaudy show dress, once a night's playing was done. "I like bright colors," was all that Max said one day when Peter had asked him about it. This annoyed Johannes and Beatrice no end, arguing as they often did that his good clothes, which were terribly expensive, would last much longer if he didn't wear them so often. But Max was impervious to their logic. He'd always select his performance clothes to wear, unless and until specifically ordered out of them. And then he'd put them on again as soon as he determined the term covered by that order had probably expired. By contrast, Peter preferred simple brown homespun, which is what he was wearing today.

Max dashed between the twin stone gateway pillars that marked the entrance to Peep lands and ran up the dirt driveway, bordered by twin rows of juniper trees. He was still carrying whatever it was he so earnestly wanted the others to see.

"Look what I found!" he shouted as he ran. "Stuck in a tree! I saw it from our wagon!" When he'd reached the others, quite out of breath by that time, he held out his discovery for all to examine. It was an arrowhead made out of iron or steel, and still attached to a few inches of broken off yew-wood shaft. The arrowhead was dark, almost black, and wickedly barbed. The bit of wood extending from it was painted dark red. Alternating bands of black and ocher thread attached the barbed head to the rest of it.

"It was stuck in a tree, but I still saw it!" Max said again, when some of his wind had returned. "Have you ever seen anything like it before?"

"Actually, no," Radulf Peep said, taking it from Max and examining it more closely. "Its markings aren't familiar to me. Not the signature of any huntsman I know around here. It almost looks foreign. Where did you find it?"

"About two miles up the road," Max said.

"Hmm, that's on my land, sure enough," Radulf said. "I don't mind a fellow taking a deer when he needs to, but the proper course is to ask first."

"What if it wasn't a hunter?" Max said. "What if this is from an advance scout for an invading army?"

"Well, I imagine that's the sort of thing that someone would notice," Radulf said. "Neighbors would certainly spread the word about armies tramping around in our woods."

"But I have heard about it!" Max said. "Lots of times!"

"I'm afraid my son has fallen in love with some wild stories he picked up in other towns," Johannes interrupted. "There are always rumors about terrible invading hordes. It's standard tavern talk by bored men who want to imagine their lives are more exciting than they are. But of course the fanciful armies have always invaded that distant town no one trades with, or that faraway kingdom that nobody ever visits. It's never anyplace someone actually knows. Finding a bit of arrow stuck in a tree is just the sort of thing to reignite his imagination."

"It's perfectly understandable," Radulf laughed. "Why, in my childhood, I can't begin to count the number of times I had to single-handedly repel foreign barbarians from those very same woods. Perhaps we should all get inside, where we'll be safe?" he laughed again, and others joined in. Then he turned to Peter and said more soberly, "I suspect you're wondering where my youngest has gotten herself off to? Well, she can't seem to pull herself away from her lambs these days, not even long enough to show basic courtesy to honored guests. She's got it into her head that every blessed one of them is this year's top prize winner. Why don't you go out behind the house and see if you can find her?"

"And save her from Max's pillaging hordes," Elfride said, which inspired more laughter.

Peter ran off around the house and everyone else began to move inside, including Max who'd turned quiet and sullen again. He trailed behind the rest of them, hanging his head and beginning to sulk at the fun that was made of him. But when he tried to enter the house behind the rest, Johannes paused in the doorway, blocking it. "Not you, Max," he said. "Not before you unhitch Bonny Lumpen from the wagon and give her a good brushing."

"Why?" Max whined. "They have servants here to do that."

"They aren't our servants," Johannes said.

"Why am I being singled out? I didn't do anything wrong."

"This isn't punishment, boy, it's duty. You're becoming a man now, and a man learns to get his work done before he rests and plays."

"But Peter got to run off and play."

"Peter's only ten years old. When you were still ten I didn't make you do such chores either. I did them. But now in my rapidly approaching dotage, I'm reminded of a rhyme someone once taught me. 'The name of my son is my work's done.' More and more each day, that's going to have to be you, Max. Think on it. And think about this too while you do your honest labor. Peter's the most gifted player of the three of us. Whether he works harder at it than we do, or it comes natural to him, I can't say. He can simply do things with a flute that you or I can't match. Which means he brings in more money than either of us. So, consider that when you're tempted again to worry about who is or isn't pulling his full weight around here."

So Max unhitched Bonny Lumpen and walked with her to the stables where she amiably chatted with the other animals — those who could talk — while he brushed her down. Reluctant though he was, he did a good and thorough job of it, because the mule could tell on him if he didn't. As he worked he stewed about the arrowhead he'd found. I did hear about real invaders, he thought. Not just rumors, because too many of the stories matched. They got lots of details the same. They should have listened to me.

And they probably should have listened. Although it's doubtful, had anyone believed him, that they could have done anything different to stave off or even mitigate the many sorrows to come.

LITTLE BO PEEP WAS STANDING in the greenest field of grass Peter had ever seen. It was a small, natural meadow set between a stand of hickory trees on one side and one curving edge of the big peach orchard on the other. Seven little white lambs and one scrawny black one grazed on the grass, keeping it cropped down so close to the earth that it looked no thicker than his father's whiskers an hour after he'd just shaved. Bo was in the yard, facing away from him, while imperiously ordering a single harried but enthusiastic sheepdog about, commanding that he not let any one of their charges break ranks and wander out of the meadow or too far from the others. The dog responded with enough "yes, missy"s and "no, missy"s and "right away, missy"s that it all strung together as one long run-on sentence.

"Bo," Peter said when he'd approached close enough behind her to be heard.

She turned around and regarded him, without expression. He knew right away it was a practiced gesture. She'd rehearsed this moment, planning well in advance exactly where she'd be when he first saw her and exactly what she'd be doing. He was surprised, realizing that it was an adult thing to do — something that should have been beyond her few years. He could never imagine arranging such a scene himself. She was a little girl on stage, starring in a play that he was also part of, except that he'd forgotten to learn his lines. Not knowing what he was expected to say next, he said nothing.

"Welcome back, Peter," she finally said, in a way that made him feel anything but welcome. "We've missed you. I'm so sorry I wasn't there to greet you right away when you'd arrived, but I've been ever so busy with my lambs. See how pretty they are?" Peter started to say that he did, but she spoke quickly to cut him off. It seems there was more to her speech. "All except the black one of course. He's sickly and doesn't eat well. He's also stubborn and doesn't know how to mind like the others. I don't know why I keep him. One shouldn't become fond of stupid and stubborn things."

By then Peter knew exactly what was coming next.

"I named him Peter," she announced.

Of course.

"After you," she added. She didn't need to. He'd fully understood her intent. Some of this play was still being written by an uncertain little girl. "I'm positive I'll win all of the prizes this year with my lambs, don't you think? I won't enter Peter the Lamb though. He couldn't win anything and would make me look bad just for having him. He'll have to stay here when we go to the fair, where he'll likely be chopped up for our dinner some night." This year, for the first time that he could recall, Bo wasn't dressed in the rough and tumble, good-to-get-dirty-in sort of clothes that she'd always favored in the past. Now she wore a pale green and tan summer dress, which should have been put away by this time of the year, but she'd probably insisted on it, and the days were still warm enough. Her long blonde hair, a bit lighter than that of her five golden-haired sisters, was tied behind her with a pretty blue ribbon. She held her own miniature shepherd's crook, made just to her size. All in all, she looked very much like a pretty little girl, and not much at all like the Bo he'd known in the past.

When enough time passed that Peter was sure she'd finished everything she'd memorized to say, he said, "I'm sorry I made you cry."

"What do you mean, Peter?" she said. "Made me cry? When?"

"Last year at the end of the fair. You kissed me and I wiped it off, and you cried."

"I never did. You just don't remember right."

"You did and I felt bad all year," he said.

"No, no, no," she said, angrily tapping the end of her crook in front of her, like a blind man tapping his cane. Little tufts of grass were torn out with every stab. "I didn't cry because of anything you did. I think a bee stung me that year, and it hurt. That's all."

"I'm still sorry and I'd like to be friends again, and that's all I had to say." Peter turned to walk back to the house, a little hurt and a little confused, because it looked like this had indeed become one of those talking-only kinds of friendships — if they were still going to be friends at all. Bo had truly turned into one of her sisters. But after a few steps, Peter paused and faced her again. "I like the little black sheep and I hope you never chop him up for dinner. And if you ever kiss me again I promise not to wipe it off this time." He went inside then, leaving her out in the meadow with her sheep.

That night, after dinner, the Pipers played again, as they did each year. But this time everyone agreed that they'd outdone themselves. Their music touched on things that were impossible to describe and seemed entirely outside the province of what mankind should ever hope to grasp, much less attempt.

When the concert ended and the last dregs of wine and beer had been swallowed, or mopped up, or poured out, and everyone had been properly wished a good night with pleasant dreams, Johannes asked Peter to tarry behind. The others were already heading up to their rooms, with candles in one hand and bed warmers in the other, the covered pans newly filled with fresh hot embers from the dying fire.

"Walk outside with me for a minute," he said, "and let's look at the stars before turning in."

They did.

"No stars tonight, Father," Peter said. "Just clouds covering the entire sky."

"That's all right," Johannes said. "I didn't really want to gaze at stars. I wanted to talk to you alone about something important." Johannes had carried his flute out there with him, as he always did. While all of their instruments were valuable enough, Mother's precious xylophone being a good example, Father's flute was a pearl beyond price. It was the single most important treasure the family owned. They never left it packed away in the caravan with the other things, where someone could come along and steal it. Father kept it with him always. Usually, when he wasn't actually playing it, he'd immediately put it away in its protective sheath of hard-boiled leather, lined with soft satin, which he wore on his belt, like a knight's great broadsword, or slung over his shoulder, like a royal courier's dispatch pouch. Tonight Father hadn't put it away, but carried it openly, and a little bit reverently. It wasn't very big – barely thirteen inches long, which was almost piccolo sized – though it played a full octave higher than a piccolo. It had a slightly flared cone at one end, eight holes in between, and a whistle-style mouthpiece at the other, which was carved so flat and thin that it looked like the blade of a knife. The small flute was pearly white, having been carved from a single piece of ivory, and then polished to a lustrous sheen that could reflect even the dimmest starlight, had there been any stars out to provide it. And like all truly important things, it had a name, which was Frost.

Johannes held Frost out where Peter could see it. He said, "How many times have I told you Frost's story?"

"I don't know," Peter said. "Lots."

"Well, I'm going to tell it again, one last time. And this time pay very special attention, because there's more to the tale that I never included before. You'll want to remember every detail, so that some night many years from now you can say the same things to your own son."

Peter felt a sudden thrill of excitement, as if he was kneeling at a lost treasure chest that he'd just unburied and was about to open. He knew instinctively that he was on the cusp of something life-altering. But it was a disturbing sensation too, and even a bit frightening, like that moment just before a dreadful lie is about to be revealed.

"Long ago," Father said, "when the world was still young, terrible frost giants ruled the far north. The worst of the lot was named Bryn the Thunderer, who'd kill and eat anyone who wandered into his domain, and would also plunder and raid down into the kingdoms of man, stealing cattle and gold, reaving and slaughtering wheresoever he went. No one could stand against Bryn, until Jorg the legendary warrior bard swore powerful oaths that he'd go north and write an end to Bryn's depredations for all time.

"Now there was magic back then in the early songs and therefore in those who could sing them. Every great hero at the age was also a musician. Jorg traveled north and stood outside of Bryn's great tower, and he called to the giant to come out and do battle."

"Which the giant did!" Peter said, too excited to keep from interrupting. This was part of the story he knew very well.

"Yes," Father said. "The frost giant came out and they did fierce battle with each other, a battle that lasted four days and three nights and shook the ice-covered lands all around them. But Jorg couldn't prevail, and the giant finally repulsed him. But that night Jorg wrote a song about the great battle and sang it to the earth and the moon and the stars, and the earth and the moon and the stars listened and took note.

"The next day Jorg went to stand again before Bryn's dark tower, and again called him out to battle. And this second great and thundering battle also lasted four days and three nights, before Jorg was repulsed once more. That night Jorg wrote another song about the second battle, and the earth and the moon and the stars listened again and took note. But Jorg was as clever as he was brave and mighty. This time he added a verse to his song wherein he promised that on the third time they battled he'd win a decisive victory and overthrow the giant, taking his head and all of his treasures. And the earth and the moon and the stars

pondered this and conferred together and decided that this must indeed come to pass, for it's been written in a song. Before that day — and remember that this happened during the early days of all things — nothing untrue had ever been written into a song.

"So Jorg and the frost giant battled a third time and it also lasted for four days and three nights, but this time Jorg won. He overthrew Bryn and took his head and all of his treasures. Now we can never know if Jorg defeated the giant solely by his own strength, or if his song convinced the earth and the moon and the stars to help, or even if the very fact of the song was itself enough to conjure powerful magic that determined the battle's outcome. But what we do know is that Jorg the Clever cut off one of the giant's fingers to roast over a fire for his dinner that night."

"And the finger was bigger than the biggest suckling pig," Peter said, jumping in with another part that he knew.

"Yes, it made a fine meal," Johannes said. Despite the interruptions, he couldn't help but smile at his son's obvious enthusiasm. He continued, "So, Jorg ate the giant's finger down to the bone, and then he took Bryn's white finger bone and carved this very flute out of it and called it Frost." He held the flute out again for his son to see. "And it had great magic in it.

"Jorg was our distant ancestor. Diluted though it may be over the generations, the blood of heroes runs in our veins. When he grew old, Jorg gave Frost to his son, Alban, who passed it on to his son, Albrecht, who passed it on to his son, and so on and so forth, for a hundred generations or more, until I received it from my father, your grandfather. We've always owned it from almost the very beginning of time and — this is important — Frost must never be lost, or allowed to be stolen, or given away to anyone but those of our bloodline, or a dire curse will befall us from now on and for every generation to come. That's the bad part of the magic that's in this thing, and part of what I never told you before. Do you think you can remember that, Peter?"

"Uhm... Yes, but..." That's when Peter began to suspect what was about to happen, and he realized something was very wrong. He knew the part about the generations and that Frost was handed down from father to son for more years than he could ever begin to imagine. And he knew this moment would come someday, but not so soon, and not to him. "But Max..." he began to say.

"No," Johannes said. "Not Max. This is for you. Max may be the oldest, so if I had any lands or high titles to pass on, those would rightly go to him. But Frost doesn't get handed off to the oldest son, it goes to the best musician. And that's you. I've known it for some time, and suspected it even longer. And tonight, when you played the way you did, I realized it was past time to hand Frost over to the next Piper to own it. Remember that it isn't a gift, it's a responsibility and a sacred trust, and sometimes even a burden. You can already play better than I ever could, or ever will, and that was while I had Frost to play and you only had your ordinary pipe, made of ordinary wood. In the days and years to come you'll discover notes you'd never imagined before and find new tunes to play that are so simple and perfect, you'll wonder how you never thought of them before.

"And there's one more thing you need to know, and this is part of the good magic that's left in the flute, even after so many ages. Because Jorg battled Bryn three times in that long-ago day, then three times — and only three times in your entire life — you can call on Frost's powers. You can use it to play a tune that will make any danger, great or small, pass you by."

"Really?"

"Really," Johannes said. "Three times only though. Remember that part. Then that particular bit of magic won't work again, until you pass it on to your son."

"And you did it, Father? You made danger pass you by?"

"Yes, and I don't mind telling you that it saved me from a nasty turn or two. But that was all in my brash youth, when I was full of pepper and aching for adventure. I don't want to scare you with the details of the first two occasions, but the third and final time I had need of Frost's powers was when I was courting your mother. I wasn't the only young bravo who'd caught her eye back then. My rival was the grown son of a landed baron, who liked nothing so much as taking offense at every imagined slight, shooting at folks with his arrows, stabbing folks with his spears and chopping with his sword into pretty-near any unwary skull that had the bad fortune to cross his path. And when he wasn't doing that, he was out riding on his chargers, at the head of armored columns, making war on his many unhappy neighbors."

"So what did you do?" Peter said.

"What could I do?" Johannes answered. "I was determined to wed your mother and that made the baron's son awfully prickly.

So I played him a sweet tune and he went away to pick other fights. If I can offer you any advice on how to make use of your three gifts, now that you own Frost, I'd caution you to choose wisely how you decide to spend them. Sometimes a situation turns out in retrospect to be not nearly so dire as it may have seemed at first, and only three turns at anything can go by surprisingly fast."

Without any further words, Johannes handed Frost over to Peter, who took it in both hands and couldn't tear his eyes off it. He'd held it many times before, but it never felt quite as heavy as it did now. For a long time no one spoke a word, until Johannes finally said, "It's grown late and we need to make an early start of it in the morning. Time to go to bed, son."

Peter had many dreams that night and all of them involved wonderful and dangerous adventures, where he had to fight valiantly against impossible odds. And Bo was in every one of them, always nearby, always waiting for him to win her from horrible barons' sons and other deadly monsters.

Chapter Three
WOLF VALLEY

*In which Bo captures
Peter and then releases
him again.*

AFTER A BREAKFAST SPENT MOSTLY IN strained silence, Peter rode with Rose Red back to the main village area, where he dropped her off before taking over the Range Rover and turning it northeast again, then east, navigating around the Farm's Great Wood, giving it a wide berth. This was the deep forest where tiny but doughty mounted knights of the constabulary rode valorous mice on patrol. Under these dark canopies Kaa lurked in the treetops, proud Bagheera prowled in the night, and the vast and barbarous Bandarlog host cavorted and pestered and performed their secret rituals, away from the sight of man.

True to his father's instruction, on that fateful evening so many ages past, Peter had the flute named Frost with him. It sat in its small carrying case on the truck's bench seat beside him. This was a new case, of course, made of modern high-impact plastic and reinforced steel. The original leather case had worn away long ago, as had many successors since. But Frost remained, unchanged by time. It looked as new today as when he first saw it, and probably the same as when fabled Jorg first carved it.

Eventually the gravel road turned into little more than an overgrown footpath, and in time disappeared altogether, so Peter had to take the truck overland, avoiding the bigger boulders he could see above the tall grass, and bouncing over small ones he couldn't. He maneuvered around stands of trees and any number of hidden culverts, ditches and sinkholes. A trip that would have taken minutes on a good road took most of an hour cross country. He kept the truck aimed more or less east, and a bit north, towards a notch between the lowest of the rugged hills girdling Wolf Valley. From a distance at least it looked like the easiest route over to the other side.

The grade got steadily steeper the closer he approached the hills, and the number of trees, rocks and other obstacles increased. Finally, when the accumulating hazards were more than the vehicle could safely handle, he parked it to get out and walk.

He zipped the flute case into a daypack, added a few bottles of water, and a light rain slicker, in case the weather turned, and set out at a brisk pace. He passed a hand-carved wooden sign that announced he was about to leave the Farm. A few feet beyond that, another sign warned him that he was entering Wolf Valley, even though he was still at least one long ascent away from anything remotely valley-like. The slope increased as he went, and in scant time he was doing as much actual climbing as hiking. He pulled himself upwards, grasping branches and rocks overhead, or anything else that looked solid enough to take his weight without dislodging. There were some evergreens here, but most of the trees were still broadleaves, and this high up they'd already turned every possible variation of red and orange. The overhead leaves stained the blue ceiling of the sky like dried blood spatter.

After some time Peter finally crested the top of the hill, only to discover that it was a false summit – a ridge that looked like the top from below, but which turned out to be just another step along the way. The rest of the hill continued upwards, following a short tease of gentle down-slope. He decided it was a good time to take a break, so he found a fallen log to sit on. No sooner had he gotten comfortable than a deep bass voice surprised him from somewhere nearby, though its owner remained quite concealed.

"You made good time," the hidden someone said. "I was just heading overhill, to meet you at the edge of my property. I thought I'd save you the tough climb."

"Bigby?" Peter said, standing up to look left and right, not entirely certain from which direction the voice had come. Then, with a soft rustle of leaves, a huge shape detached itself from the concealment of rock and root, and padded forward through intervening trees, resolving into the form of a wolf as it did so. And such a wolf it was! It was a monstrous thing, as tall as a grown man at its shoulders. Its coat was black on top, shading to gray under its belly. It had yellow-white fangs as long as daggers, and its eyes reflected the filtered light coming through the overhead canopy, amber one second and then dark red the next. This was Bigby, the legendary monster, the subject of countless nightmares, the Lord of All Wolves.

"And," Bigby continued, "I thought it best we had this conversation alone, rather than let you come all the way to the house and risk upsetting my wife and cubs. They've had their share of tough times lately and don't need a new worry to fret over. Especially when it's nothing they can do anything about."

Bigby came closer and Peter took an instinctive step back.

"Don't worry," Bigby said, "I won't eat you. Haven't you heard? I've stopped doing that, especially to those I've invited into my company."

"You didn't always behave so well," Peter said. In their first meeting, long before either of them had heard about the new world and its status as a place of shared refuge, much less before either had traveled here, the giant wolf wasn't nearly so generous of spirit. His appetites were at their height then and the encounter nearly ended Peter's life, almost before it had properly begun.

"People change," Bigby said.

"People?" Peter said.

"Sure, I'm people. At least some of the time. Hell, most of the time, now that I've taken up married life." In what was arguably the most improbable wedding in Fable history, Bigby Wolf had recently married Snow White. Peter couldn't understand the match. While it was true that the wolf had learned how to take human form, even as a man Bigby looked like a bad patch of road. In fact he looked just like the sort of fellow who was a wild animal in his real guise. The official story was that Snow and Bigby shared the truest of all true love. Peter had his doubts about that. But he didn't voice them.

"You heard that my brother Max was back in the world," Peter said, wanting to quickly conclude their business, so that he could return to his own wife as soon as possible. "How do you know? Did you see him?"

"No," the wolf said. "If I had, I'd have taken him right then and there, and we'd be having a different sort of chat right now."

"I doubt you could have killed Max, or even survived the attempt. He's grown too powerful over the ages."

"While I've socked away a few tricks of my own," Bigby said.

"Still, the question remains. How do you know that he's here in our world?"

"The information's good," Bigby said. "It comes straight from the witch. I'm not her biggest fan, but if she says a thing is so, you can count on it being so."

"She's far from all-powerful," Peter said. "She had the opportunity to fight her duel with him and lost. Remember what that cost us?" A chill wind blew down from the hilltop, causing a forest's worth of leaves to start chattering, all at once. Peter pulled the light windbreaker out of his daypack and put it on. It helped a little. The wolf seemed immune to any sort of discomfort. "And let's not forget her part in creating this mess," Peter continued. "If not for her, Max might still be — human." He'd intended to say Max might still be his brother, but stopped himself at the last moment. He'd be damned if he shared his most personal feelings with an unrepentant killer. Bigby Wolf had been a terror of the Homelands, one of the great monsters in every sense of the word. And that was why he wasn't allowed on the Farm, even today. Too many of his potential victims lived there, and many of them were certain the wolf would return to his old ways. But he'd taken full advantage of the General Amnesty — that part of the Fabletown Compact that wiped out all previous sins, as soon as you formally became part of the community in exile. All sorts of villains had snuck in under that ridiculous policy, including the witch of their discussion, who was another destroyer of ill repute. No one need repent. It wasn't required. They only needed to promise to act better from now on. Peter hated everything about the General Amnesty, especially considering how perilously close Max had once come to receiving its protections.

"It's pretty clear you still haven't warmed up to me over the years," Bigby said. "I can smell the fear and hate coming off you.

It's a strong musk I never mistake."

"I just don't trust you is all. Your past record speaks for itself," Peter said.

"Apparently not very convincingly, since my record also includes about four centuries of not only keeping my own nose clean, but keeping everyone else on the straight and narrow as well. Doesn't any of that weigh in the balance?" It was true, Peter considered, that since the very founding of Fabletown, Bigby had served as its sheriff. It turned out he was quite good at keeping the peace among many squabbling factions, still learning how to get along with each other. He seemed to like the job and only quit when he had children and got married. But all that it really proved was that Bigby was the biggest, scariest bully on the block who could effectively enforce his will over any number of lesser thugs.

Peter said, "You remind me of the killer finally captured, whose defense at trial was, 'Look at all the people I didn't kill.' Any number of good years doesn't wipe out the bad ones, in my estimation."

"Suit yourself," Bigby growled. "I don't insist anyone love me, but I do require a reasonable degree of respect, even in my retirement. In the future, if you can't summon the real thing, it's best you learn how to fake it. I set up this meeting as a courtesy. Way back when I was still sheriff, you made it clear to me that you wanted first crack at Max, if he ever surfaced again. And while I no longer have any official authority to give you that chance, I think that Fabletown's new sheriff might take my advice in this instance, seeing as how I'm the one he just asked to track Max down and do him in. If we have nothing else in common, I understand the importance of settling family business inside the family. So, even if the bureaucrats down in Fabletown bitch and moan, I figure I can guarantee you at least a week's head start. Hell, I can waste that much time just saying goodbye to my wife and cubs. But know this, Peter, in a week I will step in, and once that happens I won't let anyone get in my way."

"I understand," Peter said. "I haven't forgotten that you vowed to kill me once."

"I vowed to kill a lot of folks back in the day," Bigby said. "I was a kill-everyone sort of wolf back then. Being one of the good guys now puts quite a collar around my neck. Many oaths are of a necessity on hold, pending further developments. But chafe though it might, I think it's a collar worth wearing – for now."

"Do you know where Max is? More specifically, I mean?"

"I've told you all I know. If you need more information, ask the witch. I suspect she'll be trying to pin down his location."

"Any idea why he's here? Why now?"

"Like I said, go ask the witch."

It was cold and occasionally treacherous going back down the hill, which seemed on consideration much more mountain-like after all.

"I'll have to go to Fabletown first," Peter said. "Then I could end up going anywhere from there. It all depends on Max." Instead of returning the Range Rover to Rose Red, as he'd promised, Peter first drove directly home to his wife, to have the conversation he least wanted to have. Best to get it out of the way, he thought. The cottage was filled with the aroma of the coming dinner. Resisting the many and constantly changing influences of modern mundy culture, which had affected most Fables in more ways than they cared to admit, Peter and Bo Piper resolutely, some might say stubbornly, continued in as many of the old ways as they could, including the habit of eating their big meal in the afternoon, rather than evening. There was a fat roast, with carrots and onions, cooking in the wood-burning oven. They didn't have electricity out here and didn't particularly want it. Another pan of red potatoes, in a butter and tarragon sauce, bubbled and sizzled on the burner above. An unbaked apple pie sat on the butcher counter nearby, waiting to be popped into the oven as soon as the roast came out. Peter and Bo sat at the kitchen table, opposite each other. They'd pushed the two place settings out of the way, so they'd have room to lean on the table, or pound on it, as needs must, without fear of breaking anything. Bo always cooked a big dinner, full of his favorite dishes, when she knew they were going to fight. She also brought out the good china. It's as if she calculated that it was something nice she could do to partially offset all of the horrible things she might end up saying. Of course, like most men, Peter didn't care what quality of dinnerware he ate from, so that part of her gesture was always lost on him. The good dinners helped, though. He noticed those.

"One way or another I'll be back in a week," Peter said. "That's as long as Bigby's given me to settle the matter. I hate having to leave you, even for a short time. And I know I promised never to leave your side, but..."

"But this is the one absolute exception," Bo said, finishing his sentence for him, since he seemed so reluctant to do it.

"Yes," he said, not quite able to meet her gaze.

"You realize he's going to kill you, don't you? You won't be back in a week because you won't be back at all. We barely survived him the first time, when he wasn't nearly so powerful as he is now, and we were both fit and whole and at the top of our training in every dirty sort of business that Hamelin's underworld could teach us."

"I know."

"But you're still going to try it, Peter?"

"Yes."

Bo backed up abruptly from the table and wheeled herself over to the oven. Putting on a thick, quilted mitt, she pulled open the oven door, leaned forward in her chair to furiously and silently examine its contents. Then she closed the door, not quite slamming it, stirred the potatoes for a few seconds and then wheeled back over to the table.

"Ten more minutes," she said, as if she were an ancient sea captain pronouncing some draconian ship's punishment on a member of her crew. "Maybe fifteen."

"I'll come back to you," Peter said.

"Is this such a terrible life we have? Is it so bad?" Bo said.

"No, it's good, and I wouldn't trade it away for anything else, except — "

"Except in the fantasy version of your ideal marriage, you never imagined it would include the grotesque hell of my body from the waist down. You never thought we'd have to live strictly platonically for — how many centuries has it been now, and counting?"

"That's not what I was going to say," he said.

"Then what?"

"I was going to say: Except that I can't pass up the chance to end this with Max, once and for all. We can't just hide out here and hope he never finds us. He got close once and look what happened. In this matter, time isn't on our side. And once again, I promise you that I'll come back."

"What a grand gesture," Bo said. "That's such an easy promise to make, which is why it's both insipid and unfair. It's a no-lose deal for you. Either you do come back and you're the big hero who's kept his promise, or you die horribly, and I have to instantly forgive you, because I'd be a heartless bitch if I didn't. I couldn't even remotely resent the fact that you failed to keep your word. You get out of any consequences scot-free!"

"Well, except for the part where I die horribly," he said,

trying on a crooked smile — the one she liked best.

"Well, yes, except for that part. Don't you dare try to make me laugh, or like you again, Peter Piper. I'm not done arguing and I don't want to like you yet."

"Then by all means, please do continue."

She thought for a bit. It was obvious he was determined to leave, and just as determined not to be talked out of it. He spoke soothingly and diplomatically, but he'd already dug his heels in. Then again, there was one argument she felt would almost certainly stop him, except that it was cruel and cheap — a truly low blow. So she took a long moment, weighing whether or not she actually dared use it. Then she said, "Someone will have to come out here to take care of me."

"I know," he said. "I'll be arranging that when I see Rose Red again, before I drive down to the city."

"Some stranger will have to change me and bathe me and help me with all of my bathroom functions — all of the stinky, messy things I no longer have any control over. He'll see my shocking and lurid disfigurements — everything that no one else but you has ever seen. And sooner or later he'll let something slip. He won't intend to. He'll try to do the right thing and keep it to himself, but one day he won't be able to help it, because there won't actually be a compelling reason to stop him. He's not my husband. He's not family. He has no real obligations towards me and no duty to preserve my very reasonable shame, much less my modesty. He'll tell someone, who'll tell someone else, and pretty soon everyone will know our most private secrets.

We'll be a lovely bit of gossip then, the subject of a thousand hushed conversations. And even though I can keep hiding here — even though I won't have to go out and actually confront the effects of it — you will, because one of us still has to pick up supplies and interact with the rest of the Farm. You'll hear the sniggering and see the quick, behind-the-hands whispers wherever you go. 'Yes,' they'll say. 'He's the one. He's married to her, the living horror show. Not really a marriage, mind you. Couldn't be. Probably has to sneak out into the mundy once in a while for a little bit of the strange, just to release the natural pressures, don't you know.' And that will be our lives from now on — for every single year of every single century that we continue to exist."

  She could see right away the devastating effect her speech had on him and she hated herself for it. She'd been cold and calculating and brutal, even to the extent of intentionally using the male pronoun in referring to her unspecified caregiver, so that he'd be forced to imagine another man doing all of those things she described. She'd never before played the cripple card like this, and though she'd done it for a perfectly justified reason, to save him from throwing his life away in a noble but futile gesture, she regretted it instantly, even as she saw that she'd won. She'd defeated him thoroughly — in detail, as the military men like to say. She could see from his expression that he'd stay here now if she wanted him to, to preserve and protect the agreed fiction of their lives, even at the terrible cost of letting Max go. She'd won, unless she turned it around right now and gave it back.

Should she let him go?

Could she?

She leaned her elbows hard on the table, putting as much weight on them as she had, and clasped her fists tightly in front of her. She stared down intently at her whitening knuckles. Peter didn't try to say anything, because this was her "I'm trying to think of how to say something really important in just the right way" pose. Even while he was as miserable as he'd ever been, torn between two absolute but conflicting responsibilities, he was content to give her the time to conjure whatever it was she needed.

She looked up at him and fixed his eyes with hers, which were red and swollen with unshed tears, but there was a cold anger in them too.

"When you find him you're going to have to kill him," she finally said, low, controlled and without emotion.

"Yes, I know."

"You know, Peter, but you don't really absolutely, down-in-your-ugly-depths know. You can't hope to kill him only as a last resort. You can't try to reason with him first, or look for one tiny scrap of potential redemption. You can't even talk to him, because I know that's what you desperately want to do. You want to find out why he did the things he did and why he let himself become the creature he turned into. You want to understand him and have him explain everything in a tidy, storybook denouement. But that will never happen and you need to know it. If I let you walk out that door — and believe me, I can still stop you if I need to — then it will only be because

I have your solemn promise that you won't try to talk to him first. You'll use every dirty thing I've ever taught you and just do the bloody business and walk away."

"I think I can make that promise," he said, after considering her words.

"I think you can, too. I just wish I was more confident you will."

Peter looked down at his hands, studying them as if they'd only recently grown out of the ends of his arms. The cottage was full of the cooking aromas and he savored them for a moment, realizing that they added to the weight that held him there in their home that he never wanted to leave. Finally he said, "Who'll we get to come out here then? Who can we trust?"

"No one," she said and there was adamant in her voice. "You said you'd only be gone for a week at most? Well, I can hold out here alone for a week. It won't be pretty, and you'll have a hell of a mess to clean up when you get back, but what's left of our stunted dignity and reputation will remain intact."

He started to speak again, whether to protest or to comfort she'd never know, because she cut him off. "Not now," she said. "We're done arguing now. You've got too much to do. You have to pack and get Rose's truck back to her, before she sends her fire-breathing raven out to burn our house down. And if you think there's a chance in Hell that I'm letting you go before you do justice to this massive dinner I've cooked, then you're truly living in a dream world."

So they ate and they played at small talk, as if a silent pact had been struck to speak only of inconsequential things from now on, until he left and came back and they could take up their lives again as before.

Just before leaving, he went back into their bedroom and unlocked the one closet that was always locked and took out the small wooden traveling trunk that they'd brought with them from their old lives in the Hesse. Under her watchful eye, Peter carefully unsealed the special seals and unlocked the locks — first the obvious ones that anyone could see, and then the hidden ones. There inside were all of the deadly things they no longer had to use. Most of the knives were missing of course. Bo still practiced with them too often to go through the bother of constantly taking them out and putting them back into the multilocked trunk. Peter had already packed away her small knives for throwing and her other knives for stabbing, wishing all the while that he'd been as steadfast keeping up his practice with them as she had. So the knives were already taken, but here were all of the other small implements of murder: the vials full of poisons, those that went into food or drink and those for coating a blade or a dart. And here were other little bottles of deadly liquids to be splashed on a victim, or thicker gels to be touched onto someone's exposed skin in passing — "Only the merest drop brushed onto the outside of his wrist just so, and then hurry along quickly, so that you aren't too near when the body drops."

"How many of these will still be potent?" Peter asked.

"I don't know," she said. "I doubt my instructors ever anticipated someone keeping these things for so long. The prudent thing to do would be to test them."

"No time," he said. "I'll just take a selection and play the odds — trust that they haven't all lost their bite."

Peter took out a small metal tube — a blowgun that could fit in the palm of his hand, and whose minuscule darts, smaller than a bee's stinger, could hardly be felt. He tucked them away into one of the many hidden pockets which Bo still sewed into all of his clothes. Many of the things he ignored — innocent everyday items that anyone might carry, but which had deadly secondary uses. The problem was that everyday items of an age ago would look decidedly out of place today. But here and there he found a few things that still looked appropriate to any age: the plain gold ring with the cleverly hidden spring mechanism; the delicate ivory toothpick; the intricately woven copper wire bracelet. Soon enough he was done.

"I've got so many of your little nasties secreted about me, I feel like I'm going to clank and rattle when I walk," Peter said. "Every metal detector in the airport's liable to scream its head off."

"You'll do fine," Bo said. "All together that stuff hardly adds a single pound to your weight."

"Until I unpack your knives and other assorted hardware at the other end and add them to my ensemble."

"It won't matter. If I did my job right altering your clothing, nothing will be able to clank and scrape against anything else."

He gave her a kiss goodbye and she returned it with an unusual hunger.

Chapter Four

WHAT MAX SAW

*In which Little Bo Peep
loses her sheep and
Peter Piper picks
a pickled pepper.*

MAX PIPER WASN'T AT ALL PLEASED WHEN he went to bed that night, in Squire Peep's grand mansion. They'd played well after dinner, as well as they ever had, but once again precious little Peter got all the accolades. Peter didn't deserve the praise, Max thought, and it wasn't just jealousy, or an older brother's resentment that a younger one came along and stole all the attention. This was a matter of simple, unemotional logic.

If four musicians played the same tune, but only one of them did it well, then the bad ones would ruin any effect the good one had. It stood to reason. It wasn't opinion, but the simple and impartial calculus of performance. No matter how wonderfully the good one played, it would still come out as a mad cacophony. But, if their music did sound lovely and melodious, which it certainly had, it could only be because they'd all played well — even Peter, he reluctantly had to admit. They all did a professional job of it and no one should be singled out, except maybe Max, because he had the more difficult instrument to play. He played the large bass flute — with its deep and resonant tones — because he was the only one big enough — well, at least tall and lanky enough — to do it. His father was a short man, and Peter was still just a kid. Neither of them had a wide enough natural hand spread to cover all of the stops. Only Max's long, dexterous fingers were up to the daunting task.

And yet it was Peter they loved and complimented, and all because Father couldn't stop praising his younger son. He's the one who put the idea into everyone's minds. If Father would just shut up for once, and let their respective talents speak for themselves, then Max would be recognized as the true prodigy.

Of that he was certain.

It was a simple matter of logic.

And not only that, Peter took the best berry tart for dessert. He could see Max had his eye on it, so, just to be vindictive, the little stinker stole it right off the tray, before it came around to Max.

These were the thoughts that troubled Max's mind, going round and round, repeating once and again, as he slowly drifted off into a fitful sleep.

The sound of thunder woke him.

Max could tell many things as he struggled into consciousness, but they were all a confused jumble in his head. He could hear the distant thunder, but there seemed to be too much of it, like it was the biggest of all storms. But it was also in a terrible hurry, one thrump of thunder following right after another, with none of the usual breaks in between. It boomed in a steady rhythm, as if trying to get all of its crashing and pounding out as quickly as possible. And he smelled breakfast smells, so someone had thought to start cooking. And that was good, because if people were making breakfast, then things couldn't be too bad. No one thinks to cook when the world's coming to an end. Then again, he was almost certain he'd also heard screaming.

His first cogent thought was to go to the window and see just what was what, but he also had an urgent need to pee, as he very naturally did every morning upon waking. He sat frustrated for a moment, his pale and spindly bare legs hanging off the tall bed. Both possibilities seemed to require immediate attention. Since he couldn't decide to do one thing over the other, he compromised and did both. He grabbed the chamber pot from under the bed and took it with him, shuffling hurriedly over to the window in his nightshirt and his nightcap and his bare feet.

Out in the road, not more than a stone's throw from the main house, and therefore from his own window, Max saw an invading army. They marched in ranks, four or five abreast, down the very same road his family had traveled the day before. First, in the vanguard there were men on horseback, outfitted in iron armor overlaid with lacquers of midnight black and dusky gold and deep carnelian. Here there was a knight in armor all of green, and there was one in armor of white, decorated in twining blue flowers. And dozens more Max spied, wearing armor and surcoats and flowing cloaks of every color in the spectrum. They sat upon great chargers, with barding that matched the riders. They wore plumed helmets and had long, heavy broadswords strapped to their belts. Behind the parade of knights came the color guard, more mounted soldiers but in uniform livery, carrying bright pennants, heralding numerous past victories. And then behind the flashing color guard, the rest of the cavalry rode their war horses and carried their long lances.

Then there followed rank upon rank of foot soldiers, and these weren't even men at all! Shaped like men in only the crudest, most rudimentary way, they were huge, burly creatures with green warty skin, black animal eyes and long yellow tusks. They carried crude swords and axes and spears, some of which were still stained with the dried remains of something Max dared not contemplate. They wore armor of rough, undecorated iron, and it was the tramp, tramp, tramping of their iron boots, thousands of them marching all in unison, that Max had mistaken for thunder.

The ranks of green-skinned horrors came on and on, a never-ending column that appeared from around the same bend in the road that he'd run down, carrying his discovered arrowhead. They were divided into different groups. A company of spearmen was followed by a company of pikes and they were followed by a company of archers — all carrying quivers full of black-headed arrows on dark red shafts, Max intuited.

But it didn't occur to Max just then to realize he'd been right all along about an incipient invasion, and that he was the only one who'd figured it out, that not even precious little Peter had understood what the arrowhead actually meant, while he had, and that everyone should have listened to him in the first place. That insight would come later. At the moment Max could do nothing but gape in astonishment, watching the invaders come on and on in their endless ranks, while he stood there with his nightshirt pulled up around his chest, miserably pissing into his chamber pot.

In an awful rush, Max dressed and ran downstairs to find the entire household engaged in a flurry of activity. One of the Peep daughters — he couldn't tell which — flew by him, scampering up the same stairs that he'd descended. She was bawling loudly and trailing three or four frightened and worried household maids in her wake. Two of the hired hands, armed with pitchfork and hoe, were standing in the middle of the room, getting manure from their shoes all over one of the good rugs, loudly asking of nobody in particular, "Do we fight? Are we going to fight?" But no one answered them, or seemed to pay them any attention whatsoever. Other servants were quickly gathering silver candlesticks from off the mantle and silver serving trays from off a sideboard. Whether to hide them from the invaders, or steal them for themselves, Max couldn't guess.

None of the other Peeps were present, nor any of his own family. Not knowing what else to do, Max grabbed one of the house servants by the sleeve as he tried to scurry by. It was someone he recognized, by the name of Kurt, if one of the adults or any of the Peep daughters spoke to him, but whom Max and Peter had to address as Mr. Morganslaughtern. He was fat, old and red faced and looked like he was about to burst something. He carried a small framed portrait painting of Mrs. Cresentia Peep in one hand and a paring knife in the other. What he planned to do with either of those items no one could tell, perhaps not even Morganslaughtern himself.

"Where is everyone?" Max shouted. He hadn't intended to shout, but the army outside combined with the chaos inside made Max more frightened than he ever imagined he could be in a situation like this. He'd always pictured himself as cool and calm in an emergency, taking command, and of course he always had a sword in his hand. There was a set of decorative crossed swords mounted on the far wall, over an equally decorative console table, and he briefly wondered if he should go arm himself with one of them. Then Morganslaughtern's insistent tugging at his hand — he still had hold of the man's sleeve — reminded him of his original intent, to find someone in charge. "Where's Squire Peep?"

"He's in the kitchen, of course!" Morganslaughtern snapped.

"Now kindly unhand me, young man!"

Why in the kitchen and why "of course"? Max knew nothing of the important matters of high men of status like the squire. Is the kitchen where all great men in command of great estates naturally go in times of crisis? Whatever for? To personally guard the pots and pans? Max could make no sense of the comment, but since he didn't know what else to do, and a man like Mr. Peep certainly would know what he should do, Max headed for the kitchen.

The kitchen wasn't a single room, but a complex of interconnected chambers that took up the entire west wing of the ground floor. In the main section, the part with all of the stoves and chopping blocks and such, Max saw all three cooks and both scullery maids working feverishly, preparing the breakfast Max had smelled earlier. Dozens of eggs were being boiled and broiled and fried in skillets. And in other skillets large slices of ham and fat sausages sizzled and popped. No sooner did one cook pull pans of just-baked biscuits out of the oven than another one put new pans of dough in right behind her. And there was oat mush and breakfast cakes and thick brown syrup in glass pitchers that were lowered into pots of bubbling water to warm them. All five women looked harried and upset. The head cook had tracks of recently shed tears down her wide cheeks. And not one of them paused in their hurried efforts to shoo Max out of there, which is the very first time that ever happened — or more properly *didn't* happen. No one seemed to mind his being there, or even notice that he was, which scared him as much as anything else had this morning. If that's changed, then everything has, Max thought. And he wasn't wrong.

Through a large open archway on the far side of the room, Max saw the great wooden table, where mixes were mixed and vegetables were chopped and diced and shucked and sorted, and where sometimes breakfast could be eaten, in lieu of one of the more formal dining rooms. Additionally it was where all of the household servants gathered to eat their dinner, after the Peep family and their guests had been served elsewhere. This morning the table was occupied by strangers.

By their expensive military dress and their brusque, superior attitudes, Max surmised that they had to be officers of the invading army outside. There were seven of them and they sat all around the table, eating the breakfast that the cooks had made, more of which they continued to cook even now. Mr. Peep was in the room with them, not seated but standing nearby, meekly nodding his head as one of the officers talked around successive mouthfuls of eggs and sausages. Max's father was also in the room, standing next to Mr. Peep and looking both grim and worried.

"All of your lands are confiscated in the name of the Emperor," the officer said, "as are your houses, barns, stables and any other structures." The officer was bald, with a fringe of short black hair around his ears and the back of his head. He had giant black mustachios that drooped past his chin before turning up again at the ends, which were waxed to sharp points. He wore a red and gold uniform jacket, decorated with frills and tassels and medals and shiny brass buttons.

"Your crops will be confiscated, too, and your livestock slaughtered to feed my troops," he continued, spooning a fat dollop of honey onto a biscuit. "You will all be allowed to remain here for now. In fact you are required to do so, while we continue on to secure the town of Wesen."

"Winsen," Squire Peep corrected, automatically, and then quickly shut his mouth and lowered his eyes as the officer shot him with an evil stare.

"You'll stay here while we secure the town of Winsen," the officer began again. "You'll work hard to bring in all of the remaining crops, as quickly as you can. And mind you, I don't mean to suggest that you'll order your laborers to work hard while you oversee them. You're all of an equal status now. You and your fat wife and your skinny daughters and even your guests will toil in the fields, alongside everyone else. In a few days I'll send one of my officers from the Quartermasters' Corps to collect the bounty and evaluate the quality of your compliance.

"This land and its people are now part of the Empire, and will be so forevermore." His voice was calm and low and nearly uninflected, as if he knew he'd never have to raise it to command anyone's rapt attention. His pronunciation, while precise, was heavily accented. "Whether you're fated to serve the Empire as slaves or to be proudly numbered among its many free and loyal citizens has yet to be decided, but will largely be determined by the manner in which you conduct yourselves over the next few days."

"Yes, sir," Peep meekly said, and Max was astonished all over again. In all of their visits over the years, although Squire Peep was always jolly and pleasant, he was also unmistakably the man in charge. He told people what to do and no one ever told him what to do — except for sometimes his wife did, but Max already understood how marriages involved a private exception to many rules. As far as Max had known, Squire Peep ran the entire county and everyone in it, and now here he was, nodding and bobbing his head at the behest of these terrible men.

Max must have made a noise then, some small voicing of his surprise, because in the adjoining room his father suddenly looked his way, and transfixed Max with such a look as he'd never seen the man produce. No one else took notice of him. Peep continued bobbing his head while the officer kept issuing commands — exactly what additional commands Max wasn't able to recall later, as his attention had shifted entirely to his father's intense regard. Never taking his eyes off Max, Father slowly and carefully raised one finger to his lips, silently ordering Max to remain quiet. Then he whispered a quick word into Squire Peep's ear before excusing himself from the room full of foreign officers. No one moved to prevent his leaving. In fact, no one showed any sign that they cared what his father did, one way or another. Father padded over to join Max in the other room.

"What has happened?" Max said, in a frantic whisper, pregnant with the future possibilities of panic and weeping.

"Shush," Father said, also in a whisper, but one under rigid control. "This isn't a time for you to talk, or ask questions, son.

It's a time for you to listen and obey. Your mother and brother are waiting for us in the great hall. That's where I want you to go too. If you see Mrs. Peep, or any of the daughters on the way, take them to wait there with you. Don't go outside and don't talk to any of the soldiers. I don't think they'll hurt you, as long as you stay quiet and stay out of their way."

"What do we do once we're all there?" Max said.

"Nothing. Just stay put and try to help keep everyone calm. Can I count on you to do that, son? This is one of those moments I've told you about, when you have to step up and be a man. Can you do that?"

"Of course."

"Good. I'm comforted to hear it, Max. So, go do what I told you and in a little while Mr. Peep and I will join you there and explain everything."

Max obeyed. For the first time in a long time, he was pleased to do exactly what Father told him to.

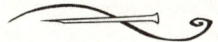

THE GREAT HALL was full of unhappy people. Most of the indoors servants and all of the outside workers were crowded in there. Mother Piper was seated at one of the benches along the wall and Peter stood beside her, trying to look brave, but mostly looking scared and uncertain. Mrs. Peep and all six of the daughters had also eventually arrived, reporting, as others had before them, that soldiers were all over the grounds and in the house. But for now at least the invaders seemed content to leave them alone here in this chamber. The girls were oddly disarrayed in small ways. One had a splash of brown mud staining her yellow dress. Another had lost one shoe and was absently holding its mate in her hands, and wouldn't let anyone take it from her, as if it was some sort of protective talisman. And the bratty little one who Peter liked sat directly on the cold flagstone floor, crying and sobbing with great, racking sobs that shook her entire body.

"They killed them!" she cried. "All my little lambs! Gerta, and funny Apfelkauph! And Peter too!" She'd gone through the list many times, over and over again. Sometimes she'd be able to name every one of them — Max gathered that there were seven or eight in all — and at other times she'd only be able to get out two or three, before the sobs claimed her again. She'd been at it for quite a while, resting between loud bouts of misery to regather her strength before starting again. Father promised Max he'd be along soon, but so far they'd been here for hours, waiting to learn their fate.

True to his word, Max took it upon himself to be the strong and steadfast leader of his father's wishes and his own fanciful imagination, whose resolutely unflappable example kept panic from spreading to the troops. Max pictured himself a solid rock of calm assurance in the storm. He circulated time and again, throughout the large room, going from one cluster of people to another, imploring them to refrain from fear, and assuring them that his father and Squire Peep would come in no time to explain everything. The trouble was that Max wasn't actually all that calm himself. His voice betrayed considerable worry, and there was a wild and unsettled look in his eyes. And since, while making his rounds, he also tried to recall and report the grim things he'd overheard in the kitchen, which were anything but reassuring, he was generally more successful at reigniting fears than at settling them.

From time to time they could hear the muted sounds of the activities outside, as the detachment of the human officers and their goblin troops — for such were the green-skinned monsters called — which had broken off from the main column and fanned out over the property, corralled animals and put them to the sword (or the axe, or club, or whatever other weapon happened to be most handy). In one truly horrifying moment they heard the pleading voices of the estate's talking animals, begging not to be killed.

"They've gotten into the Talking Stable!" Hans Kruft cried. He was the chief stable master and therefore the one in charge of the so-called Talking Stable, where those magical animals with human language were lovingly housed and cared for. "Why would they kill them, too?"

"They're all just meat on the hoof to goblins," young Manfred said, his voice unusually bitter. "I saw a few gobs off a ship once, back when my family lived at the far seaport of Land's End. Makes no difference to a goblin if a beast can talk or not. Into the stewpot they go. And not just talking beasts. Did you happen to see early this morning, when Big Jurgen and Tiny Jurgen were both cut down in the fields? None of us quite knew what was occurring yet and they just naturally resisted — you know how those two can get. Well, you can bet your last mark that they've also been stripped of their meat by now. Nothing but a few bones and red stain left of those two, because gobs take everything — the meat and guts both. Gobs will eat anything that was once alive. Even their own fallen comrades."

"Bonny Lumpen!" Peter cried from across the room. His eyes were filling with tears building enough weight to go streaming down his face.

"Your old mule's dead now, boy," Manfred said. "Sliced and hanging in the gob cook's larder, ripening for mess."

"Manfred Jakob Walder, you must stop that kind of talk this instant!" Mrs. Peep was suddenly on her feet and as red-faced as anyone had ever seen her before. "Can't you see you're scaring us all over again? Think of the children!"

Manfred had his mouth open, about to say something else, but he shut it with a loud wet smack of his lips and sat down abruptly, embarrassed and beginning to turn as red as Mrs. Peep.

"Everyone should be quiet now, until Father and the squire arrive," Max called out. It was very good advice, and might have been heeded, if Max had been older than his mere fourteen years, hadn't been so trembling of voice, or had even a portion of the authoritative qualities he desperately imagined in himself.

"You've been bleating that same tune for three or more hours, boy," another of the field hands said. His name was Wilhelm and he was a big fellow with a pudgy belly, but arms thick with real muscle. He had a long ragged scar under one eye. "Put a stopper in it, before I do a little slicing of my own." In one hand Wilhelm held up an open jar of pickled vegetables he'd been passing around among a few of the men. Certainly he didn't plan to slice anyone with that, did he? But then Max noticed Wilhelm's other hand, where he'd drawn his personal dining knife from his belt and held it down near his leg — not precisely hiding it, but not brandishing it either, the way some do who're hoping to avoid any actual knife-play by making an opponent back down. Those who're serious about their deadly intentions don't need to make a big show of it. The knife's blade was only five or six inches long, but in Max's eyes it looked as bright and deadly as the biggest sword.

Max was suddenly quite afraid, and it wasn't just the general fear he'd felt all day, when any of a hundred different unspecified dooms could have befallen him. This was a very particular sort of fear, in response to a specific and immediate threat, from a grown man right in front of him. All heroic fantasies vanished in an instant. Max wanted nothing so dearly as to run from the room, or worse, even more humiliating, into his mother's arms. And the shame of this immediate and fully potent fear hit him hard. The entire room could see him wilt like a flower. At that very moment his spirit was on the threshold of being crushed for all time.

And then, when it seemed there could be no greater humiliation than this, it suddenly increased tenfold.

"You leave my brother alone!" Peter cried. He barged forward into the middle of the room and faced the large, scary Wilhelm as if he were ready to fight him on the spot. It was a comical sight, this small boy standing up to such a big man. First Wilhelm gaped at the surprising scene, and then he laughed a great roaring laugh, and soon nearly everyone in the room joined in.

"You're quite the fierce young wolf!" Wilhelm said, a broad grin splitting his scarred face. "A warrior among men. Here, son, have a true man's treat. See if you have a taste for tough vittles." He held out the open jar to Peter, who just stood, quivering, but otherwise not doing anything in response.

"Go on. Try one, boy." The jar stayed there, suspended in front of Peter, looking less to Max like a peace offering and more like some sort of mysteriously renewed threat every second. "It'll grow you some hair down there." Even Max understood that this was now a challenge his little brother must meet. Peter hesitated and then started to reach for the jar, ready to pull his hand back at an instant.

"Hurry up, little warrior. Pick something. It won't bite. Well, it will, but not until you bite first, which seems only fair now, doesn't it?" More laughter, but quieter now, pensive as all waited to see what the little boy would do.

All at once, he seemed to screw up his courage. Peter picked a pickled pepper. He bit it hard and fast, and suddenly his eyes mushroomed with new tears and his nose blossomed bright red. His face scrunched into a mask of anxiety and regret. And then he began coughing and sputtering. Tears flowed freely and snot ran down his lip. Wilhelm and his mates exploded with renewed laughter.

"And look at that!" Wilhelm shouted, "He didn't even spit it out!" Which was true. Peter grimly chewed the pepper and swallowed it, his face a study in agony all the while. "You're a better man than I am, young hero! Even I don't eat the little red ones. We call them dragon's warts for good reason. They keep too much of their fire. I just eat around those." Wilhelm gave weeping, coughing Peter a huge slap on his back — the kind that said, "You're our friend now and equal to any of us," and that broke the last remnants of the spell of danger in the room.

Max had stood to one side during this tableau, quite forgotten by all in the chamber, which was a blessing, considering what might have happened before his little brother bravely intervened. But if so, it was a miserable blessing indeed. Once again Peter was the hero and Max was nothing at all.

But one thing saved him. Before he could sink into that final abyss of despair, the one so deep that no man could ever fully escape, Max noticed something that made him angry — very angry indeed. He'd missed it at first, because as usual, Peter was dressed in a shirt and breeches of simple brown homespun, whose color almost exactly matched the shade of the thing hanging across his back. It was a narrow tube of hard leather, just over a foot long, and attached to a strap at both ends, which was looped crosswise over Peter's back, over one shoulder and under the other. Once he actually saw the thing, Max recognized it instantly.

Peter was carrying Frost!

"Give that here!" Max shouted, startling all into stunned silence. Peter faced him, as did everyone else in the room.

"Max?" Peter said, an authentically worried expression on his tear-stained face, his eyes still watering from the harsh pepper. "What's the matter?"

"You're carrying Father's flute. That's not right. If Father doesn't have it, then I should be the one to hold it for him. You can't keep it safe. I'm the oldest, and he put me in charge." Max's face was twisted with anger, as if Peter had done something personally to hurt him. He held out one hand. "So give it to me."

"No, Max, you don't understand. It isn't Father's flute anymore. Last night he gave Frost to me."

"Liar!" Max screamed.

"He did," Peter said. "I know you wanted it, and I always thought you'd be the one to get it, but Father decided otherwise."

"He wouldn't do that! I'm the oldest! I'm the one who gets Frost and not you! You're just a big fat liar and a thief!"

"But, Max..."

"You are! You've always been a thief and you always will be! You steal everything from me and take everything that should be mine! But you won't get away with it this time! Give Frost back to me!"

Max threw himself at Peter and hit him, first once and then again. Peter staggered back, shocked into immobility. Like all brothers, Peter and Max had had their squabbles, but it had never before turned violent. Max had never hit Peter in the past, and he could hardly believe he was doing it now. Some detached part of Max realized he was out of control, but he couldn't help it. His face was a contorted mask of rage and there was madness in his eyes. He lunged at Peter wildly, hitting, scratching and clawing at him, screaming "Give it back" all the while. Peter fell to the floor, curling up and covering his face with his arms. Max dropped on top of him, continuing to claw and scratch and now also biting. He bit Peter in the fleshy part of one arm, and when he moved it out of danger, Max tried to bite Peter's newly exposed face and neck. By now Max's screams had degenerated into an incoherent wailing of pure agony.

And then, all at once, Max felt himself levitating into the air, still flailing madly, but no longer able to reach Peter. Big Wilhelm had lifted Max off his brother. Wilhelm held Max suspended in one huge hand, preventing him from doing anything but striking and clawing at the empty air and wail his frustration. Mother Piper was also standing there, looking angry and hurt.

"What are you doing, you daft child?" Mother said. "Are you insane that you'd start a fight in the middle of an invasion, where any sort of trouble is liable to inspire goblin monsters to come in here to chop us dead?"

Max only answered her with continued wailing.

"He's not a rational creature no more," Wilhelm said. And then he shook Max vigorously, still up in the air, trying to shake all of the fight and struggle out of him. "I think his mind's broken. I've seen it happen to others like this, back in my army days. They just get too afraid and something snaps inside them." Max continued to struggle in Wilhelm's arms, but weaker than before. Wilhelm shook him again, as a terrier will shake a rat caught in its mouth, to snap its neck, or at least shake the fight out of it.

"That's enough, I think," Mother said. "Please set my son down." Max no longer looked mad, just stunned and confused.

"I don't know, Ma'am. He might still have some wildness in him."

"Do as she says, Wilhelm," Mrs. Peep said. Sometime during the ugly spectacle, she'd also stepped up to the front ranks of the ring of spectators surrounding Max, Peter and Wilhelm. The other daughters were there beside her, dumbstruck by the scene, except Bo who knelt by Peter, still lying on the floor.

"Are you hurt, Peter?" Bo said. And she looked genuinely concerned.

With a grunt of disgust, Wilhelm tossed Max away from him, which wasn't quite what Mrs. Peep ordered, but which was more compliance than he desired to give. Without quite getting up off the floor, Max scuttled over to sit against one wall, where he curled in on himself, still not quite sure what had happened — how he'd let himself lose control as he had. He sat and brooded and wondered at the profound injustice of this incident. Peter had clearly caused it, but Max would surely be the one who was blamed.

"My intention," Mr. Peep said, in a booming voice, "and I believe my instructions bore this out, was that you would all assemble in this hall and wait quietly, giving our new visitors no provocation to do further harm. And now here we find you whining and squabbling like schoolboys during recess?" Radulf Peep had arrived sometime while everyone's attention was diverted by the fight. Johannes Piper was with him, looking as disappointed as the squire.

"Peter stole Frost," Max said, from over against the wall. He sat with his knees up and his arms across them, so that only his eyes and his tangled mop of hair peeked out from within his wall of protection. He sulked and steeped in the certainty of his unwarranted suffering. The entire world conspired in these terrible betrayals against Max.

"We'll talk of that later," Johannes said. "For now we've more urgent worries to attend to. Everyone here should listen to the squire."

And they did. Much of the stress and concern that had filled the room just moments before, and which had manifested itself into fights and bullying japes and angry snapping at each other, faded because here was someone who'd always commanded their respect and who could possibly provide answers, where only terrible fears occupied their minds. Bo Peep sat in the middle of the floor, comforting Peter, petting him in fact as though he were one of her lost lambs.

"It seems we've fallen under the dominion of a great and brutal empire," Radulf Peep said. "But I for one don't enjoy the prospect of spending the rest of my life in bondage to a foreign dictator. Do you?" There were a few mumbles of agreement here and there, but most in the room seemed to realize it was a rhetorical question.

"Most of the army has moved on, marching towards Winsen Town," Peep continued, "And I believe the immediate danger has moved on with them. This humble estate was not the main target of their intentions today. But a few have been left behind, no doubt to insure that we adapt quickly and meekly to our new lives.

"But almost due west of us, as the crow flies, is the River Weser and on that river is Hamelin Town, which is walled like a great fortress and garrisoned with many companies of the king's good men. We can bet that mighty Hamelin Town hasn't fallen to these scoundrels, who seem content to march along these lesser roads and take smaller, unfortified towns like Winsen.

"I don't know what you plan to do, but Johannes Piper and I have decided to take our families out of here tonight, when our new guards are asleep and make our way to Hamelin."

"How?" Someone said. "The roads will certainly be watched."

"We won't be taking the roads. We're going to cut across country."

"Enter the Black Forest at night?" another field hand said. "That's madness."

"Yes, it's a foolish act. Only the mad or truly desperate would venture into the greater haunted depths of the wood, far off the safe paths that we've managed to carve out and tame over the generations, with our patrols of armed men and spells of warding. But who's more desperate than we, who have a choice between the woods tonight, or more of this army tomorrow?

"Would you like to know how we're going to do it?" There were immediate nods and grunts of assent. "Arianne, watch that door," Peep said to one of his daughters while pointing to one of the sets of doors leading out of the room. "And Dorthe, you watch the other one. Just crack them open enough to peer out and make sure no soldiers are lurking within earshot."

And then Squire Peep spoke for a long time, and slowly a bold plan took shape, and it began to dawn on Max that their daring scheme would afford him many opportunities to set a few things aright.

Chapter Five
FABLETOWN

*In which Peter has a visit
with a beast and a witch,
but doesn't stay for tea.*

IN PAST YEARS, ONCE EVERY YEAR, PETER WOULD travel down to the city to play in the Remembrance Day orchestra. Remembrance Day was Fabletown's biggest holiday of the year, bigger than Christmas and New Year's combined — which actually isn't all that important to Fables, since the mundy world's new year didn't match up with any of the calendars they'd used in the hundred-plus worlds they'd come from. Remembrance Day was the one time of year when all of the refugee Fables, the world over, paused to lift a cup to the lands and the kingdoms and the homes they'd left behind, and to renew their promise to win them back someday. The main gala in Fabletown was a formal affair, at which there was much drinking and dancing, and for which Peter always helped provide the music. Other than that, he'd shown scant interest in either New York or Fabletown.

Now Peter was here on other business than the desire to entertain celebrants. He sat in the Woodland Building's security office, the tiny one-desk room in which Sheriff Beast worked to uphold Fabletown law and keep the peace. It was a tidy office, and entirely utilitarian, filled mostly by the one old gray metal desk that was just big enough to hold a phone and a computer, and still leave a little room for work. Other than that, there were a couple of filing cabinets, one of which had a coffee maker set on top of it, two client chairs and not much else. It smelled of stale cigarettes, though there were no ashtrays in sight, or any other indication that its usual occupant smoked. Peter sat alone in the office, waiting for Beast to arrive for their scheduled appointment. Frost sat in his lap, locked inside its carrying case.

"I'm sorry I'm late," Beast said, opening the door and stepping halfway into the room, "but I asked Frau Totenkinder to join us this afternoon. She's coming now." He was tall and heavily built, the sort of fellow who would have been called beefy in another day. And he was leading-man handsome in the same way that most Fable women tend to be "the fairest in all the land," which loses much of its cachet when you have hundreds of such beauties crowded into such a small neighborhood. "I've gotten used to taking The Witch's counsel in these sorts of matters," Beast added.

There are plenty of witches living in Fabletown of course, most of whom reside on the Woodland's thirteenth floor, which is reserved for those of a practitioner's nature. But when one speaks of The Witch, there's only one possible Fable he could mean — Frau Totenkinder, the Black Forest Witch. Beast stood half in and half out of his office, holding the door open, waiting to usher The Witch inside. Peter heard her before he saw her, from the dim tap-tapping of her cane as she approached down the hall, moving at little-old-lady speed. When she finally appeared in the doorway, Peter got up from his seat to move one chair over, so that she wouldn't have to maneuver around him in the confined space.

When he'd originally sat in the first client chair it was a spitting image of the second — a simple wooden chair with a slat-supported back piece that curved around into both armrests. But now, as he rose from his seat, it had somehow transformed itself into a sturdy old high-backed rocking chair. Peter was stiffly formal as he shifted one seat over, and he cast a suspicious glance at the old woman who entered the room.

"Thank you for moving for me, young man," Frau Totenkinder said, with a sly half smile. She looked small and frail, but Peter knew she wasn't, even though this was the first time to his knowledge that they'd actually met. All Fables, whether at the Farm or here in Fabletown, have access to the Woodland's vast library — millions of old books spirited out of the Homelands. Peter had taken full advantage of that access over the centuries, always having one bundle of books after another sent up to the

Farm on one of the supply trucks, which ran almost daily between the Farm and the city. Peter and Bo, alone out in their remote cottage, were avid readers, and Frau Totenkinder, although never mentioned by name, had appeared prominently in many of the Fable histories they'd read.

Totenkinder had gray hair and wore a print dress — lavender Pale Laurels on a tan field. She carried a wicker knitting basket that contained assorted yarns and needles. "I always prefer my comfy rocker," she said.

Peter remained standing, still formal and on guard, until Totenkinder had fully seated herself into her rocker. Then he sat down in the second client chair, which was now, one supposed, the only one. He placed the flute case back into his lap.

"You really aren't supposed to have that," Beast said, nodding towards the plastic and metal case as he moved around to take his own seat behind his desk.

"Excuse me?" Peter said.

"The flute. What is it you call it? Frost? It's magical, right?" Beast took his seat, which squeaked loudly as he leaned back in it. "By the terms of the Fabletown Compact, all magical things spirited out of the Homelands were supposed to be turned over to us, so we can safely store them down here in the business office, where they can be held in trust for the benefit of the entire community. Technically I should confiscate it."

"But Frost doesn't belong to Fabletown. It belongs to me."

Totenkinder didn't join in the conversation, or seem to take any particular note of it. She simply set her basket in her lap and took up her knitting, gently rocking back and forth in her chair, and humming a quiet, tuneless tune to herself.

"Well, see, that's the problem, isn't it?" Beast said. "If every individual Fable had the same attitude — if they were allowed to keep all of the enchanted things they brought with them to the mundy world, the things would be scattered all over the place, unprotected and uncatalogued. How long then would it be before a mundy got hold of something he shouldn't? There goes the big secret. Our magical nature would be exposed to the world at large. Or worse yet, it would be easier for one of the Adversary's agents to steal something valuable and powerful that he could use against us, rather than we use against him."

"Does he have many agents here in the mundy world?" Peter said. There'd been a few incidents in the recent past, involving the incursion of the Adversary's forces into Fabletown. Once even a full-scale battle between Fabletown and a company of the Empire's elite troops. But Peter hadn't taken part in it, and had assumed, like many others, that the so-called Battle of Fabletown had decisively taken care of any Empire interlopers.

"Officially, I'm not at liberty to say," Beast said. "But strictly between you, me, and the lamppost, what do you think? We'd be foolish not to assume the Empire has clandestine assets in this world, keeping an eye on us, just as we'd be foolish not to have our agents in place, keeping an eye on them."

"Which we do, I suppose?" Peter said. "Strictly between you, me, and the lamppost?"

"No comment." Beast said. "But to get back to the matter of

your flute, in addition to keeping bad things away from the mundys, storing everything in the business office insures that magic items of military significance don't fall into enemy hands."

"I think the argument could be made," Peter said, "that putting everything into one place is exactly the kind of policy that made us vulnerable to enemy attack. Wasn't the fact that we had all our eggs in one basket the very reason the Empire thought they could capture them in a single direct attack? Did I misread the reports on the Battle of Fabletown — the ones for public consumption anyway? They described how close the Emperor's forces came to succeeding. Were they wrong?"

"Perhaps that argument could be made," Beast said, carefully, "but I didn't write the laws. I do, however, have an obligation to enforce them." Beast's calm exterior and quiet eyes betrayed no hint of the dangerous creature that lurked within, and which could be summoned at need.

"That's all beside the point, anyway," Peter said. "Frost is barely magical anymore and has no military value. Its power was spent long ago. Neither the Adversary, nor his tame warlocks, nor any mundy could make use of it, even if they recognized it as anything but mundane and normal. But letting it out of my control could cause some harm to me, and therefore one could argue to the rest of Fabletown by extension. In addition to its long depleted positive benefits, Frost has a nasty side. If I give it away, or allow it to fall into the hands of anyone not of my blood, then I'm cursed, along with all of my descendants, until the end of time. So you can see how I'm reluctant to turn it over, despite the letter of the law."

"Let the boy keep his flute," Totenkinder said, surprising Peter with her interruption. She hadn't seemed to be paying any attention to the conversation before now. "It's of no value to us and can only harm him if we insist on taking it. I can sense that there is indeed a curse on the thing. He wasn't lying about that."

"Fine," Beast said. "I'll defer to Frau Totenkinder for now, but I promise you, Peter, we'll take this matter up again when you return."

"So you're letting me go after Max?"

"Bigby made a compelling argument, backed up by his assurance that he wouldn't be able to leave for at least a week. I gather that's something the two of you cooked up?"

"It doesn't matter. Bigby couldn't stop Max anyway."

"And you can?"

"I don't know. I hope so."

"What's your plan?"

"That's a private matter."

"Not between us," Beast said. "If you want me to authorize this stunt, or at least not prevent it, I have to know what your strategy is."

"Perhaps, but you'll have to content yourself with the understanding that I do have a strategy and leave it at that. Max has a way of finding out about things, which may be due to some magical artifice or may mean he's got his spies in Fabletown, just as you suspect the Empire has. Whatever the case, I didn't tell anyone my plans, not even my wife, and I don't intend to. This time, if Max learns of it, it will only be because he can read my mind, in which case my plan is doomed already."

Beast sat silent for a moment and then pulled open his middle desk drawer. He brought out two fat envelopes and placed them on the desk top, midway between Peter and himself.

"These are your travel documents," Beast said, "money and false ID's. We call them Legends in the spook parlance. One set is for outbound travel and the other is for your return, assuming that some of the things you might have to do while away will make it difficult to travel under the same name twice. Considering the short notice, we didn't have time to construct full, unbreakable Legends for you, but these should pass muster. Buy your tickets and everything else with cash, and don't do it anywhere near Fabletown. Do you know where you'll be looking for him yet?"

"I have an idea or two."

"Then you can be on your way, while we hope that Bigby doesn't have to follow you in a week's time."

Peter didn't stand up immediately, though it was clear the sheriff had dismissed him.

"The young man doesn't want to leave just yet," Totenkinder interrupted again, not even bothering to look up from her knitting. "He wants to have a private talk with me, but he's too polite to ask you to step out of your own office."

Peter had no idea how she knew any of that, but it was true.

"Perhaps you can find a pot of tea?" she said to Beast. "I'm certain our chat won't take long."

With a glower he attempted, but failed, to disguise, Beast stood up from behind his desk and left the office, quietly closing the door behind him. After living for centuries having to keep his beastly persona under rigid control, he'd learned long ago not to be a door-slamming sort of fellow.

"Now, what would you like to ask me, Peter?" Totenkinder said, once Beast had left. She looked up from her work long enough to face him this time.

"You're her, aren't you? You're The Witch?"

"That's what they often call me when they think I can't overhear."

"Yes, but that's not — what I mean to say is, you're the specific witch, the one who lived in the Black Forest back when my brother and I were lost there so long ago. You were the one who armed Max. You gave him the other magic flute — the more powerful one — which caused all of our problems. I've read all the books available and studied the matter extensively, for as long as I've been a member of the community, and I'm certain I've narrowed down the possibilities to one candidate. You."

"Straight to the point, aren't you, Peter? I'm not used to being spoken to with such unsoftened candor." She paused for a time and they looked at each other. His expression showed expectation, worry and under that a contained anger. Hers revealed nothing. Then she said, "Yes, I'm that same woman, but those were pre-amnesty deeds, and you're not supposed to speak of them."

"How could I not? You nearly destroyed us with what you did, not just me and my family, but all of Fabletown back during the Great War. Bigby only killed indiscriminately, but you — how could you do such a thing?"

"If you imagine you deserve an answer, strictly by virtue of the way in which you've suffered, then you're mistaken. I've never been answerable to anyone in my long life, and it will ever be so. Be careful, young man, whose toes you tread on."

"However," she continued, "though I judge myself obliged to say nothing, I am at rare times willing to explain a thing or two to those who come to me showing proper humility and deference, and who ask their questions politely. Why don't we assume, just this once, and only for the sake of expedience, that you conducted yourself in just that manner, hmm? That will save a bit of time, won't it?"

She returned to her knitting for a few moments, gathering her thoughts. And then she said, "Like so many of us, I wasn't always the same woman I am now. Once I too was ruled by my passions, and I made mistakes — some that I've lived to regret. In your brother's case I made two mistakes. I misjudged the level of depravity to which he'd sunk, and I underestimated the powers of the object I gave him. I used him to work a revenge against some people who'd done me wrong, giving him the magic flute as his weapon with which to accomplish it. But the flute wasn't something I created. It came into my possession, following several misadventures involving its previous owners. Many of the more powerful things find their way to me over time. It's one of the byproducts of the way in which I work my craft. I hadn't sufficiently studied Max's flute before I turned it over to him, thinking I had the power to call it back to me at will. Who could know how strong his will had become by then?"

"Then what do we do?" Peter asked. How do I beat it — its power?"

"I don't imagine you can. I tried once and I couldn't. Max and his flute have grown strong together over the ages, the power of one intertwining with the other, until they've become so much more than the sum of their parts. He's woven such shields and wardings of protection around himself that nothing mundane can harm him and, so far as I've tried, nothing much magical either. But I fear that he can play a spell now that will make anyone dance to his tune."

"That's as I thought," Peter said.

"And yet you still have a plan to win against him?"

"No, I have a plan to finally let myself be defeated by him, once and for all. I've had my fill of hiding from him. So, instead I plan to embrace his terrible magic and let it do its will with me. Perhaps, after all that's been done, I still owe him that much."

Peter left before the tea arrived.

Chapter Six

THE BLACK FOREST

In which the families escape from the army and a terrible thing happens in the woods.

THE WOODS WERE HAUNTED WITH EVERY SORT of malign creature. It was an evil place fit only for ghosts, bogeys and fell spirits. Of this Max was becoming more certain by the minute.

A few hours after nightfall on the previous evening, the Pipers, the Peeps and all of their servants and hired hands slipped into the woods. Not one of them elected to stay behind and take a chance with the invaders. They'd divided into three smaller groups in order to better negotiate the woods which were too thick and tangled to permit the passage of a larger company. The Pipers joined with the Peep family to form one group. The household staff formed another, and the field hands and other outside workers formed the third. Each person carried a similar bundle containing only the essentials to survive the forest: some food, salvaged from the estate's larders, warm clothes or a blanket to endure the cold of night, a weapon if they had one, and a small bag of shiny gold marks, divided equally from Squire Peep's entire cache of ready money, which had been hidden well enough that the invaders never discovered it. Peep had decided that each individual should carry his own purse, so that even if they became separated, everyone who survived the forest to eventually win through to Hamelin had an equal chance not to have to live from there on as a penniless beggar.

Throughout the remainder of the previous day, after Peep had outlined his plan, household servants plied the few soldiers left behind with wine and beer and strong spirits, which they still had in plenty, since the officers loudly refused to allow any of it to be confiscated with the other goods. It seemed they wouldn't risk an army of drunken soldiers when marching on a town to take it by force of arms.

Even after the guards had consumed their fill, grateful to be refreshed against the hot day, the house maids urged more on them, saying, "This is the season when dire infirmities are staved off only by stiff drink and plenty of it." Knowing no better in a strange land, the soldiers drank more and then more again. True to their scheme, all of the guards fell asleep even as the night fell, and the escape was under way.

The first group had set off with Squire Peep in the lead. They'd moved slowly, more slowly than the other two groups, who quickly outdistanced them to become lost from sight, because the woods were thick, and Mr. Peep was fat and old and couldn't do better. Plus the entire gaggle of Peep daughters seemed intent on tripping and stumbling or becoming entangled in one thorny stand of undergrowth after another. They cried and complained so often that Max nearly forgot how pretty they were, even in their rough, durable work clothes, and how, in the previous afternoon, three or four of them had already played a part in his private imaginings of how this escape might turn out. In each case he'd bravely rescued one of them from some fierce creature of the deep woods, killing the beast, or driving it off with his sword. Then the girl in question had shown her gratitude, flinging herself into his arms and madly covering him with unending kisses, as well as rewarding him in other ways that Max couldn't quite conjure in his mind, but knew were among the secret doings of grown men and women.

Max had his sword now, a real one this time, and not just some flimsy object mounted for display. Mr. Peep had given it to him on the very edge of the woods, just before they ventured inside. "You're one of the three men in this group," Peep whispered to him, "so we'll need you armed, like your father and me."

I'm one of the men, Max thought. That's what fat old Mr. Peep called me and it was true. He'd experienced a heady sense of elation then, which was only improved when he saw that they hadn't armed Peter in a similar fashion. I'm one of the men now and Peter isn't. Max belted the sheathed blade around his hips and decided — no, it was more of a solemn vow than a simple decision — that his true life had only begun with their entrance into the woods.

He hadn't had an opportunity at the time to take the blade out and examine it. The woods were too dark and thick. And since then his joy at having it was dimmed when the sword in its sheath seemed determined to catch on every high root or low branch. For what must have been many miles, the sword, like the heavy pack on his back, became nothing more than another burden to be wrestled through the forest. The group walked single file, and Max had been assigned to guard its rear. "Squire Peep and I will watch for dangers ahead," his father had said, "and you must look for those that might try to sneak up on us from behind. I hope you realize what a great trust we've placed in you, son." Max did. He knew his father trusted him enough to risk his life guarding a line of screeching, squabbling girls, but not enough to reward him with Frost, which was his birthright.

So Max walked in the rear, making his plans and biding his time, his resentment growing toward every one of those in front of him, who could have warned him about this root or that whipping branch, or any other of an endless number of invisible obstacles in his path. But they didn't and so he entered every further misdeed into his mind's ledger, against that time when all accounts would be balanced.

They'd walked throughout the night, and then, after too short a rest, throughout the day that followed. Day was almost as dark as night under the wood's canopy. It was ever and always a shadowed, haunted place. Max had heard every manner of hoot and caw and grunt of beasts, and once even a growl of something not too distant, which had so frightened him that he froze in place for so long that he nearly lost the rest of the group ahead of him. He only found himself able to move again when he heard the thing pad off, away from him, grunting quietly with every heavy step.

AND NOW, AT THE COMMENCEMENT of the second evening, they stopped to make a real camp, to sleep for the entire night, before setting off again with the new day. They lit a fire and built it up into a big one, to keep them warm and the beasts away, unconcerned that there'd be soldiers to spot it — not this far into the woods. "I think we're distant enough to be safe from pursuit," Mr. Peep said. "No army is likely to enter the terrifying untouched parts of the Black Forest, simply to chase a few scattered runaways. We didn't harm any of their men before we fled, and as far as they know, we didn't make off with any great treasure. I think they'll be content to let the forest have us."

Mr. Peep had also said some confusing arcane things about finding their way by examining which side of the trees had moss growing on them. This made no sense to Max but seemed to please the others that Peep knew his business. "And I can only do that by daylight," Mr. Peep said, "so we'll have to stop at night from now on. Otherwise we'd have no way of reconfirming which way is west and might become forever lost in these great woods. Remember, west to the river and then upstream to Hamelin Town. That's our plan."

While Mother and Mrs. Peep worked to fashion their dinner out of the supplies they carried, and the daughters chattered and complained and pulled off their boots to examine their poor feet, Max sat apart on a moss-crowned rock and thought his thoughts, which alternated between despair and wary satisfaction. At that moment he went over in his mind every frightening tale he'd ever heard of what lurked in the depths of the Black Forest. There were ghosts out here, spirits of the dishonored dead, doomed to spend eternity in this evil place, feasting on the souls of those who wander into it. And there were witches, who conjured evil spells and ate children as their only diet. And there were giants and ogres and every other sort of monster. What was that thing that had come so close to me in the night? Max asked himself. He could still hear every note of its rumbling growl, a noise that could only be made by something big and deadly. It was a foolhardy decision to enter this place, and his father should never have allowed it. Then again, Father's judgment had also been demonstrably faulty in other ways of late. How could he give Frost to Peter and not to him?

And then Max considered the other hand. I was reborn here in these woods, which couldn't have happened elsewhere. Before, I was only Max Piper, a simple flute player in a family of vagabond minstrels. Now I'm Max the Swordsman, who saved Arianne and Brigitte and young Elfride, with her pretty blue eyes, from any number of dangers so far, simply by guarding the rear of our line against them. I stood alone and faced down the growling thing, until the others could get away, which is how he resolved to remember the fearful incident from now on.

So he looked at the bright side, even as he looked at the bright blade of the sword lying across his lap, now that he was finally able to study it. It was thin and sharp and just the right size, almost as if it had been made for him personally. Max had never held a real sword before, but like any child of the age, he'd practiced often with sticks. He knew that one chopped with its edge and thrust with its tip. That was enough for the basics, and everything else was just a matter of practice and refinement. He would practice and grow ever more sure and deft with his blade, until every villain feared Max the Swordsman and every good man respected him. A sword this grand needs a name, Max thought, and it was then that he looked up across the fire and knew what his blade must be called.

On the other side of Max, by the light of the crackling fire, Father was showing Peter some of the intricacies of his new flute. Frost was the only item not directly essential to survival that Father or Mr. Peep would allow anyone to take with them, and then only because Father had whispered a few family secrets into Mr. Peep's ear, no doubt telling him that Peter could use the flute to make danger pass them by. Yes, Max knew that story, because many times in the past, when he was supposed to have been long asleep, Max had lain awake to hear Father and Mother murmur to each other in the night.

"In most ways, Frost is no different from any other flute," Father said. "But look here at its mouthpiece."

"It's so sharp," Peter said. "Why?"

"I'm not sure. Perhaps it needed to be carved just so in order to achieve the sweet and perfect notes that only Frost is capable of playing. Or perhaps ancient Jorg, being as great a warrior as he was a musician, thought that one should pay a price for the opportunity to play so wondrous an instrument. But whatever the reason, you have to be ever careful as you play, or Frost will cut you. See these tiny scars on the corners of my mouth?" Max had seen them many times before, just as Peter had. They were nearly invisible at all times and would be extra hard to see by flickering firelight. Nevertheless Peter leaned forward to intently study them, just as though he'd never noticed them before. Good little Peter, always quick to do anything Father asks.

"Yes," Peter said.

"Frost usually got me when I became too caught up in the music I was making to worry about my safety. Sometimes there's just no way to prevent it. You'll pay in blood for those magical moments when you're reaching for true greatness in your music, just as I have."

"Was it worth it, Father?"

"Every time."

Father continued, giving Peter his lesson, and good little Peter gave him rapt attention, as he always did. Max smiled to see Peter's bruised face, with one eye so wonderfully blackened that it had nearly swollen shut. I did that to you, Peter, Max thought, and that's just the start. And neither Father nor Peter took any notice of Max, or had the faintest clue that, just a few feet away from them, across the revealing flame, Max had just named his sword Frost Taker.

THE FIRE HAD BURNED LOW and all were asleep, except Max, who'd been woken an hour ago to replace Squire Peep as their guard. Max the Swordsman, brave wielder of fabled Frost Taker, was on duty. That's who he was now, but he'd also become something else — something stronger and more frightening than just another hero of legend.

He sat his watch and peered outwardly, to be sure, but he also observed the others as they slept under their blankets, cloaks or coats, huddled in a close circle around the fire. Mother and Father slept together, wrapped up in a shared blanket. Mother had suffered in the day and night before. He'd seen it in the weary sagging of her shoulders and in her eyes, which no longer shined with the delight she took in nearly every day of her life. Her world was gone. She lost it when they turned away from their caravan wagon, filled with drums and bells and her beloved wooden xylophone. The fact that she now carried in her purse more gold than she'd ever had in her life, more than the total worth of all that she'd left behind, and that Father, Max and Peter each had an amount to match, was of no comfort to her. That wagon was her home and it was gone forever. But she never complained, not once. Mother wasn't the type.

Mr. and Mrs. Peep also slept together. He was so large, and she was plump enough in her own right, that they could barely get their arms around each other, but somehow they managed it.

The Peep daughters slept in one great extended bundle. Some covers had been kicked off in the night, lying as they were so near the warmth of the fire. Max could see the fascinating curve of one girl's body, or the flutter of an eyelid, or the delicate quiver of another girl's perfectly formed and achingly lovely lip as she breathed in and out. Many times he reached out almost touching one of them, before drawing back his hand. Not now, he thought. I'll wait for the right time, which will be soon enough.

And here was Peter, the only one sleeping alone under his coat. Poor little Peter, who was out in the woods on a great adventure with his dear little sweetheart Bo, but unable to enjoy it. Even now he can't touch her, Max thought, like I know he wants to. It wouldn't be proper, and Peter is nothing if not always proper and good. But I could touch the little piggy girl right now if I wished. But I don't wish because she's not among the ones I want. Bratty little Bo was sleeping just a few feet away from Peter, so enticingly close, on the outside edge of the tangle of Peep daughters. How Peter will wail and cry when he sees what happens to her.

Out in the darkness the beasts were calling their calls and making every sort of noise. While here by the light Max wasn't as afraid of them as he had been just hours before, because he was now a thing transformed. He'd pondered imponderable thoughts, and come to dark decisions, as he grew more and more certain that the only way to survive in such a place as this was to become one of them. Just like the creatures beyond the light, Max was now a fell beast of these woods. And none of these foolish sleeping people knew what a terrible danger sat so quietly among them, regarding them without compassion or mercy, with his cold, reptile eyes.

WHEN ANOTHER HOUR had passed, Max gently shook his father awake. "It's your time to stand guard," Max whispered close into his ear. Slowly his father came awake, carefully extricating himself from his makeshift bed, so that he didn't wake Mother. He stood up, found his boots and his sword belt, and put them on. Then he led Max a small distance away from the others, so that their talk wouldn't disturb them.

"Can you keep watching for another few minutes, son, while I step into the woods a ways and make my water?" Father said. "And then, when I return, if you're not in too much of a hurry to get back to sleep right away, I'd like to have a private talk with you about some of the decisions I've made lately."

"You mean about giving Frost to Peter," Max said.

"Yes. That and other things."

"Of course, Father. I'll stay up as long as you like."

"Thank you. I won't be long." And with that Father turned and stepped gingerly into the darkness, pausing once at the very edge of the firelight to turn and say, "I'm proud of the way you acted today. I'm proud to see my first son grow into so steadfast and reliable a man."

Max the Great Swordsman, the hero of many a legend, would've been elated to hear those words from his father, as would simple Max Piper, the fourteen-year-old boy. But they were both absent just now. It was Max the Beast of the Woods who heard and cared not at all. He waited for a few seconds, listening to the faint sounds of his father walking off into the forest. Then he followed, stooping down once before he left the circle of firelight to pick up the biggest stone he could carry in one hand.

He stalked through the night, and being who he now was, he made little sound and stumbled not at all. He crept deftly and silently around tree and root, and ducked under intervening branches. Max found his father with his back to him, splashing his night water against the base of a tree. Max approached and his father turned, alerted by a small sound, or maybe just the presence of another creature so close to him.

"You should be back with the others, son. You're still on guard until I'm done."

Max raised the stone and struck down hard on his father's skull.

Father wobbled in place, looking at Max with an odd expression, which wasn't only due to the now distorted shape of his head — sunken and indistinct on one side. Yes, there was confusion in his expression, and maybe some pain as well — it was hard to tell for certain in the dark. But mostly Max thought he saw a look of deep regret in his father's eyes.

"Max?" Father said.

His hands lost their ability to grip the trousers he'd unlaced to make his water, so the trousers collapsed down around his ankles. The sword he'd never even tried to unsheathe clattered loudly against some unseen rock or root on the ground.

The stone in Max's hand was wet now.

He struck again, and his father fell like a dropped bag of onions.

Something warm had splashed Max's face. His father, lying crumpled at his feet reached out weakly with one trembling hand, trying to touch Max, but then it fell unmoving by his side. Max knelt next to his father and hit him again and again with the slippery stone. He continued doing it for a long time, and when he'd finished, and stood up again, his father was no longer there. No discernible man at all existed in the grim pile of ruined meat and spilled wetness at his feet.

Max dropped the stone and drew Frost Taker from its sheath, intending to plunge it a few times into the mess below. But then he thought, no, I'll wait to let Frost Taker drink for the first time from the child thief who stole my inheritance. So he turned, with the blade still in his hand, and walked back towards the firelight, which was partially obscured by the trees of the great and terrible Black Forest – his home.

Chapter Seven

PETER AND THE WOLF

In which three can quickly be reduced to two, and two can be reduced to one all alone.

PETER SLEPT, AND AS HE DID HE DREAMED. He dreamed of the woods at first, and all of the scary things which lurked within them. The forest noises, which never stopped through the night, fed into his dream, conjuring up all manner of fearsome creatures to beset him. But later in the night he dreamed that Max had spoken to him – he couldn't be sure where, because one moment they were in the Peeps' great hall, and the next moment they were riding on top of their own lost caravan wagon, swaying hypnotically with the contours of the road, as dear old Bonny Lumpen pulled them along.

"Peter?" Max said in the dream. "I'm sorry I hit you and I don't want to be mad at you any longer, even though you got my flute. You're my little brother and I love you. I'll never let anyone else harm you and I'll always look out for you, from now on."

Then Peter handed the flute over to Max and said, "No, I'm not going to keep Frost. It's yours by birthright. It was just a mistake and I talked to Father and he said I could give it to you now."

The two brothers embraced and were friends again. They talked about innocent boyhood things from that point on, about swimming holes and big green frogs and good sticks for swords, but the exact details of their conversation were a little hard to make out, because Bonny Lumpen kept interrupting from the front of the wagon, saying, "Am I dead yet? Is it time for me to be dead?"

And then there was terrible screaming.

But the screaming wasn't only in Peter's dream. It was still there when he woke up. In fact it was worse than ever. "The soldiers found us! Run away! They're here!" This is what Peter heard as he struggled to wake up and make sense of the world. It was still nighttime, but the fire had burned much lower since he fell asleep. He had trouble seeing, so he wiped at his eyes — which caused the blackened one to smart — and then looked again, but it was still too dark to make out much. All the while the sounds of fear and panic went on and even grew. He wasn't sure who was doing the screaming, but the voice sounded familiar.

Peter sat up and looked around him. Mother was already on her knees, rising to her feet, but also clutching her empty blanket to her breast and looking about, as though she were trying to spot someone in particular. Two of the Peep daughters were trying to pull Mr. Peep to his feet as well. Both daughters were screaming too, or at least crying loudly enough that it added to the indecipherable cacophony. And then Peter saw Max, standing in the firelight. He was wearing his bright performance clothes, which is what he insisted on wearing for the escape when everyone else chose rugged and durable clothes that could withstand a long journey and many hardships. He recalled the terrific fuss Max had made two days ago, until finally Father had relented, so as not to risk attracting the soldiers' interest.

Max was still in his bright clothes, but now there was something wrong with them. They'd been stained with yet a new overlay of color — ropes and curls and looping tendrils of bright red. Not only that, but the new color was all over Max's face as well, in garish stripes, and matted into his already tangled hair.

Blood, Peter realized, with a shock that made him dizzy and unable to rise to his feet. He also realized that Max was doing most of the screaming.

"They found us!" Max shouted. "The soldiers! You promised they wouldn't follow us, but they did! They killed Father and almost got me! And now they're coming to get the rest of us!" Max had a horrible look in his eyes and he was holding his new sword, stabbing it here and there, in the air, at no one in particular.

"We need to run away!"

This time Peter bolted upright, no longer dizzy and now fully awake.

"Scatter, children!" Mr. Peep called, having finally lumbered to his feet. "Scatter into the forest!"

Peter moved quickly, as the full import of what was happening began to sink into his head. Max seemed able to fend for himself. Father would look after Mother. But wait, hadn't Max just said something about Father? Never mind. There'd be time to think it through later. For now he had to move. Everyone had to move. He already had his boots on — he'd slept in them — and most of his clothes. He reached down under his coat and picked up Frost in its carrying case, where he'd slept with it wrapped up in his arms. Then he looked to his left and saw that Bo was nearest. She was standing, tears and confusion in her eyes, holding onto her own boots, one in each hand.

Peter grabbed her under one arm and started pulling her away from the firelight, into the shadows of the woods. "Hold onto your shoes for now!" Peter said to her as he dragged her along. "We'll stop to put them on later!"

At first they simply stumbled along together in the dark, crashing into bushes and trees and falling often. Each time Peter recovered Frost with one hand and helped Bo back to her feet with the other. She was blubbering steadily, but not too loudly and, more important, did what he told her to — almost automatically, as if she weren't yet ready to face for herself the implications of what they were doing.

Peter's eyes slowly began to adjust to the darkness and he could start to make out dim shapes — more solid areas of blackness in the greater black all around them. Now at least he could avoid running into the tree trunks themselves. Turning to look back, they were already completely out of sight of the fire. The terrain underfoot was sloping down and Peter went with it, thinking it was better not to fight it or take any route that might slow them. He would let the descent pull them along faster than they could run without it.

The angle of the slope increased and the density of the trees gave way to rounded boulders, covered with slick, wet moss. Peter slipped on one of them and fell hard on his rear, pulling Bo down with him. They began sliding downwards, going faster and faster. He dared not release Bo's arm or he'd surely lose her in the darkness, so he held on tight, even though he could hear her smashing into rocks and other things as they fell. In little time they came up against a pocket of larger rocks that stopped their descent hard and fast.

Peter was in terrible pain. He'd banged his knee against something, and he thought there might be a cut above his already-injured eye. He was pretty sure blood was leaking down to pool in the folds of swollen flesh. He'd finally had to release Bo, as the last smashing stop jolted her out of his grip. But he could hear her right beside him. She'd obviously been hurt too.

Then in a panic he remembered Frost! He patted frantically on the ground around him with both hands, and soon enough came across the leather carrying case. Painfully he pushed himself off the ground, into a sitting position. The first thing he did was loop Frost's strap over his neck and under one arm, so that he couldn't lose it again. Then he felt around for Bo, but she was somewhere out of arm's reach.

"Bo?" he said. "How bad are you hurt?"

"I lost my shoe."

"What?" Relief flooded through him. If that was what had her most upset, she couldn't be too badly injured, could she?

"You told me to hold onto my shoes, but I lost one of them. I think it was maybe when we fell down the hill. And they're not shoes, they're boots, and you shouldn't call something one thing when it's another. You don't know everything, Peter Piper, so don't think you can tell me what to do."

Peter felt a flush of happiness. At least Bo was still Bo, he thought. If she could still scold him, then she was all right. And if she was all right then soon enough they both would be.

"Don't worry, Bo. Your missing boot will have landed somewhere down here with us. We'll feel around until we find it. But first try to pull your other boot on, so we don't lose that one while looking for the first."

"I'm already doing that. You don't need to tell me obvious things."

"I'm sorry," Peter said. "I can't see you yet. I can only hear you, and I know I should've heard you pulling your one boot on, but I'm not very smart and I don't know what that sounds like."

Peter sat quiet for a moment, listening to Bo beside him and listening to the greater darkness, trying to hear if there were any sounds of pursuit. He didn't hear any — at least none that he could identify — but he did hear something he knew well, the constant sound of water trickling and flowing over stones.

"There's a stream down here in this gully," he said.

"I know," Bo said. "I landed in it and now my bum's wet."

It was slightly lighter here where the stream cut its way through the woods, because there wasn't as much tree coverage directly overhead. Now Peter's eyes had adjusted so that he could make out the rough boundaries of the stream — he was almost in it — and he could see the outlines of a moving shape that he recognized as Bo-like enough to presume it was her.

"Can you stand up?" Peter asked.

"Can you?"

That was as good a question as anyone might ask in these circumstances, so Peter tested it. First he pulled his feet slowly under him, noting that the one with his banged knee seemed a little more numb and more wobbly than the other. Then he pushed himself up, with one hand on a big rock, but mostly by the strength of his legs. There was some newborn-faun shakiness at first, and he was uncertain that he could maintain his balance, but eventually he realized his legs — both of them — would take his weight.

"I can stand," he said.

"Good, but you're going to have to get right back down on

your hands and knees again. I don't think we're going to be able to find my missing boot by looking for it. We have to crawl around and feel for it."

"Fair enough," he said, a phrase he'd often heard his father use with his mother.

Peter lowered himself back down to his knees and together they crawled around, going very slowly so as not to miss anything and to avoid getting further banged up. They carefully felt through wet and rotting dead leaves and over mossy boulders, squinting through the fear-weighted darkness, keeping each other in sight when they could and within easy earshot when they couldn't. It took an awfully long time to do this and without success, so that Peter was beginning to worry that the soldiers might find them. They covered the ground around them several times, but there was no boot to be found. Then he heard Bo speak from up on the hillside above him.

"I've got it," she said. "It was tucked in under a bush and mostly buried in the dirt we scooped up while we were falling."

"Lucky that we could find it at all then. Can you get it on?"

"Ick! It's full of dirt and dead leaves."

"They can't hurt you. Scrape it out and try anyway."

"Oh no! Oh no!" she screamed above him in absolute terror.

"What is it?" Peter cried, already scrambling on all fours, up the loose hillside towards her. His thoughts filled with every imaginable calamity that could have befallen her. "Hold on! I'm coming!"

"There was a snail in it!" Her voice trembled with horror.

"Is that all?" He stopped climbing.

"But I touched it! And not just the shell part. I grabbed the sticky gooey part right in my hand."

"That's okay, Bo. It can't harm you. Just put your boot on."

"Not until I wash it out, and wash my hands too. I can have a wet boot, but not one full of snail goo. Stay there, I'm coming back down."

He did and she did, and soon she was kneeling by the edge of the stream, thoroughly scrubbing out the inside of her boot. Peter crouched close beside her, trying to visually examine her for any obvious injuries. He thought he could make out a few scrapes and bruises, and one big goose-egg forming on the side of her head, but nothing that seemed to need immediate attention. "Hurry up," he said. We have to cross the stream."

"Why?"

"Because we know the camp and the soldiers are somewhere on this side of the stream, so that means they aren't on the other side. We'll be safer over there."

"But can't we just hide here until the soldiers go away and then go back to the camp?"

"I don't think so," he said. "I think we have to get farther away first, before we try to hide, and I worry that we may not be able to go back to the camp at all. If I were a soldier in the woods, I'd stay there for a long time, waiting for someone to try to sneak back to see if it's safe again."

"But my mother and father may be back there," Bo said. "What if they're worried about me?"

"They'll have to miss you for now. I'm not responsible for looking after your mother and father, but I did choose to pull you into the woods with me, so that makes me responsible for you. I have to make certain you're safe, before going back to look for them, or your sisters, or my family."

"You're not the boss who gets to decide things."

"No, but your father and my father are, and this is what I think they'd do."

And that was that.

They crossed the stream, crowded with mossy-topped boulders, which the water had to find dozens of ways around. There were so many boulders that they could've tried stepping from one to another, and never have to get their feet wet — or more wet in Bo's case. But the moss and smooth rock was slippery and Peter reasoned that it was better to walk in the stream, where the footing was surer. Better to get all of their feet wet, rather than risk slipping off of a boulder. Another fall might succeed in bashing their heads in this time. In the middle of the stream Bo stopped them and pointed upwards.

"Look," she said. "Straight up you can see stars." And it was true. In the very middle of the stream they could see a thin strip of night sky, uncovered by the accustomed shroud of overhead branches. It was filled with bright stars — the very same ones they'd known before they entered this alien world. It was reassuring to be reminded that there was still sky beyond the all-enclosing forest.

They held hands while they crossed, to help each other keep

balance, but they didn't let go on the other side, when their footing was secure again. Hand in hand they started up the other hill forming the gully. It was a large slope and very steep. It took them a long time to climb it, but it became easier once the rocks gave way to trees again and they could rest with their backs against the tree trunks, which kept them from falling back down into the gully. After resting for a few minutes they'd set out again up the embankment.

By the time they reached the top, they were back in the dense wood once more, under a canopy that deepened the shadows and blocked every patch of sky overhead.

That's when they heard the monster.

First there was a simple coughing sound, which is what great beasts sometimes make when they stalk through the night. But neither Peter nor Bo had ever encountered a great beast before, so at first they simply thought the noise odd. They grew more nervous as the coughs came initially from one direction and then from another, as if something was circling them — something very big.

Peter stopped Bo in a spot about equally distant from four big tree trunks. It wasn't quite a clearing, but there was scant undergrowth in the place. From here at least they could choose to run in any direction. Peter could feel Bo's hand trembling in his. With his other hand he slowly reached around behind his back and untied the laces that kept the flute case's flap closed. Once the flap was freed, gravity took over and Peter felt Frost slide softly out of its case, quiet as a whisper, and into his hand.

Now there was a deep grunting, growling sound from only a

few feet in front of them. They could make out nothing in the darkness.

"Bo?" Peter said.

"Yes?"

"When I start to play, you run. Don't go before that, or the thing might get you. But once I begin, run as fast as you can." He released her hand.

"But I can't leave you here."

"Yes you can. You have to. I need to stay here to keep the beast away from you, and you need to run and get help. Find your father or mine and bring them back here. I'm counting on you to run fast and find them and save me." Peter was lying. He knew that she couldn't possibly find anyone out there in the dark and then lead them back here in time to save him. But he needed to make sure she'd run as far and as fast as she could to get away, and this seemed the best way to convince her to do it. He'd hold the beast as long as he could, but he didn't know how long that might be, so he wanted her as far away from him as she could manage.

"That's a grand idea, little girl," a voice said from out of the concealing blackness. "Run fast and lead me a merry chase. You'll have as much head start as it takes me to gobble down your friend. Give me enough good sport and, even though I can't promise to spare you, I'll at least make sure you don't suffer overmuch." The creature's voice was deep and growling, like huge stones scraping against each other. With the muffled squishing of dead leaves underfoot, it approached closer, on heavy paws. It stepped between two trees and Peter could see just enough to make out the great black shadow of a giant wolf. This close its breath sounded like a blacksmith's bellows.

Even though he was no longer in contact with her, Peter could feel Bo beside him, shaking like a leaf — or like a scared deer who, cornered and exhausted, surrenders to the idea that its only remaining purpose is to be food for another. Peter was shaking, too, so much so that he wondered if he could successfully play a note.

"We don't mean you any harm," Peter said.

"Gracious of you," the giant wolf said. "But I can't say the same. I absolutely mean you harm. But there's the matter of the proper scoring to determine. You're both so small, you'd barely number one whole person added together. However, I'm so far behind on my daily tally, perhaps I should count you as two.

"Then again, I smell others nearby, and I hear them crashing about in the woods, wailing and moaning for someone to come along and end their suffering. Maybe I'll end up with my full complement for the day after all.

"What do you two think? Would you like to go down as one or two? I'm generously inclined to let you decide."

"I think you should pass us by and go far away," Peter said.

"I've already been far away," the wolf said. "That's where I came from. Now I'm here. I was following a great army, reducing their numbers every night, sowing fear into their ranks. But those clever goblins stole a march on me while I napped, and then wandered off to get my supper. They don't taste right to me, so, though I'll kill them gladly, I don't get the well-deserved feast afterwards. In any case I lost track of them."

"I know where they are," Peter said. "They're the ones who chased us into the woods. If you're their enemy like we are, then we should be friends."

"I've neither friends nor enemies, and desire none," the wolf replied. "I only have food and sport, both of which involve killing."

"But I can direct you where to find the army you seek."

"Then do it."

"And in return you'll let us go?"

"No."

Beside him, Bo seemed on the edge of panic. He had to act now or not at all.

"Remember what I told you, Bo," Peter said. Then he raised Frost to his lips and started to play. It was a simple tune he knew well. He didn't want to risk any mistake now. And as he played he thought over and over in his mind: Pass us by and go far away.

"Pretty music," the wolf said. "Possibly the only good thing your miserable race has ever done for the world."

Bo turned all of a sudden and ran. The giant wolf immediately sprang after her, but before he'd even gotten a full stride away from Peter, he was suddenly and violently brought up short, like a dog that had reached the end of his tether. Peter never stopped playing. The wolf stood where he'd become frozen in place and shook in rage.

"What have you done to me, boy?" There was fury in his voice and it rattled Peter and all of the trees around them. But Peter played on, not missing a note. Pass us by and go far away, he thought. Far behind him he could hear Bo still running away, scrambling back down the embankment they'd just climbed, splashing through the stream, and running farther away on the other side, until she'd run far away, entirely out of his hearing and possibly forever out of his life.

"Seven times seven times the ridiculous men of your race have tried to collar and chain me, coming on me when I slept or just when I felt like an interesting challenge. I snapped every rope and shattered every chain in no more time than it took to shrug them off. Now you bind me with an insipid little tune?"

Pass us by and go far away.

Pass us by and go far away.

Clearly against his will, struggling against every step, the wolf turned and began stalking off the way he'd come. Peter played on.

Pass us by and go far away.

Pass us by and go far away.

"I've got the scent of you, boy and I'll never forget it. No matter how far you send me, one day I'll track you down again and grease my chin with you and your sweetheart. Oh yes, I can smell your love for her. Maybe I'll make you watch me devour her, before I get to you. All of this I vow."

Peter played on, and gradually at first, but then in faster steps and ever increasing strides, the wolf began to run. And as he ran he howled his rage to all the world, and throughout the forest, every other creature trembled in its den. Peter heard him for more than an hour after he began playing, howling fainter and fainter into the distance. Then, when he couldn't hear the beast, he still continued to play for as long as he could, hours at least, hoping that he was truly sending the danger farther and farther away.

Finally, when he couldn't play any longer and had to stop, he noticed only then that his chin and shirtfront were drenched in blood. His mouth was cut in many places from Frost's sharp blade. The wolf had been unable to touch him, but Frost had bitten him thoroughly in return for its saving magic.

And that was how Peter spent Frost's first gift, making danger pass him by.

Afterwards he cleaned himself as well as possible in the stream, before setting off to find Bo again. But he found neither Bo nor any of the others. The Black Forest had swallowed them without a trace, or perhaps it had swallowed him. Who can say which?

Peter was lost in the forest for months. He had no gold to spend, for that was left behind, in his bundle at the camp. And besides, there was nowhere in the forest to spend it. He had no coat or warm clothes, except for what he was wearing when he first ran out of the camp, fleeing into the night, away from the attacking soldiers, whom he never saw for himself. But Max had, and his condition at the time was ample testimony that they were indeed real and dangerously close. He had only Frost and the clothes on his back.

For all of Peter's life, the Piper family had lived on the move. Traveling often in the country and through the woods (though always on the protected roads), he'd grown up gathering wild plants and mushrooms for their dinner. Mother would direct him to this tasty fungus, or that buried tuber, identifiable by its sprouts, or its color, or shape or markings. "The forest is just a book you have to learn to read," she'd say. Under her direction he'd jump down from the wagon several times a day to snip wild herbs or any of a hundred edible plants and mushrooms. This knowledge saved his life in the Black Forest.

Peter lived as a wild boy, scrounging his meager dinner in the daytime and finding a hole to sleep in at night, or climbing a tree as necessary. Once in a great while he'd catch a fat toad, or some creepy crawly thing, and the best of all prizes was when he'd come across the half-eaten carcass of some other creature's dinner. How he feasted then!

Fresh water was plentiful. Hundreds of small streams bisected the forest. One only had to be cautious of who or what else might be coming to drink.

And wherever he wandered he always looked for Bo, or his mother, or anyone else from their escape party, but there was never a sign of them. He'd daydream for hours about finding someone, and it was always Bo who was foremost in his mind, before he'd remember that there were others to look for and long for as well. He wandered so far and so aimlessly that he could have been a hundred miles or a hundred yards from that old campsite and he'd never know it. Many times he'd daydream that Max would suddenly appear, his sword flashing in his hand, and announce that he'd killed or driven away all of the threats in the forest, and he'd come to take Peter home. But Max never appeared. No one did.

Peter carried Frost with him always, but seldom played it and never to use one of its two remaining gifts of safety. The wolf hadn't returned and most other creatures seemed content to give him a wide berth. He ran and hid from the more aggressive ones. Once he'd seen a lovely dark-haired woman in the woods and he started to approach her to ask for her help, but she was naked, painted in weird red designs, and talking in a strange tongue to a coal-black goat with high twisty horns. And that disturbed Peter enough to pass her by. At another time he spied a great ogre, as tall as the Peeps' old house. The thing had its back to Peter, who watched it bite the head off a black bear with one chomp and then suck out the innards, before finishing it with another single bite. Peter made no sound, but backed away slowly and then put miles of distance between the ogre and himself.

And then long after he'd lost count of the days, Peter stumbled onto the banks of a great river, winding its majestic way through the woods, and it sparked a dim memory of something someone said: "West to the river and then upstream to Hamelin Town. That's the plan." He recalled it now! That was where they were all going to meet again, if they got split up. That's where he would find the others!

Peter followed the river upstream. It was slow going, because he'd learned over his recent troubled months that he could successfully live off the land or move through it, but seldom do both with good results.

Gradually the forest widened out from the riverbanks on both sides, as small villages and farmsteads began to appear. Peter was torn, not knowing what to do. He was filthy and cut and scraped and dressed in rags by then, and had no idea what sort of reception he was likely to receive should he present himself at any of these strange doors. At the same time, the idea of Hamelin Town had become a talisman to him — a name to conjure with. If he could only make it to Hamelin Town, all would be well again. His family and the Peep family would all be there, safe and comfortable and waiting for him. Hamelin itself was transformed in his mind to a magic place of refuge. Peter couldn't risk his welcome at any place but Hamelin, so he passed the other settlements by. He stayed at the edge of the forest, sometimes venturing out at night to steal eggs from henhouses, or vegetables from fields or gardens. And once even (oh, glorious day!) he helped himself to an entire blueberry pie that had been set out on a country cottage's windowsill to cool.

Max had once accused Peter of being a terrible thief and it seems his accusation, while false at the time, was prophetic. Peter had become a thief indeed. When he saw a new (to him anyway) set of clothes, hanging out on a line to dry, he took them to replace the rags he wore. It would not be fit to present himself at the magical city's gates as a filthy ragamuffin. Likewise he stole a bar of good lye soap from an outdoor washtub, and bathed himself in an isolated spot along the river.

Peter looked quite human again as he topped a rise one day and looked down into the valley beyond. There in the distance, spread out over two hills, and filling the lower lands between them, was the great walled city of Hamelin. The sun was out, birds sang in the forest, and all of Peter's troubles were finally over.

Chapter Eight

In Flight

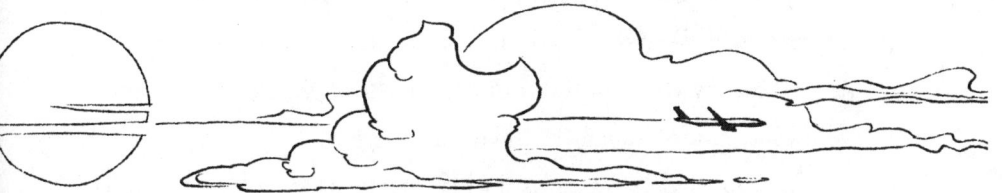

*In which we ponder
the eternal question:
How good were the
good old days?*

THE MORNING AFTER HIS INTERVIEW WITH THE sheriff and The Witch, Peter boarded an international Lufthansa flight from New York's La Guardia airport, bound for Frankfurt, Germany.

The last time he'd flown on a plane, it was powered by propeller engines, seats were roomy, full meals were served in-flight by polite and pretty hostesses who seemed genuinely glad to serve you, the napkins were cloth, the dinnerware was made of real glass and china, utensils weren't made of flimsy anti-terrorist plastic, and all of the passengers applauded after every successful takeoff and landing. Things had changed since. Now the airport was an oppressive mess, the flight crew seemed annoyed at the passengers, just by virtue of their existence, the seats were cramped, and the meal (designated a snack actually, and six dollars extra for those in coach) was a pre-packaged mystery in aluminum foil. Worst of all, no one besides Peter seemed at all impressed by the absolute miracle of the flight itself — crossing an ocean in less than a day? Wondrous!

Surrounded by grumps and the terminally jaded, he pulled out his book (a paperback detective story) and settled in for a long flight.

Chapter Nine

A Little Touch of Max in the Night

In which a terrible transformation is completed, and Max passes up a good meal.

AFTER EVERYONE ELSE HAD SCATTERED into the darkness, screaming and crying and moaning their fears, Max stood alone for a moment in the small circle of soft, flickering light given off by the dying campfire. He felt the blood drying on his face and the alarming thrill of what he'd done. He trembled with the enormity of it. There would be no going back now. Max Piper was no more. The flute-playing son of a flute player had died forever, victim of the same heavy, wet stone that had brutally transformed his father into raw memory and carcass. Max the heroic swordsman was also gone forever. Some part of his mind recognized that version of himself as nothing more than the temporary conjuration of a boy wishing to become a man. Only Max the Great and Terrible Beast of the Black Forest remained — neither a child nor an adult, not even a man, but a completely new sort of thing, ageless and eternal, and totally lacking human compassion, or love, or (most important) guilt. Instead the new Max possessed appetites, cunning and calculation, and that was enough.

He considered the various packs left abandoned in the campsite, along with the food, the blankets and most of the warm clothing. Each pack, of which there were twelve in total, contained a fat purse of gold marks, and all of it belonged to him now. But gathering his money would have to wait. There was a much more pressing treasure that needed collecting now, before it was lost forever. Frost was out there in the dark with Peter. That's what needed sorting out first and foremost. Frost Taker, still hanging heavy in one hand, was eager to be about its work and needed to drink deep of Thief Peter's innards. Only then the family treasure would be restored to its true owner. Only then would things be set right. That's what Max needed to do first, before Peter could get away. Mere gold could wait.

Max stepped into the darkness, following in the direction he'd watched Peter go just two or three minutes earlier, dragging his sobbing little sweetheart behind him. Before long Max was as lost and confused in the pitch black of the endless forest as everyone else must be. At first he thought about finding his way back to the camp and making a torch from the fire. But he quickly discarded the idea, realizing that, although it would certainly provide him greater light to see by, it would also alert others to his coming. Even someone as stupid as filthy little Peter couldn't help but easily avoid someone carrying a lit torch in the night. No, instead Max would creep silently and carefully, pausing often to listen. That's how the other night prowlers hunted, and he was certainly one of them now.

He did so and in time his practice was rewarded. Pausing at the top of a slope, Max heard the quiet murmur of a stream far below, accompanied by distant voices. Listening intently, halting his own breathing to help unmask the nearly inaudible sounds, he eventually recognized Peter's voice, along with the bratty Peep girl. It was hard to be certain, but they seemed to be arguing about her shoes, or perhaps just one shoe, along with something he couldn't fully make out about a snail.

Ever so slowly he began to creep down towards them, taking care not to slip and thereby betray his presence. By the time Max reached the stream at the bottom of the gully, he could hear Peter and Bo, quite clearly now, on the water's far side, crawling up the opposite slope. Max let them get farther up the hill, into the tree line, before crossing the stream after them. Be patient, he had to remind himself, when his every desire was to throw caution to the wind and dash boldly up the hill. Stealth and guile is what will win this night's contest. Oddly, he began to suspect that he wasn't the only one in danger of surrendering to impetuosity. Was it only his imagination, or could he now actually feel Frost Taker's intense hunger for Peter's blood? It seemed to practically vibrate in its sheath, like a prize colt being restrained from its desire to run.

After he judged that his prey was far enough up the hillside so that Max could not be easily overheard, he began to climb. It was beginning to get easier now to track them, and Max's confidence was growing to fit the new circumstances. Not only were his eyes adjusting to the darkness by now — it had been thirty minutes at least since he was exposed to the camp's firelight — but the children seemed intent on making his task easier by talking all the time. Max continued to climb.

And then he stopped.

No, he hadn't intended to stop, but he stopped all the same. He wasn't overly tired from the steep climb and felt nothing physical holding him. His desire to continue was undiminished — was growing in fact. But even so he remained still, as if rooted in place, halfway up the hillside.

Then, softly at first, Max began to hear the music. It was Peter somewhere up above him and he was playing a tune on Frost! Was the child insane? Who stops to play a flute when he's on the run from any number of angry soldiers? Did he want to be caught? The music swelled in volume, and Max's understanding grew with it. He'd heard the same tales of the ancient flute's powers that Peter had and realized that Peter was using Frost's magic to make danger pass him by. That's why Max was suddenly stuck in place. Amazing! But how could Peter have known how close Max was to overtaking them? I must have made some sound, he thought, given myself away in some small manner.

The music continued, and as it did so Max had an increasing desire to turn and retreat back down the slope and then splash his way back across the stream. But then, before he could act on the growing compulsion, he was frozen in place by a new sound.

"What have you done to me, boy?"

It was a terrifying voice that shook Max to his bones! This was neither Peter nor Bo. It was the voice of something huge and deadly, not in the normal way of fearsome but entirely comprehensible dangers, but deadly in the way the old gods themselves must have used the word.

The creature went on to say more, but Max didn't make it out, because just at that moment something came crashing down on him from above, striking him with such force that he was sent tumbling down the hillside, not stopping until he lay stunned, half in and half out of the chilling waters of the stream. Somewhere along the way he'd heard high screaming, which might have been his own, but he couldn't quite bring himself to believe it. A beast of the night didn't scream — at least not in such a high pitch.

Gradually his senses began to return and Max made out the dim figure of a little girl standing over him, holding a sword to his chest. It was Bo Peep and the sword was his own Frost Taker. That was impossible! Frost Taker would never allow any hand but his to wield it! And yet here was this ridiculous little girl, crying and shaking all the while, but definitely holding the sword towards him.

"Don't move, soldier," she sobbed, "or I'll run you through!"

"I'm no soldier!" Max shouted in return. At the same time he discovered that the spell holding him in place was gone now. Wait, that wasn't true. On further examination it was still in place, because he realized he couldn't possibly make himself return up the hill to where Peter was still playing his haunting tune. But that same spell wasn't keeping him from all movement, and did nothing at all to protect Bo, down here with him in the gully. Max could tell that he was perfectly free to take his sword back and slaughter little Bo Peep with it.

"Either my brother doesn't actually love you after all," Max said, "or the magic only works to protect him. Isn't that hilarious?"

"Max?" Bo said, and there was fear and confusion in her voice.

"Give me my sword back, girl, and I'll protect you, since Peter seems unable or unwilling to do it." Max reached out, but Bo took a step back. She still had his sword and its point remained fixed somewhere between his chest and throat.

"You look strange, Max," she said. "Sort of wild in the eye."

"Give me my sword, you stupid little witch!" This time Max lunged at Bo, who screamed once and flailed wildly with the blade, catching Max on the base of the thumb. This time it was Max who screamed in pain and rage.

That was too much for Bo. She dropped the sword and ran

off once more into the night. Max's first instinct was to follow her and gut her from neck to belly for cutting him. But then he thought he'd better first find out how deep the cut was. He stood and tried as best he could, in the nearly nonexistent light, to examine his bleeding palm.

And while he did this the music of the flute continued above him, while the forest all around him reverberated with the howls of a great and savage monster. Gradually, over the span of an hour or more, the bestial howling faded into the distance.

MAX COULDN'T FIND PETER again after that night, nor was he able to find Bo or the camp where his gold waited for him to come back and retrieve it. And who knows? Those twelve purses of good Hessian marks might still be there today, patiently waiting for someone to discover them.

Like Peter, Max had also learned enough basic woodcraft from their mother to recognize many edible plants and mushrooms, and like Peter, that was how he survived those first long days and nights following the incident at the camp. During that time, unknown to either brother, their lives paralleled each other's. Both wandered without direction, living on scavenged plants and grubs. But unlike Peter, Max didn't remain alone in the woods for long. On his fourth, or possibly fifth, day Max stumbled into a small clearing where two of the Peep girls were huddled, more dead than alive, under the half-hollowed trunk of a giant fallen evergreen.

"Look, Dorthe, Look! Here's Max come out of the woods like an angel to save us!" It was either Brigitte or Elfride who was pointing at him, as if he were a handsome prince come to take her away on a white stallion. In all of their past visits, Max had never bothered to learn one Peep daughter from another very well, and now in their dirty and disheveled state, it was even harder to tell them apart.

Both girls crawled out from under the fallen tree and clutched at him, frantically, the way a mother claws at a lost child who was suddenly restored to her, not quite willing to trust such a happy miracle.

"We ran and ran," Dorthe said, tears streaming down her dirty face. "Brigitte and Elfride and I. But a creature got poor Elfride!" That cleared up the minor mystery of which daughters he'd found. "There wasn't even any sound," she continued, hiccupping the story out in short fragments, between sobs. "I thought Elfride just tripped, but then she said, 'Something bit me,' just like that. Real quiet, as if it wasn't anything important. But then something pulled her down into a deep hole."

"A fell beast's den!" Brigitte interjected.

"Oh, then there was such screaming!" Dorthe said. "And ripping and tearing sounds."

"Bones crunching," Brigitte added. "We heard every moment of it."

"And all the while Elfride kept calling out to us. 'Don't

leave me,' she cried, over and over again."

"But we did. We ran away." And then both girls seemed to simultaneously run out of the power to continue their account. They looked up at him, whether for forgiveness or judgment, it was impossible to say.

"Do you have any food?" Was all Max said in reply.

"None at all," Brigitte managed to whisper, between great and gasping breaths, as if any additional wind for speaking had quite deserted her.

"Then what business can we have with each other?" Max said. Slowly, he drew Frost Taker out of its sheath.

DAYS LATER, AS HE STUMBLED again through the forest, lost and directionless, Max considered that he might have made a serious mistake where the two Peep girls were concerned. He'd taken their clothing, which he had every right to. He'd torn it into rags and stuffed them inside of his own clothes, for additional padding against the night's chills. But he'd left their bodies untouched. It was a waste of meat on the bone, he thought. At the time he couldn't bring himself to consider such an unthinkable sin, the eating of one's own kind. But now he reminded himself that he was no longer of any kind save his own. He was a new creature, of which there was only one in the whole wide world. He should have recalled that back when it could have helped him — back when he stood over their ridiculously available flesh. What a waste, he thought. I could've feasted, but instead I go hungry. That's what I get for clinging to compassion, which no longer has a proper place in my heart.

He stumbled and wandered, living on roots and berries, but there was never enough. No matter how much he found, he was always hungry. Then, one day, long after he'd given up keeping count of the days, Max emerged from the wood onto a small dirt road, which cut its narrow and winding way through the forest like the passage of a serpent. This was no major road, down which more invading troops could march. This was little more than a walking path. Only the smallest of carts could navigate this track.

"It doesn't matter!" Max called aloud. "Any path, no matter how small, means I'm saved!" This path would lead to places where people lived, or at least to a bigger road where there would certainly be towns and farmsteads, somewhere down the line.

Since he was thoroughly lost by this time and had no idea in which direction the path ran, Max chose a direction at random and set out following it. Night fell quickly while he walked down the lane, as it always did in the deep forest. But in little more than an hour the path led to a small and tidy cottage tucked among the trees. There was a garden on one side of the cottage, and on the other side a small fenced-in yard, containing a milk cow and two fat pigs. A low shed anchored the far side of the fenced yard. Many clucking chickens wandered here and there around the homestead. A trail of inviting smoke rose out of the cottage's stone chimney. Light flickered from the one window that he could see from the direction of his approach.

Max could hardly believe his turn of good fortune. He stepped forward at a lively, almost jaunty pace, drawing his blade as he did so. The evidence of fire made him think of cooked meals and a hot bath. While he was still at least a dozen paces away from the front door, he'd already begun to think of this place as his new home – his very private new home.

Chapter Ten
Hamelin

In which Peter learns something of the bureaucracy of conquest, commits a grave crime and then does it again.

Peter realized he was dying. Only a month ago he'd presented himself at the south gates of the walled town of Hamelin, certain that all of his trials had come to an end. But instead of reaching the glorious refuge of his imagination, he'd found a Hamelin that had already been overrun by invader troops from the far Empire. These occupiers were a strange and frightening bunch, which he was able to examine up close for the first time.

The human troops must have been the officers, because, like all leaders, they kept remote from the town's general populace. But it was the horrific goblin soldiers who mixed with the townsfolk, patrolling the streets, and manning the gates and street corners.

Hamelin was a vast walled city, home to tens of thousands. It was roughly circular in shape and pressed up like a jealous lover against the eastern bank of the Weser River, which flowed almost due north at this point in its meanderings. A deep moat had been diverted from the river to ring the town, just outside of its high walls. Three great gate towers straddled both wall and moat at three of the four cardinal points of the compass; north, east and south. To the west there were two more gates; one opening onto a wide, fortified stone bridge that spanned the Weser, leading to a separate castle fortress on the west bank, and a second gate that opened onto a smaller bridge that led to a sliver of forested island in the middle of the river, dividing the river in twain for about five hundred meters. In addition to the gate towers, seventeen tall stone towers were spaced along the wall's circumference, making Hamelin a truly imposing city.

A town like this could repel the direct attacks of any army and withstand a siege that lasted years, Peter had believed when he'd first arrived. But the enemy invaders who occupied Hamelin had apparently done so without inflicting any visible damage on its unscarred battlements.

Peter had arrived at the South Gate just as a long line of wagons, each piled high with the produce of the fall harvest, was entering the city. One of the rotund goblin guards simply waved him in as he approached, no doubt assuming he was part of the company of farmers delivering their goods. The goblin paid no further attention to him, even though he couldn't help but gape in open astonishment at the creature. Like those he'd seen only from a distance, back at the Peep estate, this one had beady black eyes and green, leathery skin. Up close he could see the thing's skin was spotted with ugly cankers and scored with deep, badly healed scars from past battles. Yellow tusks protruded from its oversized lower jaw, and its meaty fingers ended in thick, stubby claws. Its breath, even while standing more or less at rest, heaved louder than a blacksmith's bellows, and it stank of sulfur and rot. It wore black armor over a coat of chainmail and carried a long spear, which looked anything but decorative.

"Move along," the goblin croaked in a rough approximation of the Hessian tongue. "Don't clog the gate!"

And so Peter did as instructed. As much as he was tempted to flee from the city and its terrifying conquerors, the plan among the two families was that they'd all meet up in Hamelin, should they become separated. *If any of the others had survived, they simply must be here by now,* Peter thought. *Goblins or no, I can't even consider abandoning my family, or Bo Peep, or any of her sisters or parents.*

So, seeing no other choice, he'd entered.

If anything, Hamelin seemed bigger on the inside than out. And it was crowded with more people than Peter had ever imagined existing at all, much less squeezed into one place. From the bits of chatter he could overhear just by having to struggle through the crowds, he'd learned that many, or most, of them were recent arrivals and refugees, just like he was. They'd journeyed from smaller towns and homesteads all over the countryside, some of which had been burned during the invasion, while others had been forcibly taken for the sole use of the invaders.

A town this crowded will make it harder for me to find my own friends and family, he thought. Then again, it might help me stay free longer to look for them, since one small boy can better lose himself in a crowd, the bigger the better.

But Peter couldn't start looking for the others yet. He'd arrived here with only the clothes on his back, Frost in its dull, leather carrying case, and nothing else. More than ever he dearly missed those seventeen fat gold marks that he'd been forced to abandon in the deep woods. Peter was experienced enough to know one absolute and unchanging rule of any town, no matter who ruled it. No money meant nothing to eat. The first thing he'd have to do, even before beginning to look for his loved ones, was to find a tavern or guest house, play his pipe, and pass the hat. Of course that assumed he'd be able to borrow a hat. His had been left in that long lost campsite, along with the gold.

"Has the rot gotten to your head, boy?" the innkeeper said, after Peter had proposed to play for his evening customers. "There's no singing and playing allowed in public houses no more — not since the gobs took over. It's forbidden now. Are you trying to get yourself chopped into bits? Or, worse yet, are you trying to get me killed?"

"I didn't know," Peter said. "I'm new here and —"

"Well, that's no excuse, is it? Just ask those who tried to plead ignorance. You can usually find their heads lining the East Wall, provided the crows and rats haven't got to them yet. You got to learn the rules, boy, or a gob ax will fix you certain."

It was the same in every other public house that Peter had tried. One innkeeper had actually struck him just for asking, lest any of his customers overhear him even having such a conversation and think to curry favor by denouncing him to the guards.

After a night spent cold and hungry, sleeping in an alley, Peter had decided to look for other kinds of work that didn't involve playing music. He quickly found there was none of that to be found either.

"I can't let you work, young man," a stable owner named Krupf told him, "not without a pass signed by the new Ministry of Labor. Not even a single sweep of the broom can I allow you."

"How can I get such a pass?" Peter said.

"Well, that part's easy enough. First you present yourself down to the Ministry offices and tell them who you are and how long you've lived in Hamelin and answer any other questions they think to ask. Then you wait to see if they issue you a pass, or cart you off to a slave camp. I'm told a gift of some kind to the desk sergeant can be helpful in that particular."

"I don't have anything I could offer as a gift though," Peter said.

"No matter," Krupf said. "Even if you could get a signed pass, you'd never find a job anyway. They're all gone by now. I can't spare a bit of work, or even a crust to pay you with. Mostly now I think the Ministry only keeps its doors open to lure in the less wary vagrants and street tramps. It's the labor camps for you, I fear."

"But if I don't find a job soon, I'll have to leave the city in order to feed myself."

"You can't do that either," Krupf said, "unless you get a different pass from the Ministry of Travel. The new overlords don't want people just wandering free and unregistered about their countryside, now, do they?"

"But I got into the city without a pass."

"I'm not surprised. They want you in the bigger cities and towns. Easier to scoop you up then. No, young fellow, I fear it's the camps for you. Best turn yourself in now and get that first bowl of dinner all the sooner."

And so it went.

Peter had no documentation, but documents of some type or another were required for anything he might try to do to stave off hunger. Even begging was regulated in this strange new empire. Beggars required their own brand of written license to do so, which were issued by the Ministry of Charity. Unfortunately the Ministry of Charity was no more charitable than any other of the town's uncountable regulatory offices. Hamelin was limited to no more than thirty such passes, and the waiting list to get one was already over a thousand names long – or so Peter had heard. He wasn't willing to enter any government building to find out for himself.

With no other recourse, Peter turned to eating garbage, but in a city as crowded as this, there was precious little of that to be found. And what he could find was often difficult to keep. Usually he had to be willing to fight others for it. Scavenging turned increasingly difficult as the days went by. Most of the other vagrants, finding themselves in the same position as Peter, formed gangs of desperate ruffians, all the better to fight off other gangs for the few scraps that could be discovered. Peter refused to join one of the gangs, since the standard rite of initiation required killing some smaller, weaker street-dweller to prove one's will and ability to do all to serve the gang and to survive.

He continued to sleep in alleys and gutters, but never for more than an hour or two at a time. Patrols of the goblin nightwatch regularly searched likely places where street tramps might be found. Some of the bolder gangs were even worse, routinely killing those they could find still living on their own, so as to keep its reputation growing, its members in fighting trim, and to reduce the number of mouths competing for the available food trash.

The rat populations were increasing too, as they always did in a place where the human population is so much greater than the available food supply. The dead and dying may have been too terrible a food source for most of the town's starving people to yet contemplate, but they proved a wonderful feast for rats. Turnabout being fair play, many of the street-dwellers started hunting rats. Peter tried it with limited success.

On most days Peter was too weak from hunger to succeed in catching and killing one of the big Hamelin rats with only his bare hands and teeth as weapons. They were tough, fast and fought viciously when cornered. On those rare occasions when he did triumph, Peter ate the thing raw, meat and guts both. Then, strengthened just a bit, he usually celebrated by taking the rest of the day off to search for his lost friends and family. His reasoning was sound for the most part. If one or more of them had survived to make it here, there was a chance, slight though it may have been, that they'd done so with their gold in hand. Peter's greatest fantasy in those rough days consisted of finding his mother, or Max, or any of the Peeps, and discovering that they lived like kings, with plenty to eat, surrounded in fact with every type of treat one could imagine.

He seldom thought of Bo, or at least tried not to, because he no longer felt worthy of her. He couldn't bear what he'd become — a human version of vermin, a filthy rat in the streets — and knew that she'd be justifiably shocked and appalled by him now.

Sometimes he thought of his father, and when he did he imagined a terrible sight of many scarred and bearded soldiers standing over an unrecognizable thing on the wet forest floor. They wore his father's blood, spattered over their face and skin and clothes, and didn't mind it. Each one of them looked as frightening as Max had on that unspeakable night so long ago.

When he could, he went from door to door in one of the town's sixteen distinct residential neighborhoods, asking after his lost ones. Most of the time he'd had the door slammed in his face, before he could get his story told. The residents of Hamelin were learning not to talk to strangers for any reason. None of the few willing to listen to his plight had ever heard of anyone named Peep or Piper. No one he spoke to ever had a crust or a scrap to spare, and most were shocked to see someone beg without a license.

In addition to the residents, any one of whom might think it prudent to turn him in, he had to be careful to avoid the guard patrols. On more than one occasion they'd tried to run him down. So far he'd managed to outrun them, scampering into the hidden warrens and shadows that any big town offered, and which he was learning in minute detail. But he was getting weaker, and therefore slower, by the day, while the goblins, though not as fleet of foot as the average human, were always well fed. Sooner, rather than later, they'd catch him sure enough.

Once recently, one lucky gob had actually gotten a hand around Frost's carrying case, which Peter still wore slung over his back. When he could feel the strap slipping, about to hitch up to where it would either come free of his head, or choke him around his neck, Peter had suddenly stopped running, turned and kicked the massive goblin in his large round belly. His attack couldn't possibly have hurt the creature, but the gob was so surprised by the bold act that it let go of Frost's case, and Peter got away. That sort of miracle wasn't likely to happen twice.

When nearly a month had passed since his arrival in town, Peter had to admit to himself that he was dying, slowly to be sure, but dying just the same. The days had steadily grown colder and wetter as winter approached, and he'd grown too weak to succeed much longer in avoiding or outrunning each one of the many dangers in this very dangerous place. In desperation, he considered his remaining options.

First, he could turn himself in to the occupying soldiers and be taken off into one of their slave camps. He knew that in his frail condition he probably wouldn't last long, but at least he might get to eat something close to a real meal again before the end.

The second option was to try to steal the food he had no way to pay for, or earn in any other honorable way. The idea was abhorrent to him, especially so in light of his brother's past accusation that he was nothing but a dirty thief all along. How long ago was that? It seemed so distant, but it couldn't have been much more than two months past. How odd back then that Peter hadn't any idea he'd ever want for enough to eat.

The third option was the most alarming to imagine. He could try to find some way to sell Frost, his only thing of value, or trade it for something to eat. But even in his terrible state, knowing full well he was dying, the idea seemed monstrous to him. He'd promised to guard and cherish Frost always, ultimately surrendering it only when he had a son he could pass it on to. It was the first oath he'd ever taken as a man. He'd sworn a sacred vow to his father, only two nights before his father was slaughtered at the hands of the very invaders who were killing him now in dull and numbing increments.

No, he couldn't do it. No matter what else happened, Peter couldn't willingly dispose of Frost and thereby bring a dire curse down on all of his surviving family, and their offspring, until the end of time. If Peter were doomed to die, he'd have to devise some clever, solitary way to do it, whereby Frost would be buried with him for all time, never to be discovered by another. By keeping Frost with him, even after death, he'd stave off any chance of the curse falling on others.

Devising such a plan would take time and require a clear mind, so first he'd have to try just once more to live. Since he couldn't part with Frost, and since turning himself over to the soldiers would also result in losing the magical treasure, Peter would attempt the only remaining option. He'd fulfill his brother's prophecy and become a thief.

Halfway along Fish Door Street, just before it jogged north towards the city wall, which was called The Wall of Chestnut Trees in this section, was the public house identified by the sign of the red mare, rearing over a coiled green serpent. Most people simply called it The Horse and Snake. Like most public houses, several sections of its front wall, that part directly facing the street, could be removed during the warmest part of a sunny day, so as to keep the interior cool and to be more inviting to potential customers. Also like most such establishments, The Horse and Snake always had a big cauldron of stew simmering near the street. Such stews were commonly called Belly Vengeance, because it was a cheap and horrible concoction, made up of rotting wastes and leftovers. It was constantly added to throughout the day, replenished with anything that could possibly go into the pot, including the dirty scrub water and the sweepings from the floor. A public house's vat of Belly Vengeance was sold for a halfpenny a bowl. Often the 'bowl' was actually a hollowed crust of stale bread, so that no one had to worry about recovering and cleaning the dishes. Only the town's most wretched souls would buy it, as the single daily meal they could afford. This was why the stewpot was commonly kept out close to the street, since no decent pub owner wanted such disreputable scum entering the actual establishment, where the more respectable (meaning wealthier) customers dined.

Peter examined the exterior of The Horse and Snake from his vantage point, a dark and narrow alleyway across the street and not three doors down from it. He watched several customers come and go, paying their halfpenny to an old man stationed out on a stool, near the pot, which simmered over a wide, flat, iron pan of hot coals. Most of them would take their time, selecting the biggest, most bowl-like crust available, to dip as deeply as they could into the Belly Vengeance. Then they'd continue on their way, walking as they ate. If they dared try to linger too near the pub to eat, the red-faced manager would quickly rush outside to shoo them on their way. When too long a time passed between customers, the old man guarding the pot would often begin to doze on his stool, his back pressed against that part of the pub's street-side façade still in place.

Now that Peter had the old man's pattern down, he got ready to move. As soon as the fellow began to doze again, he sprang into action, dashing as fast as he could, out of the alleyway and across the street. Almost without pausing, he grabbed a crust from out of the big half-barrel, shoved it deep into the stew — almost scalding his hand in the process — and ran off with his stolen treasure.

Peter immediately began eating as he ran, pouring the hot stew into his open mouth as fast as it would go. It was glorious! It might have been the finest meal he'd ever enjoyed. Most of it was brown, greasy broth, but the broth was thick, almost as thick as a proper gravy, and he was almost certain he'd gotten a chunk of potato (or perhaps it was a rutabaga) and there was most definitely some bit of meat.

Peter heard a yawp of surprise behind him, as the old man snorted and sputtered back to wakefulness, but there was no chance he could catch Peter, who'd carefully chosen just this pub, on just this street, because of how winding the serpentine street was, with many a dim and narrow alleyway leading off from it. Peter chose an alley more or less at random and disappeared into it, giggling with delight as he sucked the last dregs of stew out of the bread. Then he paused to scrape every bit of cooling broth off his face and then lick his fingers clean, before turning to the bread itself. It had been dry and several days' stale, but the hot gravy softened it just fine. Peter ate it in three huge bites and it was better than the stew itself.

He walked deeper into the alley, grinning with pride at his accomplishment. Great Jorg himself, heroic warrior-bard of old, would have been proud of his mighty deed! He was tempted to pull Frost out of its case that very moment and compose a song in praise of his daring exploit on the spot. He almost did it.

Almost.

Over the next few days, Peter struck time and again, swooping down on a badly guarded stewpot, two and sometimes three times a day. It was easy. He never got caught, because he was always careful to scout the area thoroughly before he struck.

If there were goblin patrols anywhere within two city blocks, he'd wait. If one of the public house's legitimate customers looked too fit or, in some other way, able to give pursuit, he'd move on and select a different location. There were perhaps four hundred cauldrons of Belly Vengeance brewing on any given day, and Peter was determined to sample each and every one of them in time.

Now that he ate several times each day, his health was coming back. And as his strength returned, he grew bolder. With the winter rapidly approaching, there was more than food on his mind. One afternoon he stole a warm, woolen shirt off a clothesline. The next day he returned to take an even warmer cloak from the next yard over. What a luxury it was to sleep warm at night, for the first time in months, and on a full stomach to boot.

Eventually his taste for variety resurfaced with his restored health. He began to recognize just how grotesque the flavor of Belly Vengeance could be. That's when Peter began stealing fruits and whole vegetables from the open stands on Market Day. He enjoyed whole apples and pears, and once even an actual orange, which had to have been shipped in, at great cost, across the seas and down the Weser, from some distant shore. And he also cursed himself for not thinking of this sooner, for, with the first winter snowfall, Market Day would be discontinued until the following spring. It wouldn't be long at all before the remaining fruit and vegetable supply was stored away in deep cellars and stout, wooden lockers, where he couldn't get at them.

For the first time he began to think of some way to steal a larger supply of food all at once, more than what he needed for just a single day's repast. Surviving the winter would largely depend on whatever he did now, to store enough supplies to last him through the cold months to come. There were two problems to overcome: how to steal a large provision all at once, and where in the city to hide his food cache, where it would be safe, both from city authorities and others like him.

He considered his dilemma as he surreptitiously stalked an onion-seller, who'd lost half of one leg in some previous misadventure. Stealing a few of his onions would be easy enough, but his stand was deep inside the market grounds that some of the other vendors might try to intercept him in his getaway. There was one idea he'd been holding in reserve for some time, because it was likely to work only once.

Pausing at still a dozen paces distant from his intended target, Peter suddenly pointed due south, towards the Cathedral Wall, and shouted in panic.

"Soldiers! Goblin troops, coming up the Street of Bakers in great numbers! They're killing all they catch!"

It worked marvelously. Some vendors and shoppers surged towards the southern boundary of the market square, crowding each other to see if the warning were true. The remaining vendors tried to flee in every possible direction. In the first surge of panic, no one seemed to be watching Peter or the produce stalls immediately around him. Almost leisurely he filled his pockets with sweet onions. Then, perceiving that he had more time, he stepped over to another stall and filched three fat potatoes, and (wonder of wonders) an entire slab of uncut bacon.

Hiding all of his loot inside his jacket, which in turn was concealed under his cloak, Peter made his way slowly through the crowd, which was still entirely focused on locating where the danger was.

Ten minutes later, he was outside of the market square, free of the crowds. He walked west, towards the waterfront, along the Street of Boats, changed direction as soon as he could, north along Theatre Street, and then doubled back on himself, turning east along the short and narrow Barrel Maker's Street. He began to relax just a little, certain that he hadn't been followed.

He was wrong of course.

ON THE LAST SUNNY DAY OF THE YEAR, Carl the Arrow watched Peter from a distance, not knowing who he was, and not much caring. It was enough that Carl had seen him before, and on that past occasion, as in this one, Peter had been engaged in the act of bold and open thievery.

He observed from a distance, and noticed, not without admiration, as Peter threw the entire market crowd into a panic, with only a few well-chosen words. When Peter had completed his theft and had worked his way free of the market area, Carl followed, always at a discreet distance, and always so slyly that Peter never suspected he was being followed.

When Peter entered the narrow Barrel Maker's Street, Carl let a short but heavily weighted wooden truncheon fall into his palm. When Peter turned a sharp corner into an even darker and narrower side avenue, Carl rushed forward, silent as a monk's prayer, raising his truncheon on high.

Peter had only begun to sense his danger and turn around when Carl the Arrow struck hard.

After an indeterminate time, Peter began to awaken, slowly and with great effort. He was dizzy and nauseated, and there was a vicious pain thundering in his head, pounding over and again like the unstoppable beat of an ironsmith's hammer. He was lying on a stone floor, covered with old, damp straw. He could feel the scratchy, prickly straw ends sticking into his face. He reached for his head and felt dried blood in matted hair. His face and neck also seemed to be crusted with dried blood.

How long have I been here, he silently asked himself. And where exactly is the "here" that I've landed myself in?

He raised himself up a bit on unsteady arms and looked around. He was in a small, dark room, but not so dark that he couldn't make out any details. The floor and walls were made of dressed stone. There was partially dried vomit and the smell of urine mixed in with the straw directly beneath him.

Both from me, he thought, recognizing that there was an acid taste in his mouth and a dampness in his clothes to match the smell in the straw.

There were no windows, but there was a single stout wooden door set within one of the walls. The little light that was in the room entered through a small window cut high into the door. It was only a short narrow slit, not nearly enough to escape through. He thought of escape, because it was all too clear that he was trapped in a prison cell.

"The gobs finally got me," he said, aloud this time, in a voice that cracked and strained to summon barely a whisper.

Taking an infinite amount of time, Peter struggled to sit up and place his back against the far stone wall, where he could sit and regard the single locked door. He knew it would be locked with the same certainty that he knew day followed night. He didn't need to further pain himself making the useless effort to test it.

After sitting for a long while, listening to the pounding behind his forehead and letting his vision drift into and out of focus — but gradually more into focus than out — he thought to examine himself. He knew he'd been whacked solidly in the head, but there might be other injuries. He felt here and there over his aching body and in so doing made a surprising discovery. Everything he owned was still there, including Frost in its case — he opened it to make sure — and even the six onions, three potatoes and large slab of bacon he'd pilfered. Everything.

Why would the gobs let me keep my stolen goods, or anything at all for that matter?

In one corner there was a small wooden pail he hadn't noticed at first. Crawling over to it he found it full of pure, sweet water. Realizing only then how thirsty he was, Peter drank deeply.

Later he slept.

When he woke again, he first noticed that the small shaft of light coming through the door's slit window had moved considerably. Its angle was much higher in the tiny room, indicating that the sun outside was much lower in the sky. Even later he woke again to find the room was completely dark, not recalling that he'd slept again. Sometime during the night, someone had come in to refill his water pail.

Much later still, when the diffused shaft of light was once again present in his cell, they came for him.

"So, what do you think?" Someone said from the open doorway. There were two of them, just vaguely man-shaped silhouettes, backlit by the grey daylight. "Are you going to live?" He could hear the soft sound of rainfall behind the two men.

"I think so," Peter answered, "though my head doesn't agree."

"My fault for that," the same man said. "I didn't want to have to hit you more than once, but still make sure you dropped without a sound. Perhaps I overdid it. Can you stand?"

Peter didn't try to answer, since speaking audibly was still difficult. Instead he simply tried to stand, using the wall behind him to brace himself. It took some time and there were a few false starts, but eventually he succeeded. Somewhere along the way the realization sank in that he wasn't a prisoner of the goblins, and probably not of any other civil authorities either. Who then?, he wondered.

"I see you've drunk your fill a time or two, but have you eaten anything yet?" Once again it was the same fellow speaking. "I noticed you were fully provisioned when we first met. Of course we couldn't allow you a fire in here to cook some of that delicious-smelling bacon, but some of the other things stashed all about you looked tasty enough."

"You didn't take any of it," Peter said. His voice was less of a discordant croak by then, but only just so.

"No, of course not. Why would we? It's one of the cardinal rules of the Brotherhood. Thieves don't steal from each other."

"He's no brother of mine," the other one spoke for the first time.

"Not yet, Josef. And maybe not ever. We'll see."

"We'll see," Josef echoed.

Taking Peter by each arm, Josef and Carl, as the other fellow introduced himself, took Peter out of the cell, supporting him when he needed it, but not dragging him or treating him roughly. They stepped outside into a yard that had been used during the year as a vegetable garden, judging by the patches of open dirt, dressed into a series of long, narrow furrows. It was raining, but only lightly. A glance up at the grey sky, full of darkening clouds, promised harder rain to come. The yard was enclosed by a high wall, built out of the same stone as the small outbuilding that Peter had been kept in. Across the yard was a larger limestone building, with an outwardly curving wall and a high, domed roof that supported a spired crossing tower in the center of it.

"A church?"

"That's right," Josef chuckled. "You're going to church. To give your confession and then be judged," he added, which seemed to further amuse him.

"It's not a church any longer," Carl said. "The Empire's soldiers closed them all down when they took over. Well, most of them anyway. They couldn't completely close the two major cathedrals, could they? Not without riots. But these smaller churches now sit empty, until the big powers back in wherever they came from decide whether or not to allow our religion and our gods on their list of approved deities."

They stopped under the sheltered entryway into the main building. Now that Peter's eyes had adjusted to the daylight, he could see that Carl and Josef were hardly the grown men that he'd first thought them to be. Though both boys were clearly older than he, it was clear that they were still boys, fifteen or sixteen years at the most. But both of them looked prematurely hardened by the lives they'd led. Both were dressed in rude, unremarkable clothes like his, but theirs were better mended. Carl had reddish hair and blue eyes. Josef's hair might have been dark blond, or maybe light brown. It was hard to determine while it was wet with the rainfall.

"With all these fine buildings lying empty," Carl continued, "it seemed a shame to let them go unused, so the Brotherhood moved into this one."

"And a few others," Josef added.

"But here's the important thing," Carl said. "We're gathered today in this place to hold a trial. Your trial. You're going before the king, and he's going to decide if you can continue to live among us, or if we have to kill you. Those are the only two options."

"Trial for what?" Peter said. "What crime?"

"Thievery," Josef said.

"But you said you were thieves too."

"Correct," Carl said. "But we're sworn members of the Brotherhood, aren't we? We pay our tributes upwards and properly split our takes into the prescribed shares, don't we? You didn't do any of that."

"Unauthorized thieving is your crime," Josef said.

Carl kept talking before Peter could ask more questions. "What's your name?" he said.

"I don't want to say."

"Well, you should," Carl said. "If I'm going to speak for you, I'd better be able to act as if I know you well enough to trust you. And I'll have to call you something, won't I? So tell me your name, or I'll consider standing silent."

"I'm Peter."

"It's fine to meet you then, Peter," Carl said. "So listen close. We can't keep you out here all day answering your questions and giving you advice. The king won't abide waiting, nor should he, right? Otherwise, what's the advantage of being king? Here's what you need to know. The moment we walk in there, the trial has started. Don't speak to anyone but the king, and then only to answer his questions. Don't try to lie to him. He always catches the lie and never forgives it. If there's something you simply refuse to answer, then just say so and pray for clemency. It's rare that he grants any, but not unheard-of. Now, are you ready?"

"It doesn't matter if he is or not," Josef said. "It's time."

They opened the door and ushered Peter in to see the king.

Chapter Eleven

In Transit

In which Peter closes in.

THE LUFTHANSA JET TOUCHED DOWN AT Frankfurt am Main airport just after ten a.m., in the pouring rain. The time in flight was just right for Peter to finish his mystery story, a real page-turner featuring a spunky young female detective operating out of Las Vegas. By the time they started their final approach into Germany's busiest airport, the detective had identified the killer. While they taxied towards the gate, she'd smartly listed all of the clues that led her to the thrilling denouement. In hindsight

Peter realized he should've seen it all along. This being a fair-play mystery, all of the clues had been there for him to recognize. Peter was vaguely disturbed that he hadn't been able to solve the murder. He silently hoped it wasn't an ill omen for the success of his mission.

When they arrived at the gate, he stood up and took Frost's hard plastic case out of the overhead compartment. He also took the paperback with him when he left the plane, even though he'd finished it. Bo will want to read this one, he thought. She's always able to put the clues together.

He walked directly to the baggage claim area where, after not too long a wait, he was able to retrieve his single suitcase. Then, with both cases in hand, he followed the signs that read "Zoll duane," directing him to Customs. The grey-uniformed Customs officer asked him a few perfunctory questions about the nature and duration of his stay. Then he asked Peter to open the smaller case, which Peter did, revealing Frost.

"Is this an antique?" the officer asked. Peter recognized the German language, and mostly understood it, as it was close to the Hessian tongue which he'd spoken back in the lost and ancient world of the Hesse, and which he still spoke with Bo in their current home at the Farm.

"Yes," Peter said, in a rough approximation of the German language. "But not so old that I don't still play it. I'm a musician, and this is the instrument I play to make my living."

"You'll be performing here?"

"Yes, in Hamelin. For their autumn festival and concert

celebrating the Pied Piper. As you can see, I'll be playing the Piper."

"Ah. Well then, I hope you brought bright clothes."

"Actually, someone else is bringing the costumes."

"That's fine then," the officer said. "As long as you aren't attempting to smuggle museum treasures." The officer then waved Peter through the line, after wishing him a pleasant stay in Germany.

Peter breathed a sigh of relief, glad that the Customs official hadn't requested to search his larger bag, which contained all of the deadly devices that he couldn't bring aboard the plane in his carry-on luggage. Of course, they weren't just dropped willy-nilly into the open bag. Each weapon was secreted in hidden pockets, behind a false bottom. Anyone who found his weapons would have to have been already suspicious enough to conduct much more than the standard random search.

Before leaving the terminal, Peter went down a flight of stairs to the ground level automobile rental kiosks, where he rented a car. His false documentation included a current international driver's license. Then he collected his car and drove into the city, getting turned around once or twice in the crowded urban traffic.

After finally making it through the city, he drove on into the nearby Rheingau Region, where he found his hotel, the opulent five-star Schloss Reinhartshausen, situated directly on the Rhine River. Since I'm likely to die in the next few days, he thought, I might as well try my best to live it up in the meantime.

He ate dinner in the hotel restaurant that evening, where his waiter suggested the house specialty. "It's a hunter's stew," the waiter said, "though it also includes lamb, which is hardly a creature one need hunt." He laughed at his own comment.

"No, thank you," Peter said. "I lost my appetite for any sort of stew long ago. I think I'll try the rolladen."

"A fine choice," the waiter said. "We make that exceptionally well here."

And it was good. So good in fact that Peter not only ate the rolls of tender spiced beef, but the pickles at the center of each roll, which were, strictly speaking, only intended to flavor the beef as it cooked, and not meant to be consumed themselves.

Later in his room, before retiring for the night, Peter retrieved the many weapons from their secret locations in his suitcase, and installed them into their secret locations in the suit he would be wearing the next day, for the long drive to Hamelin.

Chapter Twelve
The Trial

In which Peter plays for a king.

T HE INTERIOR OF THE FORMER CHURCH WAS large and drafty. The room was circular, with vaulting archways at several stations in the curving wall, leading off to other sections of the building. Fluted columns lined the curved walls, bracing the first indented cornice overhead. Then there was another eight or nine feet of wall above that, elaborately decorated with intricate moldings and relief sculptures, depicting scenes Peter couldn't begin to interpret.

A second level of cornices supported the high domed roof, the interior of which was carved into rectangular coffers with stepped frameworks. Peter had played in many churches in the past, always with an appropriate sense of awe at being allowed inside such places.

Three or four dozen people were gathered into this chamber, which wasn't nearly enough to fill it up. Most of them were boys, some younger even than Peter, some older, while a few were young men. There were some girls too, but not many. They stood here and there, in no discernible organization. Any seats or benches that may have once been present in the chamber had long since been removed. There were only two plain, wooden chairs in the room, both of which were occupied. A man sat in one and a woman in the other. They were two of the only three full adults present.

Carl and Josef escorted Peter to the room's center, to stand before the two people who were seated.

"Can you stand on your own?" Carl whispered into his ear. "No, don't answer. Whether you can or you can't, you have to, so do it. The good news is, one way or another, this won't take long."

Carl and Josef released Peter and stepped back a few paces. Peter was wobbly on his feet, but was able to remain upright.

"Let's begin," the seated man said. "I don't like having this many of us gathered here all in one place." Peter couldn't begin to guess how old the man was. He could have been twenty or sixty. He was thin, but beginning to get a belly. He had dark hair, darker eyes and a short beard in good trim. An old scar slanted down one of his cheeks. He wore rough homespun, like the rest of them. His were dyed in green and ochre.

"This boy is called Peter," Carl said, turning this way and that as he spoke to address the entire assembly. "He's accused of unsanctioned thieving. Now he stands trial before Erwin, unchallenged King of all Thieves in the Town of Hamelin and its environs. Here also is Gisela, his advisor and his queen, and Hagan of the Lowenbrucke, Master of the Touch, and also a trusted advisor to the king." Carl's gesture indicated the other grown man standing in the room, among all of the children and young men. He wasn't tall, but was nearly as thin as Peter's lost brother Max. What hair Hagan had was also dark, but it was just a fringe circling around his ears and the back of his neck. He had bright green eyes that were fixed on Peter, seeming to pierce him, looking past his rude flesh and plunging deeply into his most private thoughts.

Gisela, the queen, seated beside King Erwin on his right, had reddish hair like Carl's. In fact she resembled him so closely she could've been his elder sister. She wore a brown dress of wool and a tan-colored blouse made of the only bit of linen evident in the room. She was pretty, but had a severe look on her face.

"Carl tells us he caught you stealing in my town," Erwin said to Peter, indicating that the few formalities had concluded and the actual trial had begun. "Is that so?"

"Yes," Peter said. He didn't know if he should call the man 'sir,' or 'king,' or any other form of polite address.

"And does anyone here recognize this boy as our brother?"

No one spoke.

"All right then. He's guilty of thieving without my permission, for which the punishment is death. Carl, since you caught him, you can kill him. Your prize is whatever he has — yours alone in this case, with no need to share it among us."

And with that, the trial seemed to be over. The king of thieves brushed his hands on his knees and began to rise, but he was interrupted when the queen leaned over from her seat and whispered in his ear. He abruptly sat down again.

"Hold on a moment," the king said. "My lovely bride reminds me that I skipped a step. Does anyone assembled here wish to speak for this boy?"

"I will," Carl said. Peter noticed that Carl hadn't tried to speak up, or hadn't even looked at all distressed, when the king had pronounced his quick judgment and started to leave.

"My young brother-in-law wishes to delight us again with his gifted tongue," the king said, proving that Carl was indeed related to the queen. "What do you have to add, Carl?"

"Two things, King. First, Peter didn't know he was breaking the laws of our Brotherhood."

"Ignorance of the law is no excuse," the king said, "as our current oppressors are so fond of reminding us."

"True, King, so then to my second observation," Carl said. "Peter proved to be a careful and inventive thief. I believe he can be trained to make a clever and useful addition to our society."

"He wasn't so clever as to avoid being captured by you," Hagan said, speaking for the first time.

"True, honored Master of Thieves," Carl said, "but no one can avoid my notice, or ever outwit me. I'm simply too skilled to be held up as an example to measure others against. Otherwise, no one here, not even the gloried king himself, could pass muster in our fine company." That brought a short round of snorts and chuckles from the gallery of young thieves in the room.

Hagan looked slightly vexed by the remark, but curiously the king didn't. Instead he smiled for the first time.

"Peter," the king said, "is what Carl tells us true? Are you fit to join our Brotherhood, knowing that it commits you to a life spent among us, sharing your wealth and marrying your sacred honor to us for all time?"

"Yes, King," was all that Peter said, knowing that he had no choice. The life as a thief, in the company of same, had to be better than the alternative. Peter correctly guessed that saying as much would do him no good, so he refrained from pointing out so obvious a fact.

"Then I'll defer my mortal judgment until we see if you can indeed impress us," the king said. "But you still have to pay for your crime, so, not only will you have to perfect your art quick and sure, you'll have to do it with only a single hand. My new decision is that you have to lose one hand as just payment for your previous misdeeds. Carl, be sure to find out which limb he favors, so we don't deprive him of his better thieving hand."

Once again the king started to rise. This time it was Peter who interrupted him, surprising all in the room at his temerity, Peter included.

"But, King, I'm not actually a — " Peter began, but then reconsidered his words, knowing it was a time to be most careful. "What I mean to say is, in addition to being a skilled thief, I'm also an accomplished player of the pipes. With only one hand I won't be able to do that any longer."

"So? What's that to me?"

"I'd like to request an entirely undeserved favor, King Erwin."

"This child has no right to ask favors from the king," Hagan said.

"Of course not," Carl jumped in. "Who does? I believe that's why it's called a favor and not an obligation." There were more soft titters of laughter in the room.

"What is it you'd like to ask?" the king said. "Maybe I'll consider it."

"Since I'm about to lose one hand," Peter said, "and will never thereafter be able to play, I'd like your permission to play my flute for you one last time, here in front of this company, before your fair sentence is inflicted on me."

The king considered for a long time, a frown creasing his face. No one dared speak while he did so, until the queen, his wife, grew weary of the protracted silence and unrelieved tension.

"Oh, let the boy play," she said aloud. And a smile touched her face for the first time, brightening it considerably. "It's been too long since we've heard any music in this dull town."

"Because it's been forbidden, dear Queen," Hagan offered.

"So what if it is?" she said. "Aren't we criminals? What's the use in breaking the law at all, if not to enrich our dull lives? A little flute music isn't likely to pierce these thick walls and betray us to the gobs. If they're close enough to hear that much, then they've already got us surrounded for other reasons. Play on, young Peter, and show us what you can do."

"I believe my queen just gave you a command, boy," the king said, settling back into his chair with a look that said, "you'd better impress me."

Which is exactly what Peter did.

First he removed his cloak and let it fall on the floor beside him. Then he began removing the various market items he'd stolen, beginning with the thick slab of bacon, which had been stuffed down the front of his jacket. He followed that by digging out the onions and potatoes from his various pockets and makeshift caches. As he did this, laughter began to build once again in the chamber.

"So, is it to be music and a juggling act as well?" the king said, laughing along with the others.

Peter didn't answer, unable to think of any retort that could do anything but make his position worse than it already was. Instead he finished divesting himself of his edible goods, carefully placing each one on the floor, on top of his cloak. Then he unlimbered Frost's case from around his shoulder and removed the bone white flute, handling it with care and reverence.

"Now there's a treasure I think I'd like my share of," Hagan said, in a whispered aside to the king and queen.

Peter placed the flute to his lips and began to play.

He selected a soft, slow lovers' song that he'd last played for a bride and groom on their wedding day. And as he played, for the second time since he'd come into ownership of the magic instrument, he devoutly wished that the danger would pass him by. As the melody increased in cadence and volume, members of the audience couldn't help but start tapping and clapping along with the tune's merry rhythm.

He ended with a flourish, and as he lowered the flute he noticed that there were tears in the queen's eyes.

"We can't deprive this artist of his hand," she said, her voice catching on pent-up emotions she tried, and failed, to conceal. "Not when he can do such wondrous things when he still has both of them."

"True," the king said, in a hushed and awed tone. "I thought I'd heard music many times before, but in truth I never did. Not before today."

Peter replaced Frost in its case, and then wiped two trickles of blood away from either side of his mouth, where Frost had again cut him.

"Your hand is given back to you," the king said, "as reasonable and just payment for your second job among us. For, in addition to joining our Brotherhood as a fellow cutpurse, you're appointed Royal Troubadour to this august court."

And that's how Peter Piper became a thief in earnest, far exceeding in every respect his long lost brother's most adamant accusation.

Chapter Thirteen

Fire Time

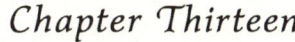

In which Max lives well, then not so well, encounters three knights and a witch, and receives a gift beyond price.

Max Piper stayed in his cozy cottage for several months, clear through the harsh winter, eating his fill every day and keeping warm by the crackling fire. Having gone hungry for an extended period of time, exposed all the while to the bitter elements, warmth, comfort and enough to eat became the sum total of Max's ambitions. It's entirely possible that he'd never have wanted to leave, if not for the deceit and low actions of Mr. and Mrs. Schoep, the cottage's previous owners.

At first Max had planned to simply kill anyone living in the home, going so far as to unsheathe Frost Taker for instant action, as he pounded boldly on the cottage's single door. But when the door finally opened, he saw that a timid old fat man and his old fat wife were the dwelling's sole occupants. He reconsidered the need for murder. Neither looked as if they could possibly offer him any harm. Better to question them first, at least long enough to find out how far away the nearest neighbors might be, and what dangers might lurk in this neck of the woods.

"Who are you?" Max shouted into the old man's face. Not waiting for an answer, he pushed past the fellow and entered the little home's single room.

"I'm Gerwulf Schoep," the old man said, "and this is Claudia, my good wife." Palpable fright was evident in Gerwulf's voice. Max recognized the tone as one of instantaneous and complete surrender. He'd have no trouble with these two — assuming there were only two of them.

"Who else lives here?" he demanded.

"No one. We're all alone," Claudia said. She'd been sitting in a wingback, densely upholstered chair by the fire. There was a bowl full of potatoes in her lap, which she'd been peeling with a paring knife. When Max burst in she seemed to shrink farther into the chair's cushions, as though hoping to flee by disappearing into them. "Our daughter from town visits us once a week to see that we're still well," she continued. "At least she used to, but she hasn't come in three weeks now."

"She was probably killed by the invaders," Max said.

"Invaders?" Gerwulf said, his wide eyes growing wider still.

"We'll talk about that later," Max said, "after I'm fed and rested. I've been days alone in the woods and suddenly find myself nigh exhausted. You'll cook my dinner and then stay quiet while I sleep by the fire."

"Lost in the woods?" Claudia said. "Oh, dear! You poor young man."

"Of course you're welcome to the hospitality of our home," Gerwulf said.

My home, Max thought, as he settled by the fire. But he didn't say it aloud. Better for now to let them think I might be willing to leave once I've recovered, just in case they conjure enough courage to try slitting my throat while I sleep.

After that long night, once Max had wakened to find his throat uncut and the Schoeps still cowed and deferential, he described to them, in no uncertain terms, the new pattern their three lives would take from that day forward. From now on Max was master of the house and the Schoeps would be his servants. Claudia would cook his meals, wash and mend his clothes, draw his baths and generally keep the home. Gerwulf would chop the wood for his fire, butcher the livestock for his meat, and generally do everything that needed doing outside of the home. Max explained that he never wanted to venture outside again – at least until new warm days arrived with next year's spring – and expected never to have to.

This worked well for a number of weeks. Max seemed content to sit by the fire all day, eating every meal there as Claudia brought them to him, and only moved when it was time to take to the cabin's only bed at night. He had no idea where his servants slept, since, at his insistence, they never retired at night until after he had, and always rose in the morning before he did. He never even stepped outside to use the outhouse — tucked almost invisibly back in the woods — but made his wastes in one of Claudia's treasured porcelain bowls. After all, it was their job to clean up after him and dispose of his messes. The Schoeps settled into their new life without a complaint and Max seldom had to correct them.

"You two are eating too much," he said one day, when the first snowfall of the year had begun to drift down from a dark sky.

"Excuse me, Mr. Piper?" Gerwulf said.

"We're nearly finished with the first pig you've butchered," Max said. "And there are only two pigs left, plus the cow. But once we kill that for its meat, we'll no longer have its milk. If we keep eating at this rate, we'll never have enough to last us through the winter. Now, as the master of this house, I can hardly be expected to do with less, but you and your wife aren't eating as lowly servants should. You're feasting every day as if this is your food, and not the bounty I've generously provided for you.

"But Mr. Piper — "

"Don't try to plead with me. You're both too fat anyway. Fat servants are an indictment against their lord. It shows others that he's not truly in command of his own household — that he lets even the lowest minion get away with stealing from him. Eat less, or I might be tempted to cut by one the number of mouths I have to feed. The two of you are barely doing a single man's work anyway. I'm too soft and indulge you too much."

From that day on, Gerwulf and Claudia were only allowed a single meager bowl of porridge in the morning and another at night. For the afternoon meal Max allowed them a small serving of bread, cheese and meat. When Max reckoned later that this new plan would insure a surplus by winter's end, he decided to increase his own portions, so as not to risk wasting any of it. Three times a day, every day, he tucked in with gusto, but remained rail thin.

The days accumulated along with the snow. Winter set in with grim intent.

Then one afternoon, when the snow had drifted high and the days had grown short, Max realized he hadn't seen Gerwulf all day.

"Where is he?" Max asked of Claudia, who looked nervous and flighty, like a quivering young faun ready to bolt at any provocation.

"There are many chores to be done outside," she said.

"Always, but he usually comes in three or four times a day to get warm. Has he suddenly discovered a reservoir of endurance and a sense of duty he never had before?"

"We're low on firewood," she said, "and I saw him earlier with the ax. Perhaps he's wandered afar in search of the right trees to fell. This deep snow makes for slow going."

That was a perfectly reasonable explanation, as Max had not the slightest idea what the true state of their wood supply was, seeing as how it was stored outside, under the same low shed that housed the animals in winter. But something seemed false in the way Claudia acted.

"You look nervous, Claudia, dear. What are you not telling me?"

"Nothing at all, sir. Only – "

"Yes?"

"Well, like you, I'm naturally nervous, because it has been some hours since Mr. Schoep's been gone. Though he's made his life as a woodcutter, he's not as young or strong as he was. And there are fell creatures in the woods."

"You're offering up a number of good reasons why poor old Gerwulf might be tardy," Max said. "But now I wonder if you might be providing too many."

"Never, sir!"

"Just the same, your worry has now become mine. I think I'd best go out and see if some harm has befallen the man."

"But, sir! You never go out!"

"And I shouldn't have to. But like you, Claudia, dear old Gerwulf is under my care, and a good shepherd doesn't neglect his flock. Besides, at least once before the season passes I should try out the new coat you've sewn for me over the past two months."

After Claudia had finished cleaning and mending Max's performance suit of bright colors, seeing how deft she was with a needle and thread, Max asked about the possibility of a coat to match. Claudia practically leapt at the idea, thinking that a warm coat might inspire him to once again venture outdoors, and doing that might inspire him to move down the road to oppress other homesteads. Claudia only had bits and pieces of cloth to work with, the scraps of a lifetime of sewing not only her own clothes, but finer dresses to sell at market each year. That suited Max's tastes just fine. A coat of diverse colors and patterns would be a delight.

So Claudia made Max a pied coat of bright yellows and cheerful blue stripes, and silky vermilions, and a dozen shades of verdant. There were bold reds offset by somber browns and amber checkerboards. Fine needlework designs tied it all together in a festive theme. It was a coat like no other, and Max loved it.

Then, in order to further encourage Max to leave, she sewed him a warm liner for his coat that could be buttoned in or removed at need. In his younger days, Gerwulf had been a hunter, as well as a woodcutter. He'd provided Claudia with many a fur pelt from which to devise expensive winter coats for rich townsfolk. Claudia used the many leftover scraps of treated pelts to form the liner, sewing them together any which way. She didn't worry about matching one type of fur to another, since Max reveled in the chaotic jumble of different shades and napes. Joined with the outer coat, it was a mantle that could keep a man warm on the coldest day.

Claudia made it all to encourage Max to leave, but now she acted as if that was the last thing she wished him to do.

"Don't worry, old mother. I'll bring Gerwulf back, sound and safe."

Claudia couldn't answer. Max put on his coat, with its fur liner, a pair of the couple's old fur snow boots, which turned out to fit his feet just fine, and then buckled his sword belt outside the coat. After he left, walking resolutely through the drifts, she tried to keep from weeping, but ultimately failed.

Maybe Husband left in time and is too far ahead to be caught now, she thought. And maybe Max will give up and turn back around, which, considering his past inclinations, seemed entirely likely.

Outside of the cottage, Max was nearly stunned by the intensity of the cold. His first instinct was to turn around immediately and go back in. But then he saw the tracks Gerwulf had left from earlier in the morning. It had snowed all night and not since then, so there was only a single set of tracks leading away from the cottage and they were as clear as could be. When he'd left early this morning — long before Max had awakened — Gerwulf had made straight for the forest path and then down it. There was no indication that he'd wandered the yard at all first, as someone setting out to do the day's chores might do. The tracks never diverted close to the trees lining either side of the forest path, as someone looking for wood to chop would need to do. It was instantly evident that Gerwulf was attempting to escape — no doubt off to seek armed men to bring back for a daring rescue of his tired old wife.

Max's long dormant rage ignited and grew into a strong and steady fire all in a single moment. Max the deadly forest predator was suddenly alive again and spoiling for the hunt. Without pausing for any further consideration, he set out at a run, following in Gerwulf's tracks.

Despite the snow's impediment, he made good time. Small, fat Gerwulf didn't have Max's long and lanky strides, and he'd had to cut a new trail through the fresh snow, which had accumulated belly-high in the relatively cleared area of the forest pathway. Max only had to follow in the trail the fat old man had already cut deep for him. He ran and then rested and then ran again, surprised to discover that he was enjoying himself. In fact, he was having fun. Now that he'd adjusted to being outdoors for the first time in months, he was perfectly warm in his long pied coat.

Max ran and ran, as the weary sun dropped closer and closer to the horizon.

Even in the dead of winter, the sun's setting was gradual enough that Max was surprised when he realized it had actually turned dark. He'd chased Gerwulf for hours, but now it was time to turn back. He'd learned his lesson months ago that attempting to navigate the woods at night was a fool's endeavor.

Then again, this was an odd sort of dark, for though the woods were black indeed, as was the sky overhead, the trail through the woods was still plain to see, draped as it was with a vast blanket of pure white snow. Even at night, the white snow stood out brightly, in stark contrast to the woods. He could continue on and still find his way back home without fear of losing his way.

And then, while Max was still dithering, trying to decide which way to go, he spotted a faint flicker of yellow light in the distance, like a single candle flame as seen from across a large hall.

"That's a fire," he said aloud.

So Max trudged onward. And in little time at all he came up on a humble campsite, pitched just off the side of the trail. Gerwulf was seated alone in the camp, close to the fire he'd built, but still shivering in his winter coat. He saw Max walk up on him, but made no attempt to flee, or grab for his ax, which was set into the same fallen log he was using for his seat.

"I thought you'd never try to follow me," he said.

"I almost didn't," Max said. Frost Taker rose slithering from its sheath, thirsty and eager, hardly helped at all by

Max's guiding hand.

"Four more miles and I would've made it," Gerwulf said. "But I got too tired to continue tonight."

"Bad luck then," Max said.

Frost Taker struck. Then it reared back and struck again, and again. It was all Max could do to hold onto it.

CLAUDIA DIDN'T LAST LONG after that night. She didn't need to be told a thing when Max returned to the cottage, early in the following morning. His grim face told the story entire. She tried to carry on and keep working, hoping that her daughter would arrive some day, with a company of hard men, to put things right. But the life had simply drained out of her with Gerwulf's loss. It was as if she had been stricken with the same thrusts of Frost Taker's blade that had killed her husband. Within two weeks she passed away in the night, leaving Max entirely on his own once again.

Max deeply resented the betrayal.

"I protected them and cared for them," he grumbled to the walls, "and they paid me back by abandoning me, just like Father and Mother did. And so did filthy Peter and all of the Peeps. They all ran off and left me in the woods to die like an animal."

After Claudia died, after he'd dragged her body to the edge of the woods and left it there, food for whatever sort of thing that might happen to come along and take it, Max had to fend for himself. He wasn't very good at it. He couldn't figure out how to coax milk from the cow and finally decided just to butcher it for its meat. But the cow didn't cooperate at all, finally running off down the snowy path, bleeding from a dozen minor cuts and lowing angry insults into the cold air. After killing four chickens, cutting them into useless jumbles of blood, gore and feathers, he finally managed to get one more or less intact onto a roasting spit. He did better with the pigs, having learned his lesson from the mess he made with the cow. He reached in and cut its throat first, before trying to cut or stab the animal anywhere else. Then he could chop at the dead pig all he liked, hacking off ragged chunks of meat as he needed them. But then, on the sixth day in a row that he trudged outside to cut his daily chunk of pork shoulder off the nearly frozen pig, he discovered that some beast had come in the night and dragged the remainder of its carcass away.

"That's not fair!" Max shouted up to the indifferent sky. "There was so much left!"

As the early spring rains came to start washing the snow away, Max killed the last pig, and this time he cut every bit of meat he could get off it all at once, taking all day and half the night to complete the bloody work. Then he hauled all of the meat inside the cabin, where it would be safe from predators in the night. It took him several trips to tote every piece inside and he piled it on the table and counter and on the top of the sideboard, after he'd cleared all of Claudia's fancy serving dishes off it. Within a month the cottage smelled like a charnel house, and Max was sick in his belly from rotted pork.

Aching and half delirious, he tossed the remainder of the rotting pig meat out off the front door, hurling each piece as far from the door as he could. Then he took to his bed and stayed there for eight days, writhing in a deep fever, until it finally broke and he felt well enough to get up.

The next day he trudged out to the animal shed again, empty now except for the chickens and a few remaining sticks of firewood. "Gerwulf lied about the firewood too," Max said, perhaps talking to the chickens. Perhaps not. "There was plenty. Didn't he realize that would be the first thing I'd check?" Max chose to ignore the fact that he hadn't actually checked. Then, with nothing more to say about the wood, Max gathered the eggs which had accumulated over the past eight days and brought them back into the cottage, where he boiled them all in Claudia's biggest copper pot. While the eggs boiled, he gathered up the remaining potatoes, carrots, onions, oats, sugar, salt, yellow cheese, and other sundries, and dumped them all into a single burlap sack. He didn't take the flour, because he had no idea how to turn it into bread, or piecrusts, or any of the thousand other wonderful things traitorous old Claudia was able to do with it. When the eggs were boiled, he added those too to the sack. Then he filled the pockets of his coat with plenty of flint and tinder for starting fires, after which he was more or less ready to be on his way.

He donned his warm coat of diverse colors, to which a goodly amount of pig's blood had recently been added, buckled on his sword belt, took up the sack of victuals. Then he stepped out the front door for the last time.

Patches of snow were still nestled into the crooks and crannies of the earth. The air was filled with the sounds of ten thousand trickles of water, melting off the remaining snow, running downhill, where it accumulated into the forest path, which acted as a makeshift drainage ditch, turning its ground into a soup of slick rocks and mud. "Better than struggling through the forest though," Max said. Then, once again picking his direction at random, he set off down the wet path, leaving the ruined little cottage in the deep woods forever.

Early in the spring of the new year, a dark and lovely young woman of the ancient craft walked down a wide forest road, in the company of a coal-black goat with high, twisty horns and eyes of red fire. She wore a dress of fine linen, dyed carnelian. Golden needlework in the pattern of leaves and twining thorn branches decorated its collar, sleeves and hem. A girdle of woven hemp enclosed her waist. From her belt dangled two daggers in bejeweled sheaths, one curved and the other straight. Also hanging from her belt was a small leather pouch of casting stones, with many an occult symbol inscribed on them. Her hair was long, black and silken. Her skin was pale and unblemished. Her lips were red. She chatted with the goat as they walked together. Her feet were bare against the road's hard-packed dirt and embedded stones. The goat wore no leash or tether.

Max watched the girl and her goat from the concealment of the woods. He'd wandered through the forest for days, having been scared off the previous small path by the passage of a company of goblin foot soldiers. They'd come marching single file down the same narrow path he was on, no doubt on their way to expand the extent of their conquest into the smaller side roads and remote corners of the territory.

Spotting them before they spotted him, Max had scrambled into the woods just in time to avoid their notice. Now, days later, he'd thrashed, cursed and stumbled his way to this much larger woodland avenue. He was about to step out onto it when he spied the girl and her companion goat walking towards him, approaching the place of his concealment.

What to do about her, he wondered? The last of his boiled eggs had run out a week ago, closely followed by the remaining cheese, carrots and potatoes, leaving him only a few overripe onions to sate his hunger. The goat might make a fine meal, he thought. And the girl? What might I do with her? Intriguing ideas began to occur to him, while he hid in the underbrush. She was indeed a pretty one, he considered, and I'm now, by any honest measure, a man grown. It's well past time I began to do things with pretty girls.

Max was in the process of screwing up his courage, preparing to step out into the road to block the girl's progress, when a new development interrupted his plans. The heavy sounds of approaching horses rose from behind the girl, farther down the road.

Only a moment later, three riders appeared from around the bend. They were three knights of the gentry — that much was immediately obvious. They were dressed in armor of shining plate over chain mail, and wore bright surcoats over that, decorated with complex heraldic devices on their breasts. The warhorses they rode were huge and intimidating beasts, snorting and thundering.

The dark girl turned to watch them as they rode up to her. She seemed unconcerned, only mildly curious, and made no move to flee, or even step off the road. The riders reined up next to her. Their horses' great hooves kicked up mud in their efforts to stop, spattering the girl's white legs and the hem of her fine dress.

"Well, here's an unexpected prize on a dreary day," one of the knights said. He was clean shaven and fair haired. His device was two golden gryphons, addorsed, with their wings abased. "What's your name, girl?" he said, unsheathing his most dazzling smile.

"I have many names," she said, "and I change them often, lest I begin to think of myself by one of them more than another. Then one of my rivals might learn of it and use it to conjure against me."

"Many names is fine," a second knight said, "as long as I can steal a lusty kiss from each one." That earned a laugh from the first knight, but the girl and the third knight remained silent and unimpressed by the jape. The third knight wore a deep scowl.

"We're wasting time here," the third knight snarled. "I want to be under good cover before the rains come again." He had dark hair and a dark beard that was cut into a single point that jutted from his chin like a dagger. His armor was enameled in a midnight blue, and his device was a red falcon at prey, against a field of vert. "You, girl. We're on our way to Hamelin Town to reinforce their imperial garrison."

"To greatly improve it," the second knight interrupted. He had long and curly brown hair, but a darker beard and mustaches.

His device was a purpure vine against a barry of twelve in argent and azure.

"Tell us if we're on the right road and how far away it is," the third knight continued.

"You're on the right road," the girl said, "and going in the proper direction. You'll reach Hamelin before nightfall if you continue to ride with a purpose. But I can't say if you'll get there before the rain resumes."

"I can," the goat said, startling all but the girl. Even Max in his hiding place was surprised. "The rain will certainly catch you before you can reach your destination. You'll arrive drenched to your new duty station."

"Blood of the gods!" the second knight said. "I can't abide animals that pretend to a man's speech." He dismounted, tossing the reins of his charger to the knight with the gryphons on his crest. "I'd thoughts of making my dinner out of this beast, but a talking one is unnatural. I won't have it." He drew his long sword.

"Stop!" the girl cried. "How dare you?"

But it was too late. The Knight of the Vines struck once and then twice. With the second blow the goat's head was separated entire from its body. Both parts splashed into a brown puddle on the muddy road. There was surprisingly little blood, but a dark and grainy mist seemed to rise from the carcass for just a moment, before fading into the afternoon's breeze.

"Nicely done, Sir Diederick," the Gryphons Knight said. "But I venture I could've done as much with a single cut."

"No," the girl said. "This wasn't nicely done at all. It's a fearsome power you've released back into the wild world this day. It took me a dozen lifetimes to bind it safely into so gentle a form. I'll have recompense from you three!"

"The only payment I'll award you," the Knight of the Vines said, "is a little bastard to round out your flat belly."

The girl said nothing to this, but backed away from the dismounted knight, placing a hand on the hilt of one of her daggers.

"It's not your place to demand anything from sworn officers of the Empire," the scowling Falcon Knight said. "You should take care, girl, lest we take you to trial as an unauthorized witch. You've already admitted as much."

"The trouble with witch trials," she said, "is that once in a great while you actually capture a real one. And then the spectacle never turns out the way you anticipate. Often the one who ends up hanged, or drowned, or burned, isn't the one in the docket."

The girl and the Falcon Knight glared at each other for a long moment. A few small raindrops pattered against armor and mud, advance skirmishers for the vast army to come.

"Mount your horse, Sir Diederick," the Falcon Knight said, breaking the brief contest of wills. "I told you we were wasting our time here."

The Vines Knight slowly, and some might say insolently, cleaned his blade on the goat's black coat. Then he sheathed it, took the reins back from his fellow knight, and mounted. He smiled one last smile at the dark girl, and blew her a kiss, before the company spurred their horses and rode off along the forest road.

Max stayed in his hiding place, determined to remain quiet as a mouse. Any thoughts he'd entertained about confronting this dark girl had fled. His new plan was to wait where he was, until, like the three imposing knights, she too had continued on her way.

The girl stood over the goat's black carcass for a long time, as the rain gradually grew more insistent. Then once again she said, "There will be recompense," as if making a promise to the dead animal.

After a while she resumed her way, apparently not minding the rain, which had begun falling in earnest by then. When she was directly across from Max's hiding place in the underbrush, just inside the tree line, she paused in the middle of the road and looked in Max's direction, as if she could see him, or at least knew he was there.

In his hiding place, Max was frozen in fright. Though he was certain of his concealment, she was looking directly at him. What should I do, he frantically wondered?

Then, never having spoken to him, the girl turned away and continued down the road. Soon enough she'd disappeared around a bend. Max stayed in place for many long minutes afterward, hardly daring to make a sound, and trying to understand what he'd witnessed. After a time, getting wetter all the while, he recalled his original desire to help himself to some of the goat's meat for his dinner.

The animal's of no use to anyone but me, he reasoned. So I might as well cut myself a roast. It's newly dead, so there's no chance it will be rotted like the last meat I had the misfortune to eat. And I'd best build my evening's fire soon, before there's no wood dry enough to light.

Timid as a deer, ready to spring away at any provocation, Max ventured out into the road. He walked a few paces up its length, to the goat's carcass, where he used his sword to hack and chop at it. In little time he'd cut himself several strips of meat. He brought the smallest one up to his lips to taste at it, never having tried goat before.

He nearly gagged.

"This wretched thing's flesh tastes of ashes and dust!" he said aloud.

He dropped the slice of goat's meat and looked all around him accusingly, though there was no longer anyone there to complain to. Out in the middle of the road, he was getting wetter under the more direct rainfall. He needed to be on his way. But first he needed to pick a direction in which to continue his wandering. He considered something the knights had said. They were on their way to Hamelin Town, and now Max remembered that he'd once undertaken a journey to the same place. That was where his family and the Peep family had agreed to rendezvous, should they become separated in the Black Forest. More important, if Peter were still alive, that's where he'd most certainly be.

Frost Taker practically hummed in its sheath.

"Peter has my inheritance," Max said. "The dirty thief stole it from me and thinks he got clean away with it. Time to set things right."

Frost Taker silently agreed.

"I can easily avoid any number of soldiers and silly little girls along the way. And Hamelin will certainly welcome someone like me – a fierce warrior, and a hunter of men." He thought of the warm beds and cooked meals that are always available in towns. So, like the three knights and the dark girl before him, Max set off in the direction of Hamelin.

AN HOUR LATER MAX WAS DRENCHED and miserable again. The cold rain had steadily increased in intensity until it had become a downpour. The day had turned dark, either with the coming of night, or by the heavy rain's shroud, or both combined. He thought about seeking shelter, until the worst of the rain had passed, and there, like an answer to his wish, he spied a house in the distance.

This was a cottage even smaller than the Schoeps' humble home. My former home, he corrected himself. Its four walls were made of wood planks on top of piled stones. Its roof was made of straw and it had a stone chimney. Its single door was made of stout boards and there was the face of a lion carved in it, with its jaws wide open. A wind chime dangled from one of the eves, with the shapes of stars and crescent moons carved out of copper. Against one wall there were set many clay and porcelain jars, of all different sizes. Some had lids fastened down on them, with wax sealing the rims, while others were left open and were now collecting rain. One jar had a picture of an ancient warship, engaged in a fierce battle, depicted on it. Many seashells were tacked up on the wall, above the jars, arrayed in a complex pattern of shapes and colors. Indecipherable runes had been inscribed all around them, in white paint against the wall's natural brown. To one side of the cottage, large rounded stones, each one draped in a cloak of deep green moss, were set out to enclose a rectangle of yard, which was filled with smaller pearl-white pebbles. There was the skeleton of a great beast lying in this enclosure. Max couldn't tell what sort of creature it had been, but in life it would have been large enough to swallow Max whole without the need of any of the many long fangs in its jaws. A hundred tiny green lizards sat on rib and skull, or scampered along the other parts, making their home among the bones. Welcoming light shone from the cottage's one visible window, which had real glazing fitted into its frames. A fat toad of many colors sat on a stump outside of the door, and watched Max as he approached.

"Croak," the toad said.

Max ignored it.

"Dinner's almost ready," the toad said next, which Max couldn't ignore.

All of a sudden, Max realized where he was. This must be the strange girl's house, and he turned away from the cottage, determined to be on his way again, despite the cold and rain. But before he'd made more than a few steps, the lion-faced door opened to reveal the dark girl standing in the threshold, silhouetted by warm and inviting yellow light.

"I was beginning to worry you hadn't received my invitation," she said, to Max's retreating back.

"Huh?" Max said, turning to face her.

"Won't you come out of the rain?" she said, stepping to one side, to wave him in. "Fafnir was right. Your supper's almost done."

"My supper?"

"Yes."

"For me?"

"Exactly so, though I hazard there might be enough for me as well."

Max stood in the wet yard, staring at her, mouth agape.

"If you can't conclude whether or not you're hungry, you might as well debate the matter in here, where you can at least get warm and dry while you decide."

After another moment, Max shrugged and entered the cottage.

"Welcome to my home, Max," she said, as he passed over her hearth.

"How do you know my name?" He stopped again, ready to bolt away.

"A simple working. You don't change your name often enough to hide it from one such as I."

Dinner consisted of plum pudding, a mountain of green peas, and a score of plump stuffed baby quail, baked into a flaky pie. Then there were buttered new potatoes and a dripping red roast, which the truly lovely girl invited Max to carve at as often as he liked. There were brown rolls just out of the oven to dip into the gravy or sop up the meat drippings. After all of that, there were fine cakes and golden mugs of beer, which, in the years before, Max had only been allowed to try once in a great while, on special occasions. But the girl, who would never speak her true name no matter how often Max asked, allowed him to drink as much beer as he liked. "I'm the Black Forest," she'd said once, in reply to his oft-repeated question, but that answer only confused him all the more.

"Are you married?" Max said, after taking a long draft of beer to wash down a mouthful of cake.

"Never," she said.

"I could marry you," he said, in a calculated offhand manner, as though he were willing to do her a favor in return for her kindness. He reasoned that he could do a lot worse than wedding a girl this young and pretty, who was also enthusiastic about feeding him. "I'm a man grown now and at an age when I should begin to think of such things."

"And perhaps we can talk about that someday, Max, but not just yet. You've so much to do for me first."

"Like what?" He began to look suspicious.

"Before all else, before you even take your revenge against your younger brother, for his sins against you, you will first become the instrument of my revenge against those who've so gravely insulted me today. You'll punish those three knights of the road, and all of their comrades in arms, and perhaps even the entire Hamelin Town, which they claim to rule. That's why I summoned you here tonight."

"How did you know about my brother?"

"I discerned ever so much about you when I first saw you in the woods. Your hatred and desire was a beautiful fire in the rain. How could you hope to hide among mere leaves and branches, with a flame that burned so brightly? And oh, Max, such a consuming will you have. By the terrible power of your will alone, you've managed to imbue a dull and lifeless blade with a modest touch of real magic, even though you've no understanding or practice in the craft. You've impressed me, Max. I've never seen such a thing done before, and would have considered it impossible before today."

"Frost Taker will help me get my inheritance back from Peter."

"Perhaps so, but consider some of the other artifacts and instruments here in my home. Some of them have much greater powers than a mere magic blade, the most powerful of which can still only destroy one soul at a time. There are better things here you could learn to use."

Max looked again about the cluttered room. Her cottage was bigger inside than out, which had disturbed him at first, until he'd decided that he must not have gotten a good look at the place in the dark and pouring rain. There were many more jars inside than out. Most of these were small ones, full of all sorts of tinctures and powders, the girl had said. Max didn't know what a tincture was, but knew that things in such tiny jars are usually women's stuff, so he didn't concern himself with them. There were also uncounted weapons in the place, stacked and leaned and placed everywhere, without rhyme or reason. He saw many more daggers, hanging from thongs, or sitting on tables, or stuffed into bookshelves to separate one book from another, and to mark a place that she intended to return to again. There were swords too, most of them so much finer than Frost Taker. And there were spears, and slings, and arrows, and other things that he didn't recognize, but which she assured him were absolutely instruments of mortal intent. She also had more books and scrolls than he'd ever seen, outside of the one time he'd been allowed inside the great stone library in Old Heidelberg City, when the Family Piper had played there one year. There were a hundred or more dolls, and the girl had said they were powerful conjuring devices, not meant for playthings. But Max assumed she was just embarrassed to still have them, after she was no longer quite young enough to keep such things.

 A fat yellow tomcat, covered in old scars, and missing one eye and most of its tail, stood up from the chest of drawers it had been sleeping on. It leapt ponderously down to the floor, to chase a mouse. When it suddenly moved, Max's eyes naturally followed it, and so alighted on the top of the chest and the shelves it

supported. On the second shelf up, he saw a long wooden flute, which he hadn't noticed before, embedded as it was among all of the other clutter.

"I can play that," he said.

"The flute?" she said, following the direction of his gaze. A sly smile began to grow upon her lips. It was the sort of smile from which devils and hauntings and deadly secrets are born.

"Yes, that's what I do." And then after a sullen pause, "Well, that's what I used to do, back when I was young, before the invaders came."

"Then that's what you shall do again," she said, taking him by the hand and leading him over to the old chest and its shelves. She picked up the flute and handed it to him. It was a few inches longer than Frost and made out of a deep red wood, polished to a remarkable finish. "There's powerful magic locked away in this thing," she said. "I've been meaning to learn to play a pipe someday, so that I could explore the uses this might be put to."

"I'll find its power," Max said, never taking his eyes off it. "What's its name?"

"I don't know," she said. "It came to me long ago, delivered by the trembling hand of a dying prince, who claimed to be the last of a dying race."

"Fire," Max said. "Its name is Fire."

And so it was.

Chapter Fourteen

The Piper at the Gates of Dawn

In which Peter returns at long last to a town he'd never been to.

It was less than two hundred miles from Frankfurt to Hamelin, as the crow flies. Unfortunately the proverbial crow didn't design Germany's autobahn system, which refused to provide Peter with any clear way to drive due north, the direction in which Hamelin was located. The best he could puzzle out, examining his map, was to circle way out and around the Hamelin area, by first going east or west, and eventually tacking back in towards his goal. In his many centuries in the mundy world, Peter hadn't had much experience driving modern automobiles at all, much less in mundy traffic, and never before on any of Europe's roadways. Shortly after leaving the greater Frankfurt metropolitan area, he became thoroughly lost.

Part of the problem was the lack of a speed limit on the autobahns. Keeping up with the traffic flow, which resembled a modern racetrack more than anything else, sent Peter off course much faster than he would have liked to drive. Every time he took a wrong turn on the autobahn, he'd be twenty or more miles down the road before he could get himself turned around. But when he finally abandoned the autobahn all together, deciding to proceed on the much slower, and much saner, backcountry surface roads, he ran into another problem. In mid October, Germany was in the waning days of Oktoberfest, a nationwide celebration that seemed to be dedicated to the single proposition of keeping everyone as gloriously drunk as possible. In every small town and village where he stopped to ask directions, the happy townsfolk would press giant complimentary mugs of beer on him, as an essential prerequisite to even the most cursory of conversations.

He drove past farmlands and through forested valleys in a pleasant, if occasionally frustrating fog of steady, low inebriation, eventually finding his way to Hamelin by late dinnertime.

The modern Hamelin of the mundy world turned out to be quite different from the sprawling, medieval version of the same town of his youth, back in the lost world of the Hesse. It wasn't just a matter of the streets full of cars, the ubiquitous electric lights and modern construction, though that was certainly part of it. It was more the attitude of preserving the old ways by fiercely embracing the new. When Peter found a restaurant near the gates into the old part of town that looked like it might provide a decent supper, he quickly discovered that there was literally no place to park. Parking wasn't allowed anywhere on the street — in order to preserve a more picturesque downtown, he later learned — but there wasn't a parking garage to be found either. Eventually a policeman directed him to the nondescript entrance of what turned out to be an underground parking facility where huge, computer-powered robot arms took his car and stored it in a tiny metal slot, which was one of hundreds of such slots in what looked like a giant, subterranean missile silo. The complex was more than twenty levels deep, and Peter stood at the top of it for more than an hour, watching in fascination as the robot arms slid up and down the sturdy central rail, continuously storing and retrieving cars, never making an error, never so much as scratching one of the vehicles.

"I thought I'd be coming home in a way, but this version of Hamelin is no place I ever knew," Peter said, watching the slots loaded and unloaded in a matter of seconds.

"Excuse me?" the garage's computer operator said.

"Nothing. Never mind."

After dinner, Peter retrieved his car and drove to the hotel he'd booked the night before from Frankfurt. It was located just a block outside of the walled old section of the city, on the eastern side of town. It was a four-star hotel called The Mercury, and was reputed to be the most elegant place to stay in Hamelin. But, as Peter discovered when he drove into its lot, it looked like a jumbled, haphazard construction of a learning-disabled child's building blocks.

"Too much modernity for me for one day," Peter explained to the desk clerk, when he stepped inside to cancel his reservation. He had the clerk book him instead into the best room available at The Hamelschenburg, a converted medieval castle, just a few miles out of town.

"This at least resembles the other Hamelschenburg Castle I remember from my home world," he said, while driving into its courtyard, with no one else in his car to overhear him and perhaps wonder at his meaning. "Maybe a touch smaller though."

That night Peter had trouble falling asleep, despite the room's overdone luxury. After a time he gave up and spent the rest of the night writing a long farewell letter to Bo, in care of the Woodland Building in Fabletown, and only to be hand-delivered to her once it was certain he was dead and never to return.

When he was done, he showered and dressed, carefully secreting all of his diverse instruments of death and mayhem into the various hidden pockets of his best brown suit. Then he checked out of his room, still in the dark hours of the morning, asking the night clerk to provide him with an international stamp and then post his letter for him. He retrieved his rental car from the very ordinary countryside parking lot and drove into Hamelin, where he once again surrendered it into the care of the all-night robotic underground automobile storage silo.

Taking Frost in its case with him, he walked the half-block to the high-arched gateway that separated modern Hamelin from the oldest part of the town. Just at the first light of dawn, Peter Piper stood outside the gate, looking up at the bas-relief sculpture on the gateway arch over his head. It depicted an ancient scene of the infamous Rattenfanger, the Pied Piper, leading a parade of ensorcelled children out of town.

Chapter Fifteen

The Pied Piper

In which Max perfects his craft and then visits Hamelin, where he does wondrous and terrible things.

From that day on, Max lived alone in the Black Forest, wearing not a stitch of clothing, and dwelling under no roof save the canopy of green branches overhead. His only possession was the flute named Fire, and if he hoped to stay warm, he'd have to learn to play a tune that would in fact conjure fire. Likewise, if he wished to stay dry, he'd have to devise a different tune that would make the rain pass him by, just as he'd have to compose a song of summoning, to draw the beasts of the woods to him, if he ever wanted aught to eat.

"Why can't I stay here?" Max had said to the Black Forest Witch (for a witch indeed she proved to be), when she'd ventured to turn him out of her home.

"Because," she said, "when you live in comfort you become lazy and indolent. The Max of old returns, the whining, human boy, who only wants all things to be provided to him. But when you face privation, when you're forced to live rough, in the deep of the woods, the other Max comes alive. That's the creature I want to know and encourage, the merciless beast in the night who never was a man but is a new thing all its own. That's the Max that might someday learn to tame the powers hidden in Fire's depths."

"At least let me take my clothes and my sword."

"Never," the witch said. "You've accepted my gift, and all else belongs to me now. You may get them back someday, when you've unlocked Fire's secrets. And even then you must first prove to my satisfaction that you can wear the things of man, and dwell among men, without becoming man again. Only then will you be fit to enact my chastisements against those who've so grievously tasked me."

"How long will that take?"

"When has the passage of time ever mattered to me?"

Max knew that there were some questions to which an answer was neither expected nor desired. He suspected this was one of those. So, with nothing more to discuss, he took up Fire and went naked and alone into the forest, where he lived a long time.

ONCE A YEAR, ON THE EVENING OF THE HEXENNACHT, Max was allowed to return to the witch's house. On his first visit he demonstrated how he'd learned to set fires and control the rains, making them appear and dissipate at his desire, all at the command of the many haunting tunes he'd crafted. He could make any animal of the forest flee from him, or else come to him, and sit passively, within arm's length, while he took up a sharp stone and killed it for his supper. This too he showed to her.

"I'm not impressed," she said. "Where's the true mastery? Why is it you need to take up a stone to kill and strip the flesh? Why haven't you composed a more subtle tune that will not only cause the animal to come to you, but to expire at your feet, and then to be magically cleaned and cut for your cooking spit?"

So Max went dejected back into the woods.

On the second year's encounter, Max showed how he could make a full, prepared dinner appear out of nothing at all. He sat at an elegant table, covered with a white cloth of fine linen, and dined on a dozen gourmet courses, served on platters of pure silver.

When he was done, and the table and the silver and all of the scraps vanished into the nothing it had once been, all she said was, "You look silly, sitting naked and filthy at a fine table.

Pick the twigs out of your hair. And is that supposed to be a beard trying to dress your chin?"

And so it went. Year after year he presented himself at the witch's house, but each time she turned him away on some pretext or another. Then, when seven full years had come and gone, Max returned once more to the witch's dwelling. He was still naked and his flesh was pale in the moonlight. His hair was long and tangled, as were his whiskers. His eyes were dark and shadowed. He held Fire in one hand and it seemed by then to be a piece of him. He appeared out of the dark of the woods, but he didn't knock at her door, nor did he call out.

Sitting by her fireplace, in the comfortable chair of which she was most fond, reading by the fire's homey light, an odd feeling came over the witch. She marked her place in the book and set it aside. Walking to the door she said, "Be on guard," to the fat yellow tom, with its many scars of battle. Opening the lion-headed door, she looked out to behold Max, standing in the middle of the road, regarding her with terrifying eyes.

"I'm finished dancing to your tune," Max said.

"Then why are you here?" the young girl said. She sensed many shadowed things at the edges of the forest. Large and deadly shades, not entirely part of this world, lurked just out of sight, hungry, restless and straining to be set loose.

"I've returned for my things."

"And so you shall have them," she answered, "for you've finally become all that I'd hoped. Now, at long last, you can reenter the world of men and conduct my mortal affairs."

"Do you think so? After so long?"

"Of course. All three knights of the road are still in Hamelin, where they've flourished, rising to diverse positions of power and authority over the city and its outlying districts, for leagues in every direction. My many spies have kept them under close scrutiny for all these years. They've each married and sired children, on whom they dote. And this is where my vengeance will fall, because simply killing them long ago wouldn't have done. They wouldn't have suffered near enough. Instead I will now deprive them of that which they love most."

"You misunderstand me," Max said. "I was asking how you can still expect me to do your dirty business after so long. I've learned too much from Fire – perhaps more than you'd anticipated. Now I control powers and forces from far beyond the lands that we know. How do you imagine you can continue to bend me to your will? What can you possibly do to threaten me now?"

"Nothing much, I suppose," she said. For the first time in countless years, the witch felt the alien touch of concern for her own safety. He has indeed surpassed all that I'd expected, she thought. How much power is bound up within that one small device?

"But here's one talent I wonder if you've managed to master," she continued. Her calm voice masked her unaccustomed anxiety. "In all the years you've played with Fire, and played upon it, have you ever tried to use it to locate Frost, and the brother who keeps it from you? And, if you've tried, have you ever succeeded?"

"What are you getting at, woman?"

"Only this: I know where Frost is. For all these years that you've been learning the ways of Fire, I've been doing the same with Frost, always from a discreet distance of course. It's a wonderful and ancient thing and, for all its raw power, Fire will never be able to find it, because Frost, though less powerful, is more ancient and more cunning. Peter and his flute are forever invisible to you."

"But not to you."

"Exactly so."

"And therein lies our new bargain?"

"You've unearthed the full measure of it," she said.

At the height of summer, in the ninth year of its occupation by foreign invaders, a stranger presented himself at Hamelin's easternmost gate and demanded entrance into the town. He was dressed in a feathered cap, a newly cleaned and mended suit of bright colors, over which he wore a long, pied jacket, all of which seemed much too much of a muchness, both in its riot of color and the sheer totality of stifling cloth, for this was a very hot day. But the man appeared not at all affected by the heat. He had long hair and a long beard, both of which were all a-tangle. And he had wild, angry eyes that were never the first to look away. He carried a long red flute and nothing else.

"I'm Max, the Piper," he boldly announced to the guards at the gate, "and I've come to confer with your town fathers."

Now, by this time, the freedom to hear and play music had been restored to Hamelin, among various other liberties. Things had settled down over the years, as things will. Day by day, and year by year, the townspeople gradually grew more cooperative, as they acclimated to their new lives, lived in service to their new lords. In time, the new way seemed to become the natural way. In response, the ruling authorities had rightly calculated that their iron grip over the day-to-day activities of the indentured populace could be relaxed in some areas.

But Hamelin was still governed by a military bureaucracy, so there was a certain way everything had to be done. Those minstrels wishing to ply their trade in the city first needed to seek the proper permissions, pay the prescribed fees, and obtain the appropriate passes and licenses, from each of the many civil ministries who shared oversight of such activities. And all had to be undertaken with a respectable measure of humility and deference. One didn't simply march up to the nearest city gate and boldly announce one's intentions, demands, or grand expectations. It just wasn't done.

And yet that's precisely what this arrogant, or foolhardy (or perhaps suicidal) pied piper did.

Grubel Kaidan was a goblin who knew his place in the grand scheme of things. He was a soldier of the celebrated Twenty-Third Horde. And he intended to remain such, until a glorious battlefield death claimed him, or he'd reached the age where mandatory retirement would send him packing. He always did his duty, never shirked, and looked out for his troops as much as he could within the strictures of good military discipline. He made it a point to always know what his superiors expected of him, just as he made sure those under his command always knew what he expected of them. "That's the only way to run an army," he'd often opine. He didn't much care for garrison duty, preferring the joys and terrors of frontline combat. But he did it, and without complaint, because any gob who thought he should be the one charting his own course in life wasn't fit to be a soldier. On this particular day Grubel was serving as the Sergeant of the Guard for that section of the town which included its Eastern Gate.

"What's all this uproar about?" he said, when summoned to the East Gate.

"These creatures are attempting to keep me out," Max said, before either of the goblin soldiers could report.

"Then you'd best be on your way," Grubel growled in reply, "before I allow one of my troops to chop you into tidy pieces for the enlisted gobs' stewpots."

Max only smiled.

Without further discussion, he stepped back a pace or two, raised the flute named Fire to his lips and began to play a simple and cloying tune. Grubel snorted once and blinked hard and rapidly, to clear the tears from his suddenly burning eyes. He wiped furiously at his eyes and runny nose with one of his large, meaty fists. His two goblin troopers also seemed to be suffering from the same malady, as they too sneezed, squinted and frantically rubbed their faces.

Then, just as suddenly, the awful feelings passed, even though the piper played on. Grubel felt fine again. In fact, he realized that, for the first time in a very long time, he felt truly marvelous.

"Who was it you wished to see?" Grubel respectfully asked the piper.

Max stopped playing then and lowered Fire once more to his side. "The top man," he said. "Whoever's actually in charge. I've no patience for clawing my way up through the usual layers of underlings."

"Then do please follow me, sir," Grubel said. He snapped to attention, executed a perfect military about-face, and began marching off into the city. He marched proudly, happy to be of service in any possible way to this wise and wondrous man, determined to see that nothing stood in the way of whatever the pied piper desired.

Max followed, after politely acknowledging smart salutes from the two guards.

"Mere quarters won't do," Max said, "no matter how lavishly appointed. I want an entire house, all to myself, and make it a fine one — the best that the town can provide. I'll expect servants, including butlers and valets, maids and housekeepers, and coachmen of course to operate the expensive coach you'll also provide. And what else? Oh yes, I'll require only the best cooks, exclusive to my needs." He could of course continue to magically summon the most exquisite food for each meal, but that seemed a waste of Fire's many abilities. Each time he drew power from Fire's deep well, it wearied him, often for hours afterwards. Better that he learn to save Fire's miracles for more important tasks.

"Excuse me," Lord Diederick interrupted, when it looked as if the oddly dressed stranger seated in his office was about to continue listing his incredible demands. "Why would I even consider providing any of these things to you? I'm still not sure why anyone even agreed to show you in here."

This was the same Sir Diederick that was one of the three knights of the road, so many years past. But, as well as being a knight of the Twenty-Third Horde, he was also a Baron now, and in charge of the city's civil administration. He wore a fine suit of imported green silk, which had his nobleman's crest of vines sewn on its breast. In addition to Max, fat old Wenzel, the town's civilian mayor, sat in the room. The Empire liked to leave cooperative local officials in charge, whenever they could, to preserve the illusion of local autonomy. Mayor Wenzel turned out to be so completely cooperative with the invaders that he was allowed to sit in on important meetings and even administer some civic duties on his own.

"You'll provide me with all of these things and more," Max said, "because I'm a powerful sorcerer. I can do many things of benefit to you and your empire, and should be rewarded in kind." Without consulting the Black Forest Witch, Max had decided to defer her vengeance, for a year or two, so that he could first sample the various luxuries that only a fine city like Hamelin could provide. She'd made such a point about hardly noticing the passage of time, he thought, that she wouldn't mind waiting a little while longer.

"But then you'll have to wait all the longer to have your own reckoning with Peter," is what Frost Taker would have whispered to him. But Max had elected to leave the blade behind, in the witch's care, thinking that Fire, being so much more powerful, would be all the weapon he'd ever need from now on.

"The Empire already has sorcerers aplenty," Diederick said. "Every horde has a company of them, to enchant hardness into our blades and armor, courage into our troops, and true flight into our arrows."

"And can any one of them also make an opposing army surrender en masse," Max said, "or cause them to simply die in the field, without a single blow being struck, or an arrow fired?"

"Of course not. No one can."

"Except me," Max said.

"Nonsense! I'll hear no more of this!" Diederick was ready by then to have Max thrown into the streets — or better yet, the city dungeons — along with whoever played a part in allowing him to get this far. But something in Max's eyes made Diederick pause. Mayor Wenzel seemed to sense it too, because he spoke up for the first time.

"Perhaps if you could prove your extraordinary claims," Wenzel said.

"Name it," Max said, "and I will accomplish it."

"Impossible," Diederick said. "I can't send an untested sorcerer out on a military mission."

"Then choose something less martial for my first task," Max said. "What do you need done? What dire problem needs fixing?"

"There's always the rats," Wenzel offered, in his customary cringing and wincing way, as if he expected to be struck for the simple impudence of proffering one of his ideas. But he didn't get struck. In fact Lord Diederick seemed to brighten at the suggestion.

"True," Diederick said. "Get rid of Hamelin's rats. Those vermin are everywhere, spreading filth and disease. Even with a generous bounty offered on every one, we still can't make a dent in the problem. They breed faster than we can kill them."

"They fight the dogs and kill the cats," Wenzel added. "And bite the babies in their cradles."

"An easy task," Max said. "By the power of my smallest

charm, I'm able to draw after me all creatures living beneath the sun, that creep or swim or fly. By breakfast tomorrow, there won't be a rat in all the town." Max rose to his feet. His fingers seemed ever to stray over the length of his wooden flute, as if he were constantly eager to be playing it. "And in return I'll expect at least a thousand silver marks."

"Only that?" Wenzel said. "Do all that you say and we'll give you fifty thousand."

"Then we have a deal," Max said. Tipping his colorful, feathered cap, he left.

When it was clear that Max was safely gone from the building, Diederick said, "I do believe you let your enthusiasm run away with you, Mister Mayor. Just where do you expect to conjure up the fifty thousand marks you promised that man? Your salary, combined with your office's entire annual budget, doesn't come to that much."

"But the treasury — " Wenzel began, his face a sudden study of despondence.

"The treasury isn't available at your whim," Diederick said. "You'd better hope the man turns out to be the charlatan I suspect him to be."

"But — "

"After all," Diederick continued, "You were the one who proposed the rat-clearing task. I didn't. I can hardly be expected to pay for your unsanctioned exuberances." Diederick thought he could hear almost inaudible keening and moaning from the fat old mayor, as he ponderously removed himself from the Baron's suite of rooms, clutching his ermine-lined robe of office tightly, almost protectively, around himself as he went.

THAT NIGHT, WHILE PEOPLE LAY ASLEEP in their beds, the sound of music drifted like a fine mist through Hamelin's countless alleyways and thoroughfares. The enthralling tune seeped everywhere, through shuttered windows and iron sewer grates, over each rooftop, around each garden wall, and under each stone footbridge. Slowly at first, in ones and twos, and then more rapidly, in great, undulating carpets of filthy, wet fur, the rats began to appear. They swarmed up out of basement and sewer, and into the cobbled streets. Down out of every attic and loft they came, frantic in their need to find the source of the music and follow it.

A young thief in the night, out at his prowls, spotted the vast, swarming miracle that filled every street, and he marveled at it. He was called Cort and was one of King Erwin's secret brotherhood of cutpurses. He sat atop one of the high walls surrounding the grounds of the Cathedral of Saint Nicolai, watching the endless parade of rats and listening to the soft tune that seemed to come from everywhere and nowhere. *It reminds me of Master Thief Peter's playing*, he thought, *except that Peter's music always makes me feel glad to be alive, whereas this tune makes me feel odd and wary.*

A peddler boy named Till Eulenspiegel, who was too poor to afford a roof to cover himself, was sleeping in the street, under his pushcart, from which he sold rolls of bread baked into the shapes of monkeys and owls. His deep slumbers were abruptly and violently interrupted, when an army of rats overran him. They scampered across his body in wave after wave. Not a one of the vermin paused to take so much as a nip out of him, but still young Till screamed and screamed, for an hour or more, until long after the last of the rats had come and gone.

The rats swarmed southward and eastward, along every avenue and byway, filling each street by the tens of thousands, until they congregated in the great open square where three major avenues converged at the Western Gate. That was where Max stood, in the very center of the open gateway, playing his compelling tune on the pipe named Fire. A vast and wriggling pile of rats was forming around Max, as the ones in the rear scrambled and surged forward, to be nearer the source of the commanding music, while those in the front kept a respectful distance of at least three feet all around the sorcerer. Small mountains of living beasts kept forming and collapsing around him, until Max finally turned and led the way through the city gate and out onto the broad stone bridge that spanned the mighty Weser River.

The rat army followed Max out onto the bridge and then midway across the wide Weser, they felt compelled to hurl themselves over the low stone railing and into the dark waters down below. Rats great and small gladly killed themselves, all at the musician's command. Brown, black and grey rats eagerly jumped to their doom. Lithe young friskers leapt over grave old plodders, in order to drown all the more quickly. It took hours for the last of the rats to jump to its destruction.

When it was all done, and he could finally stop playing, Max was tired, as tired as he'd ever been. He thought briefly about turning back into the city, to magically force someone out of his home and hearth, so that he could collapse into the commandeered bed. But the thought of even that much extra expenditure of Fire's powers was beyond his will to contemplate. Instead he continued across the rest of the bridge and into the forest that girdled the far bank. It's the full flush of summer, he thought, and I'll be warm enough in the open. As soon as he was just a few paces into the woods, where he was sure to be unobserved by any passerby, he dropped like a stone into the underbrush and fell fast asleep.

Eighteen days and nights passed before Max woke and presented himself once again at Hamelin's City Hall.

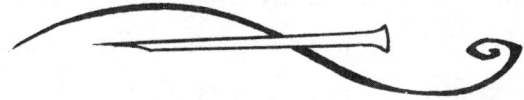

"Gone?" Max shouted. "What do you mean my money's gone?"

Mayor Wenzel fairly quivered with fear, but somehow summoned the courage to answer the mad-eyed piper. "When you never showed up to collect it, the money went back into the city treasury. Since then it's been spent on other vital necessities of the community." Baron Diederick sat silent in the room, behind his big oaken desk, perfectly content to let Wenzel spin his web of lies and impromptu fabrications. In fact he almost admired the old man's alacrity at being able to create so many reasonable-sounding falsehoods so quickly. Then again, Diederick reminded himself, to keep this moment in mind the next time Wenzel came to him with his usual excuses and prevarications for things not done.

"But I'm here to collect my reward now!" Max yelled.

"Too late," Wenzel whimpered in reply. The documents have already been filed and the accounts closed. You should've been more prompt, young man. There's simply nothing we can do. If you still feel you have a grievance, it's a matter for the courts now. But of course you'll have to wait for an opening in their schedule, which is always quite full. I think early November is the soonest they might possibly fit you in."

"I'm supposed to sue you?"

"Not me personally. It's the City of Hamelin you need to contest against, which of course is part of the Weser Mountains Region, which is part of the Greater Southern Saxony Administrative District, which — well, your lawyer will explain all of that to you. Basically it's the Empire you have to sue, but I caution you to proceed most carefully, young man, because those who undertake legal actions against the Empire tend to wind up in dank dungeons — or worse." Wenzel's voice dripped with sincere concern over Max and his dilemma.

"I have no intention of suing you!" Max said.

"As unfortunate as this situation is, I think that's the wisest choice."

"I intend to destroy you!"

"Now see here! There's no cause for that sort of talk! We're all civilized gentlemen and — "

"Wrap this up, Mister Mayor," Diederick finally interrupted. "I have other appointments waiting." And when Max turned his evil glare towards him, he said, "And you'd better watch what you say. Threats against public officials are a crime against the Empire, even those directed against useless ones like our dear mayor. And see that you don't darken my door again. This trick you did ridding our town of rats was sweet enough, and you should be commended for it. But I don't see that it has any military applications. So, in short, we've no further business with each other."

Max was silent for a long time. Then he said in a low voice, almost imperceptible, even in a room as quiet as this, "You too,

Baron So and So. You don't escape blame in this matter. After tonight you'll both regret the despicable way in which you treated me today, for I realize now that it's high time to enact the witch's vengeance after all."

"Get out now, or I'll call my guards!" Diederick fairly screamed.

"Call whomever you wish," Max said. "It makes no difference to me." But he left all the same.

Wenzel was surprised to see the usually bold Baron Diederick do nothing but tremble behind his desk for some time – whether from fright or rage was beyond his powers to discern. Something in that odd boy's eyes though, he thought. There was definitely something troubling there.

THAT NIGHT, LOW, SORROWFUL MUSIC played again in Hamelin, filling the enraptured air. But this time no rats responded to it. This time it was the town's children who were affected. Before the third note sounded, a child stepped out of his mother's house, into the street. Then another. And another.

There was a rustling throughout the city as first one door and then another creaked open. There was the slithering sound of leather slippers sliding over the hard surface of the streets, and also the sharp "tock" of wooden shoes against the cobblestones. Tallow-haired boys and rosy cheeked girls walked serenely, or scampered excitedly, or even skipped merrily. The smaller ones ran to keep up with the larger ones.

Till Eulenspiegel rose up from under his pushcart and joined the throng. Once more out and about on his nightly rounds, the young thief named Cort hopped down from a rooftop and skipped along with the others. And by extra special invitation, woven into the drifting notes of the piper's tune, the children of the three former knights of the road stepped out to join the eerie parade. Here were Beatta and little Ulrich, who were the Baron Diederick's children. And there walked Thorben, the proud falcon knight's only son and heir. In little enough time they were joined by Alban, Erich, Frauke and Gretchen, the gryphon knight's two sons and twin daughters. Finally, darling little Erna, the old mayor's only granddaughter, took her place in the ever-growing procession.

The same magic that compelled the children kept everyone else frozen asleep in their beds, undreaming and unaware of the evil deed that was occurring just outside of their doors and hearths.

In all, one hundred and thirty boys and girls followed the piper out of town. They were never seen again, unto the end of days.

"Leave two of the youngest here with me," the Black Forest Witch told Max. "I need to put them under my knife, to keep my powers strong through the coming year. The rest are yours to do with as you will." Max had marched the children out of the city and down mile upon mile of winding forest roads, until they'd arrived here at the witch's cottage in the deep woods. The sun had risen high in the sky by the time they'd come this far. Max had played the entire time, leading the company of doomed children ever onwards.

"I intend to take them far away," Max said, "to lands beyond the fields that we know. I have old debts to pay among the principalities and powers of other worlds, for the things they helped teach me during my years in the forest. Our journey will take some time — years perhaps — for I must rest often and make them sleep when I sleep, and I must play always when they march."

"And will you ever return?" she said.

"Once and once only," Max said. "To learn of Frost's location from you. After that we need never see each other again."

The witch could only hope that turned out to be true.

Chapter Sixteen

CLOAK AND DAGGER

*In which a humble
churchman's home
is invaded,
Peter meets a dark
figure from out
of his past, and then
writes a letter.*

A LITTLE MORE THAN A YEAR LATER, THE good folks of Hamelin were still in a collective misery from the horror of their stolen children. The town's military occupiers, some of whom had also lost sons and daughters that night, were also stricken and resolved to do something to insure future safety and security.

Rules that had been relaxed were strict again, curfews were rigidly enforced, and punishments for even the most trifling of crimes were both draconian and severe.

The public outcry, once people had woken up on that fateful morning to find more than a hundred of their children missing, was directed at both the town's puppet government and at the actual military rulers, who preferred to work behind the scenes, but whom everyone knew really pulled the strings. Riots were barely averted, but only through the dual practices of a rigid and brutal crackdown, accompanied by profuse promises of widespread government reform at every level.

Prior to the invasion ten years ago, Hugo the Charitable was the Bishop of Saint Nicolai's Cathedral, and official shepherd over all of the souls of Hamelin, the Weser and of Lower Saxony. And like most high-ranking ecclesiastical fellows of his time, his interests weren't limited to the spiritual realm. He was knee-deep into every aspect of secular politics, pulling the strings of the mayor and his cronies back then, much the way their occupiers did now.

Since the invasion, Bishop Hugo had been kept a prisoner in his own house, not allowed to set foot outside the doors of Saint Nicolai's, against the promise of instant arrest. This was deemed necessary by the town's new rulers, at least until such time as the Empire decided its official policy regarding the Hesse's predominant religion. But when the tragedy of the Pied Piper occurred, and Hamelin's beleaguered townsfolk turned away in disgust from the mayor and his foreign masters alike, it was only natural that they would turn once again to the repressed church with renewed vigor. And even though no final word had come back from the worlds-distant capital of the Empire, it was obvious to Baron Diederick and the other local military rulers that something had to be done quickly to avert a disaster.

Secret meetings were held. Negotiations were undertaken. Plans were hatched. Agreements were reached.

Two months after the night of the Pied Piper, all of the closed and abandoned churches throughout the town were approved to be reopened and rechristened, causing more than one set of illegal squatters to have to vacate those places in an awful hurry. Priests and churchmen who'd been imprisoned over the years of the occupation were released, free once again to take up their holy vestments. And then, miracle of miracles, Bishop Hugo was once again allowed to step outside of the cathedral and openly walk the streets of his city. He appeared in all his finery, and such a grand procession it was that formed behind him! The impromptu parade lasted all day, and noble Hugo looked like one of the mighty kings of ancient legend surveying his realm.

A month later town criers wandered through Hamelin, announcing the Occupational Government's official apology for those church officials who never survived to reach their prison cells, due to the overly enthusiastic nature of some of the sword- and ax-wielding troops sent out to capture them.

In succeeding weeks other announcements were made. From now on, church attendance would not only be tolerated, it would be encouraged. All enforced labors, even for convicted prisoners, would cease on Sunday. The promised reforms were proceeding apace.

Finally, just a few weeks ago, the big announcement came. In a month's time, on the one-year anniversary of the Night of the Pied Piper, all of Hamelin would gather in the cathedral square, to remember and mourn the lost children. And then, at the conclusion of the solemn observance, the mayor and officers of the Occupying Government would officially hand over the reins of local rule to Bishop Hugo. In return, or so it was widely rumored, Hugo would immediately decree that Hamelin Town, its environs, and all of its people were now, and would forever be, loyal subjects of the Empire, whose existence had been approved and ordained by almighty God Himself.

Peter Piper celebrated his twentieth birthday only four days before the big event. The party was held in the underground hall of the Brotherhood's new headquarters, since they'd recently lost their old home to the citywide restoration of the church. After the toasting and feasting, and after Peter had gifted them all with a wild and raucous concert on his flute, Erwin, king of all thieves, took Peter aside for a private chat.

"I fear our beloved Bishop Hugo the Charitable has been a little too generous in his charity giving," Erwin said, once he'd gotten Peter away from the chance of prying ears. "I fear he's given all of us away, into the hands of the enemy, in return for his personal freedom and getting his power back. He's sold us down the river, you and me, and everyone else for a hundred leagues in every direction."

"True enough, I suppose," Peter said. "But what can we do?"

"He can't complete the dirty deed unless he presides over this ceremony in a few days' time. So what do you say we put a stop to it?"

"How?"

"You're my Master of the Touch now. So you'll sneak into the old bastard's house, the night before the big to-do, and lift his signet ring. That's the absolute symbol of his authority. Without it he can't appear in public, or do anything official."

"I don't know," Peter said. "This is awful short notice. A touch like this takes time and preparation. You taught me that. The Bishop's residence in the cathedral is like a fortress, with all of the protections that implies."

"I've already had a chat with Lukas, our Master Caser, and Carl, our Master of Bribes. All of our top brothers are working on this one — you included."

Carl the Arrow, King Erwin's brother-in-law, and Peter's closest friend in the Brotherhood, had been first in line to become the Master of the Touch, the most prestigious honor and exalted office among thieves, short of being the king himself. But an unlucky ax cut three years past, on a job gone horribly wrong in both planning and execution, had left Carl crippled for life, with a limp that would never fully heal. An unhindered ability to move silently and lithely through the shadows, over walls and along rooftops, was essential to anyone who hoped to excel in the art of the touch. With Carl's blessing, Peter moved up to take his place, while Carl went on to distinguish himself in the tricky business of bribery, a talent for which it turned out he had a heretofore unrecognized gift.

"This is a huge score," Erwin continued, as Peter persisted in looking dubious. "Three thousand marks, of which you get the lion's share."

"Who's the client?" Peter said.

"I guess that would be me," Erwin said. "But don't you never tell nobody. Everyone would think I'd gone soft."

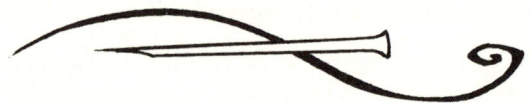

ON THE NIGHT BEFORE the memorial ceremony, Peter crouched on the high-peaked roof of Dempter House, a four-story mansion that had once belonged to the richest merchant in Hamelin, but which now served as the Bachelor Officers' Quarters for the most senior members of the Empire's Twenty-Third Horde. It was located directly across Market Street from the cathedral and afforded Peter an unobstructed view past the high churchyard walls, into the cathedral's grounds. The deep shadows cast by Dempter House's street-side crenellated façade insured that Peter could lurk there all night without fear of being observed.

The cathedral proper occupied the northernmost section of the grounds, but it was one of the other buildings that commanded Peter's interest. Directly south of the cathedral, attached to it by a covered stone walkway, was the Bishop's personal residence, a many-gabled stone structure called, humbly enough, the High Holy House. Peter crouched motionless and watched for hours, until he'd recognized and memorized the pattern of the elite Cathedral Guards as they made their rounds. He wanted nothing to do with them. Though they dressed themselves in effeminate-looking liveries of fine silk and linen, their brightly polished, jewel-encrusted weapons weren't just parade ground showpieces, and they had a reputation as fierce and fanatical warriors. Peter's only weapons were two daggers secreted within the folds of his clothing — one for throwing and one for stabbing. But in ten years in the trade, he'd never had to resort to using them. As in every other touch he'd made in his long career, tonight he planned to avoid dangers rather than confront them.

Of course, as always, he had Frost strung in its case across his back. True to his long-ago promise, he kept Frost with him always. When Peter was inducted into the Brotherhood of Thieves, Hagan of the Lowenbrucke, who was then the Master of the Touch, and therefore second in rank among all thieves, argued that a portion of Peter's flute should be shared among the brothers, just as any other take from a job — just as Peter had already surrendered a portion of his stolen bacon and market produce.

"How can we divide pieces of a flute into proper shares?" the king had asked.

"Break it apart," Hagan said.

"But then we'll have no more sweet music from it," the queen said.

"Unfortunate, perhaps," Hagan replied, "but there's a principle at stake."

"I think dour Hagan is jealous of Peter's talent," Carl said. That made Hagan color with anger, which only increased when he heard many a snigger and titter of laughter throughout the chamber.

The argument went round and round, until Peter, almost afraid to speak in his own defense, pointed out that Frost wasn't part of the take from any act of thievery. "It was given to me by my own father as an inheritance," he said.

"That settles it then," Carl spoke up, loud and confident, in contrast to Peter's mumbled entreaty. "What was never stolen, but is privately owned by one of us, isn't subject to division, either for the king's rightful tithe, or the share that's given out among the brothers. That's our law!"

"But how do we know he's telling the truth of it?" Hagan said.

"Dastard!" Carl said. "An accusation against a brother requires either undeniable evidence or blood! Since you've none of one, I'll take a full measure of the other!" Carl drew his dagger against Hagan, a bold act that surprised everyone in the room, since Carl was still a child, while Hagan was a man grown and as deadly a man with a dagger as ever there was.

"This child hasn't been a brother for all but a few seconds," Hagan said, and eagerly drew his own knife. He stepped out into the center of the room, and began to circle around Carl, a hungry, wolfish look in his eyes. The rest of the company assembled there, moved back, to give the fighters room.

"Put down!" the king cried. "Put down, I say! I'll decide when there's blood to be spilled! No matter how recently it was done, young Peter is one of us now, and deserves every advantage of our laws and traditions. His flute belongs to him alone, and that's my say in the matter. Anyone who disputes it further will taste my knife today." He looked at Hagan as he said this.

With obvious reluctance on both sides, Hagan and Carl put away their blades. But from that day forward, it was clear to anyone with eyes to see it that each hated the other. A year later the matter between them was put to rest when Hagan was caught by a lucky arrow between his shoulder blades while making his getaway with a sack of jewels formerly belonging to a renowned cavalry officer's mistress. It was said that Carl visited poor Hagan's head every day, at its resting place on a spike atop the western wall, to put fresh daisies behind each ear. But, though the daily flowers were always there, no one ever actually saw Carl do it.

Now, ten years into his career, and widely recognized (among those in the know) as the boldest thief in the city, Peter crouched in the shadows and felt Frost's reassuring weight across his back. At exactly the stroke of three in the morning, precisely as it had been arranged, he spied a door come open in the side of the Bishop's residence. A man in guard's livery stepped out of the building, looked once to the left and once to the right, and then went back inside, but leaving the door cracked open just a sliver. It was the signal Peter had been waiting for.

Quick as a wealthy man's prayer, he made his way down from his high perch and across the street, keeping to the deepest shadows at all times. Over the wall he went, confident from his earlier observations that there'd be no guards on the other side to greet him. Then he crept forward to find the side door open, unlocked and unguarded. Our ever-reliable Master of Bribes did his duty again, Peter thought, happy that his dear friend Carl was an important part of this job. Silently, he closed and locked the door behind him. Then, moving out of the lighted hallway, into the shadows of a recessed alcove, he reached inside his vest for a small bottle that had been provided to him by a potion maker well known to the Brotherhood. It was an expensive potion he carried, and usually only used in the most dire of emergencies, but the king had agreed that this time, owing to the hasty planning of tonight's touch, its expenditure was well justified.

When he opened the bottle, the liquid inside would blossom from it in the form of a mist that would spread out into every nook and cranny of the building, quickly putting all within it into a deep and dreamless sleep. Peter would be immune, having already sipped the antidote up on the rooftop across the way. But then, just as he was about to pull the stopper, something stayed his hand. The air already smelled of sticky, burned cloves, mixed with an underlying odor of rancid meat, which is exactly the odor his potion would cause.

Someone had already released a sleeping mist, he realized. And it was done only seconds ago, or else the smell would have dissipated by now.

Doubly on his guard, already half-determined to abandon the job as too risky, Peter crept down the hallway, letting the smaller of his two daggers fall silently into his hand as he went. He quickly found the guard who'd unlocked the door for him. The man was fast asleep in the mansion's small mage-room, having extinguished, as he'd promised to do, the night's spell-candle, which insured there would be no active security or warding spells to interfere with Peter's work.

Having been thoroughly briefed by the Brotherhood's Master Caser, who'd uncovered detailed designs for its construction in the city archives, Peter knew his way around the building, as if he'd lived here all his life. He could have closed his eyes and found his way to the Bishop's luxurious second floor bedroom. But for all their careful preparation, no one anticipated having to deal with a second intruder — one who seemed as schooled in the

Brotherhood's methods as Peter was.

As he proceeded through the house, Peter encountered one sleeping guard after another, as he'd planned all along. But he'd never suspected someone might do the job for him. He went upstairs, using the smaller servants' stairway in the back of the house. As he turned the corner, where the narrow flight of stairs doubled back on itself midway through the ascent, he thought he saw a shadow flit out of the doorway above. He hurried faster, as fast as he could move and still remain relatively silent. He emerged onto the second floor hallway just in time to see a vaguely human shape duck into the very bedroom he was headed for. He rushed down to the open doorway, but paused at its threshold. The bedroom was dark, too dark for Peter's faded night vision to penetrate, which had been spoiled by even the soft light in the hallways. If he entered blind into the darkened room, there was a very reasonable chance he'd stumble right onto a knife blade held by whoever was already in there. Peter was certain that the other intruder was standing just inside the doorway, pressed against the other side of the same wall he was facing, ready to ambush him, because that's what he'd do in the same situation.

He waited where he was, barely daring to breathe. At the same time he imagined that he could almost hear the other man's breathing on the opposite side of the wall. Peter had no idea what to do. None of his training or past experience had prepared him for such a situation as this. *Was it possible there was a second thieves brotherhood operating in Hamelin, which until now was completely unknown to us? No, that's not possible. So then, what* could the answer be? Lacking a better idea, Peter finally decided the best solution to the mystery might simply be to ask his questions aloud.

"I suppose we can both stand here all night," he said, in a low murmur, "waiting for the other one to do something. If your sleeping mist is as effective as the one I carry, we don't need to worry about anyone waking up for hours at least."

For the longest time there was no answer, but then he heard, "It's good enough. No one will wake, even if we screamed at the top of our voices." The other intruder had answered Peter in a similar whisper, but there was something odd about his voice, as if it were muffled through a thick cloth. "I wouldn't be surprised if we purchased our potions from the same vendor."

"Possibly so," Peter said. "Old man Konstantin couldn't live as richly as he does, strictly on the trade that we give him."

"That's his name," the other voice said. "So what are we going to do? Though the magical sleep may last, the morning's sun won't tarry an extra minute. I need to finish my business and be on my way, while it's still dark out."

"And what business would that be? I dearly hope you're not also here to rob our slumbering Bishop. My Brotherhood doesn't allow competition within the city, and I'd be expected to do something permanent about it. But I'd really like to avoid sticking a knife into anyone tonight. My heart's never been into such things."

"Well, you can turn around and go home in peace," the other man said. "I've no intention of robbing tonight. My contract is to kill the Bishop."

"In truth?"

"Yes."

"You're an actual killer for pay? Before now I'd never have believed we had a nest of assassins in Hamelin. I'd think we'd have run across one of you long ago, if that were the case."

"My society isn't based in Hamelin, or any other town. We find it more suitable to live in a place far removed from outsiders."

"Sensible enough," Peter said. "Of course, being thieves, my people are pretty much required to live where the people are. How do clients find you then?"

"You'll have to ask one of my superiors."

"But someone definitely hired you to come here and kill poor Bishop Hugo?"

"Yes, and if you don't mind, I'd like to be about it. He needs to go tonight, before he can make his speeches tomorrow."

"Ah, well, see? You and I have the same mission, except that my people have worked out a much less bloody way to accomplish it. I'm simply going to steal his ring and then he can make any sort of speech he wants, but it won't matter. There won't be any authority behind it. Doesn't that seem a more elegant solution? No blood spilled. No fancy bed sheets ruined. So why don't you be on your way and leave the job to me?"

"I can't do that. I have to either kill the Bishop tonight, or kill myself. There's no other alternative, once I've accepted a mission. We've a strict code about such things."

"Well, then we have a problem," Peter said, "because I can't let you kill the Bishop tonight, or anyone else in his household. If the word got out that I needed to butcher my target, just to get a ring off his finger, my reputation would be ruined among my peers. I've never so much as had to scratch a man in order to make the touch on his valuables, much less kill him. And no one would ever believe that the murder was actually done by a mysterious assassin who just happened to be in the same house on the same night."

"By the same token, I can't let you rob him. An adept of my society who stooped to rob his victim would be considered nothing more than a cheap thug. I'd be slain by my own masters if I let that happen, and rightly so."

"Then it looks like we've reached an impasse. I don't know how to resolve it."

"You'll just have to think of something, Peter. You always did consider yourself most clever."

"Peter?"

"Yes, you're Peter."

"You know who I am?"

"I recognized you the first moment you spoke, and it's breaking my heart that you haven't recognized me."

"But I – I don't – "

"It's me, Peter. It's Bo Peep."

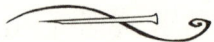

Peter and Bo talked in the Bishop's bedroom, sitting on the edge of his huge bed, while he slumbered away, snoring quietly, somewhere in its vast middle. In the ten years since he'd last seen her, Bo had grown into a beautiful woman. Like a vision in a dream, her features slowly revealed themselves out of the shadows, as Peter's eyes adjusted to the dark. He held her hand tightly as they talked, afraid that she might fade away into the insubstantial vapor of dreamstuff that he still worried she might be.

"What happened to you," Peter said, "after that night with the wolf?"

"I got hopelessly lost," she said. "I wandered for three or four days, and then a terrible man found me. He kept talking about all of the things he might do to me, if I wasn't good enough to pass muster with the Rowan House."

"What's that?"

"One of the names by which we're known to outsiders. He sold me to them, which was a blessing, considering some of the alternatives he'd described, and they raised me to be what I am now."

"A killer."

"Yes, just like everything else in this terrible world, except that I finally resigned myself to becoming good at it, perhaps so that I'd have a decent chance not to be the victim of the next monstrous thing that found me."

"So what do we do now, Bo?"

"About the Bishop?"

"No — well, yes, about him too, but also about the rest of our lives. We can't just resolve our business here and then go on our separate ways again. I've found you at last — or maybe you found me, but I'm not about to let you go again, after all these years."

"I'm afraid you'll have to," she said, her voice breaking with insistent emotion that refused to be entirely suppressed. "I've sworn binding oaths. I can't leave the Rowan House, and you can't come back there with me. Outsiders simply aren't allowed to learn our secrets and live."

"I've had to swear a binding oath or two myself."

"Then it seems we're both stuck."

"No, I can't accept that. There has to be a way. Let's start with the determination that somehow, some way, we're both going to stay together from now on, and work our way backwards from there."

They sat silent for a long time, before Bo said, "It seems that the only fair and honorable way out of a binding oath is if we'd each sworn to an earlier one that conflicts with the others."

That's when Peter became truly excited, grabbing Bo by each arm. "Bo, you're a genius! I could kiss you!" And then he did.

Hugo the Charitable, Bishop of Hamelin, the Weser River Valley and Lower Saxony, woke with a pounding ache in his head and a foul taste on his lips.

"That's the taste of the antidote," Bo said, in reply to the sour faces the Bishop made. "It's not pleasant, but it does overcome the sleeping mist, and we needed you awake sooner than you'd have done so naturally."

"What's the meaning of this outrage?" Hugo sputtered, trying to sit up in his bed. It was hard to be sure in the room's darkness, but he thought he could see two strange figures looming over him, a man and a woman, both dressed in dark clothes, such as what low villains and night skulkers might wear.

"We need you to marry us," Peter said, with a broad grin splitting his face.

"And be quick about it," Bo added. "The sun will be up in another hour, which means we'll need to be gone in half that."

Hugo was still half asleep and couldn't understand what was happening to him, but even in this state he knew the solution to his anxieties. "Guards! Guards!" he called.

"Scream all you like," Bo said, "but no one's going to come save you." She placed the tip of a very sharp knife under one of his quivering chins. "Now please get on with the ceremony."

The dagger's point helped Hugo wake up more quickly — instantly in fact. "Why? What do you want with me?" he cried, tears forming in his eyes. It was stifling hot in the room, but still someone had started a fire in his fireplace. Why light a fire on a hot summer's night? Nothing made sense in this madman's nightmare.

"The only way to cancel an oath is to act on a previous one that supersedes it," Bo said. "Long before I ever took my vows among the masters of the Rowan House, I swore I'd marry Peter some day. It turns out that someday is today."

"And I made a similar vow," Peter said. "True, I didn't specifically swear to marry Bo, but long ago, after I'd made her cry one day, I felt bad and did promise myself that, from now on, if Bo ever agrees to talk to me again, I'd do whatever she told me to do."

"That sounds like a solemn oath to me," Bo said, smiling wider than Peter, if that were possible. "In any case, my society doesn't allow us to marry."

"Nor does mine," Peter said. "At least not outside of our Brotherhood."

"So, unfortunately and reluctantly," she said, "we both have to resign from our respective professions."

"It can't be helped," Peter said.

"So hurry up and say the words, old man, before I add a bright new smile to your face."

Bishop Hugo said the words.

Though his life was spared and his ring not stolen, the good Bishop Hugo was nevertheless unable to make his scheduled speeches the next day. He was discovered late in the morning, in his bed, bound by velvet curtain ropes and screaming in pain, by his sleepy guards and servants who couldn't understand what had come over them in the night. Those same guards and servants, good churchmen all, were shocked to also discover that infernal markings had appeared on the Bishop's face in the night. There was the bleeding outline of a goat's head burned into his forehead, and twin upside-down stars, burned one-each into either cheek — clear indications that the Bishop had entered into foul pacts with creatures of the pit.

Hugo loudly protested, to anyone who'd listen, that he'd been the victim of an evil act from two very human intruders. They'd forced him at knifepoint to wed them, after which they twisted normal copper wire, such as can be found in any household, into the semblance of goats and stars, which they heated up in the embers of his own fireplace, and then used to burn these brands into his innocent flesh. Some believed the Bishop's bizarre story and some didn't, which is the way of people anywhere, in any time.

Regardless of anyone's belief, one way or the other, the Bishop couldn't be allowed to preside over important matters of church and state, from that day onward. Nor could he remain a Bishop.

He was stripped of office and cassock, and bound over for trial, as a consorter with unsanctioned fiends and devils. His own servants testified as to how they'd been ensorcelled into a diabolical slumber, while the Bishop crafted his infernal bargains in the night.

The judge found the evidence against Hugo compelling, though slight enough to warrant sparing the man's life. Hugo ended his days in a distant world, in a forced labor camp, where he was once congratulated by his goblin overseer for fashioning better bricks than most of the other slaves.

THAT SAME FATEFUL NIGHT, wherein Hugo was framed for witchcraft, Peter and Bo Piper were never seen again in Hamelin Town. But Peter's private strongbox in the Brotherhood's Hall was discovered the next morning, unlocked, open and empty of all of its jewels and coin. A letter to Carl the Arrow was the only thing found in the box. This is what the letter said:

Dear Carl,

I've gone to find this world of sanctuary of which we've heard so many whispered tales. I was skeptical before, but I have to believe now that it exists, because my lovely new wife and I find ourselves in need of it. Feel free to follow, if ever your spirit grows restless, or the thieving life gets too boring or dangerous. Give my best to all of my former brothers and to your dear brother-in-law, our king. He turned out to be a good and honest one, which seems an odd thing to say about so accomplished a criminal.

Your eternal friend,
Peter

Chapter Seventeen

A Festival of Vermin and Lost Children

In which the rats come home to roost.

OUTFITTED WITH HALF A DOZEN HIDDEN daggers, and at least twenty other concealed implements of murder, carrying Frost in its hard plastic case, Peter entered Hamelin's Altstadt, the old town, and almost left the modern mundy city behind.

Almost.

The cobbled streets were similar to the medieval town of his youth, and many of the oldest of the old buildings, constructed in the over-ornamented Weser Renaissance style, looked vaguely familiar, if somewhat smaller than he remembered. But no matter how deep into the past he'd seemed to regress, at any time, all he had to do was to look up and see the sky punctured on all sides by a small forest of massive steel construction cranes, completely surrounding the old town section, busy adding new towers of chrome-tinted glass and brushed steel to the greater metropolitan skyline.

And of course this version of Hamelin, even in the old section, was much too clean to truly reflect the Hamelin of his past, or any medieval era town for that matter. These cobblestone streets were swept. There weren't corpses set out into the thoroughfare to be removed. There were no piles of human waste and discarded refuse rotting in every alleyway, which in turn meant that there weren't the attendant clouds of gnats, fleas and flies everywhere, or the ubiquitous rats. In the lost Hesse's version of Hamelin, even after the Pied Piper's miracles, the rats eventually returned, though the stolen children never did.

Granted, there were plenty of rats to be found here, but they were artificial. The good people of mundy Hamelin seemed to have embraced the rat as a beloved symbol of its history and heritage. One of the bridges spanning the Weser River had a huge, gold-plated statue of a rat mounted at the apex of its overhead suspension superstructure, standing astride the two center tower supports like a vermin colossus. One of the local ice cream shops (where one can purchase ice cream dishes formed into the convincing likenesses of various popular restaurant entrées, such as steak and potatoes, or spaghetti and meatballs) had a brightly painted plastic statue outside of its main entrance, depicting a giant ice cream cone of many flavors, which had somehow spilled into the shape of cyclopean rat. There were little, plastic wind-up rats, plush stuffed rats, and articulated wooden rats in the windows of every one of the numerous toy stores. Carven stone rats decorated every fountain and building cornice, and painted rats were included in the composition of every bit of commercial signage. Children could ride spring-mounted rocking-horse rats in tiny play parks, scattered liberally throughout the town, or the larger, plastic green, pink, or purple galloping rats in the Market Square's gigantic motorized carousel. After a battle that lasted centuries, the rats had finally conquered Hamelin town, much to the approval of its citizens.

At this early hour, Peter nearly had the town to himself. Only a few deliverymen, hand-carting crates and boxes from their large panel trucks, were also up with the dawn. They were busy restocking the many shops and restaurants, helping Hamelin make its final preparations for the first of its big festival days, which would begin as soon as the town could rouse itself from its nightly slumbers.

Peter walked towards the center of town to the open market square, where a hundred bright tents, in every color of the spectrum, had been erected to shelter the visiting food vendors, gaming hosts, and souvenir merchants who would come to occupy them in only a few hours' time. And then, past the carousel, which was permanent and operated year round, he could see the grand old Saint Nicolai's, which also turned out to be smaller than the Homeland's version of the same building of his past. This one wasn't even a proper cathedral, but only a very large, though still impressive, church. This one was also attached to a smaller copy, though no less ornate, of the Hochzeitshaus, the High Holy House, where, in a different world, Peter had helped to force a frightened and outraged Bishop to wed him to Bo.

Peter turned away from the church and strolled down Market Street, which had been converted into an open-air walking mall, where no motorized vehicles were allowed. Restaurants, small diners and snack stands lined the street, which also had tables and chairs under shady umbrellas set out in the middle of it. Peter sat down at a random table, to wait for one of the restaurants to open up and provide him with breakfast. And even though he was quite alone in the street, he resisted the urge to constantly pat himself down, to make sure that all of his deadly secret weapons were still in place. He set Frost's case on the table in front of him, and wondered if he shouldn't open it up and play himself a tune. *Perhaps the last song I'll ever get to play on it,* he thought, *a sad and simple little farewell requiem just for myself.*

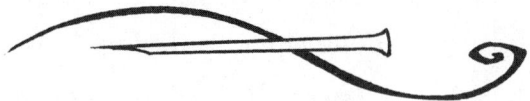

Peter looked out of the restaurant window as he finished his breakfast, and noticed that the town had woken up at last. A man in a Pied Piper costume strolled past the window, playing merrily on his flute, and followed by a half dozen happy tourists, busy snapping pictures of him with their digital cameras. The Piper was dressed in a red and purple tunic, over tights of orange, green, yellow and white. He sported a cape of many colors and a cap with a trio of two-foot long pheasant feathers arcing out from it. He played a modern style metal transverse flute. Then, less than a minute later, another Pied Piper passed by, going the other way. This one was dressed identically to the first, but played a modern clarinet instead of a flute. In addition to his modest flock of tourists, this one was followed by a troupe of children dressed in gray mouse costume pajamas, with long cloth tails and hoods that had plush, pink and gray mouse ears sewn onto them. There were at least thirty children in the procession, and they followed their Piper in pretended enchantment, dancing and prancing along to his tune.

Peter hadn't been able to finish his bacon and eggs. He was too nervous about the coming confrontation to do justice to a full meal. Placing a twenty-Deutschmark note on the table, for the check, plus a nice tip, he picked up Frost and left the restaurant. Market Street was crowded now. Hundreds of early-bird tourists had turned out to soak up every atom of the day's celebrations, which might begin slowly, but would end tonight in grand, drunken feasts, public concerts and exploding fireworks. Peter turned south, away from the center of town and the largest mass of crowds.

Almost immediately, just outside of the old town's post office, around a gradual bend in the street, Peter encountered a large stone fountain depicting the Pied Piper of legend. This was the particular fountain he'd been looking for, the one that appeared, as if by strict regulation, on the cover of every tourist brochure. It had a five-sided base, which enclosed its main pool. A pillar rose out of its center, which blossomed out into a cup-shaped upper pool that was decorated all around its circumference with carvings of parading children, along with the required rats. A life-sized bronze statue of the legendary Piper stood up from the stone cup's center, looking nothing at all like his brother Max. This one at least was depicted as playing on a front-held, flair-ended flute, similar to what Max had actually played, so many years past.

Peter sat on the fountain's edge, setting Frost's case down beside him. There were many coins in the fountain's pool. He dug into his pocket and came out with a copper ten-pfennig piece, which he threw into the pool, making a wish as he did so.

And almost at once, perhaps for his many sins, his wish was granted.

"My dear, long lost brother!" Max Piper cried in delight. "How extraordinary, and how absolutely wonderful to find you here!"

Chapter Eighteen

Frost and Fire

In which Peter puts his wife in a pumpkin shell, and tries to keep her very well.

PETER AND BO CROUCHED TOGETHER, BELOW the low green hedgerow that bordered a gently winding country lane. In the three months since they'd escaped Hamelin, retrieving various stashes of Peter's loot from scattered hidey holes, and an equal number of Bo's hidden bundles of exotic weapons from secret caches, they'd made their way nearly four hundred leagues, south and westward, across the Hesse, to the outskirts of a southern little seaport town called SonnenSee. Even in October, this was a pleasant, summery land of rolling golden pastures and rich farmlands, occasionally separated by miles-long stretches of high granite hills, on the lower slopes of which could be found the only substantial stands of uncleared woodlands. Both of the fugitives were more than happy to have left the deeper, more primeval reaches of the Black Forest far behind.

They hid on the landward side of the hedgerow, in order to avoid detection from a solitary farmer who was leading a creaking old donkey cart down the road. The ponderous two-wheeled cart was piled high with fresh produce. No doubt the farmer was bringing his harvest goods into SonnenSee, to sell in the public markets that sprang up in every town and village during the harvest season.

This close to the sea, bright white gulls dotted the wide azure sky, their wings tipped with black or gray. Some drifted high, riding the lazy thermals that rose up from the chalky seaside cliffs and inland granite escarpments, while others dived and banked closer to ground, on the lookout for their next scavenging opportunity. Always they squawked and scolded and called to each other, being a very chatty sort of bird.

When the farmer had come very close to their hiding place, Peter and Bo vaulted lithely and easily over the hedge and confronted the man, who was an older fellow and scrambled backwards, all the while clutching at his chest.

"I'm sorry, Grandfather," Bo said. "We didn't mean to startle you. We just needed to make sure that we'd be able to talk to you with no other witnesses. Be assured that we mean you no harm and we're not thieves."

"Well, to be perfectly honest, I am," Peter said, "but not today. In truth we're here with gold in hand, willing to buy what we want."

"At a very good price," Bo added.

"What sort of people hide behind bushes, only to jump out at innocent, hardworking country folk?" the old farmer said, looking suspicious, accusatory and still breathing hard, if no longer quite showing a danger of some sort of imminent collapse. "What exactly is it you want from me?"

"Everything," Peter said, flashing a jolly smile. "The donkey, the cart and everything in it. Think of a good price for the lot, and then double it. We're feeling particularly generous today."

"And add to that," Bo said, "the cost of insuring that you'll go straight home from here, back the way you came, where you'll stay for at least a week before venturing to go to town again."

"What do you need my cart, my crops and my Gertraud for?"

"We've got it in our hearts to be simple farm folk for a day," Peter said.

"For the past three months we've been every other sort of folk," Bo said. "We've been an old grandfather and his old wife. I've been an old woman with her grown son. And Peter's been an old man with his grown daughter. Once even, lacking time and materials to fashion disguises, we even traveled as a young man and his wife. Now it's time to be something else."

"To be perfectly candid," Peter said, "the gobs, and their wicked masters who now rule this land, may still be looking for a young married couple traveling together, so we tend to avoid appearing that way."

"You're villains on the run?" the old man said.

"Hardly villainous," Peter said, "but you've deciphered the crux of it."

Bo started pacing around the cart, closely evaluating its bountiful contents, quietly murmuring "hmmm" and "ah" as she made her examinations.

"I can't lose my Gertraud, for any price," the old man said. "She's become part of the family."

"She talks?" Peter said.

"No, but – "

"Good," Peter said, "because we can't risk anyone speaking up and giving us away, as we pass through that rather imposing guard tower – no doubt garrisoned by a squad or more of bloodthirsty goblins – which straddles the last high pass, leading down to SonnenSee Town. Still, I had a beloved family mule of my own once, back in a more innocent age, and I know well the reluctance one might have to part with such a creature. So, I'll tell you what; we'll still pay you double a good sell price for your dear Gertraud, but only to rent her for a week. When next you come to town, you'll find her fine, fit, and nicely fattened, at the public stables. And we'll pay for that too."

The conversation lasted a good while longer, but eventually

the old man, whose name turned out to be Meinard, by the way, gave in, unable to turn down the small fortune in silver and gold that the (almost certainly) insane young couple pressed upon him. While Peter handled the bulk of the negotiations, Bo kept a wary eye out down one direction and then the other, knowing that any passerby at this point might ruin their plans. After a while, a considerably happier, and richer, old Meinard went back on his way, down the country road, and entirely out of our story.

Once he was well out of earshot, Peter said to his lovely wife, "Okay, that's done. Now will you please tell me why we let three perfectly respectable grocery wagons pass us by, but absolutely had to procure this one?"

"Because lovely old Gaffer Meinard had the best pumpkins," Bo said. "Look at the size of these giants — this one in particular." She indicated the biggest, fattest pumpkin in the cart, and Peter had to admit that it was truly impressive.

"So Meinard had good results from his pumpkin patch this year," Peter said. "Good for him. Perhaps I'm not as clever as you are, because I don't divine the necessity of big pumpkins among the crop we use to explain our way past the guard post. As long as we appear as humble farmers — "

"That's what I've been thinking about, while we hid among the hedges," Bo said. "So far, we've always appeared as two people together on the road. But, if the military authorities are still looking for us, or if agents of your former brotherhood, or my former society still hunt us, they'd all be looking for a man and a woman together on the road."

"True," Peter said. "In hindsight, we shouldn't have written farewell letters to our respective masters."

"No, it was still the right thing to do, seeing as how we're both still clinging to the notion that we found the only honorable way to resign from our professions. I've scant eagerness to spend an eternity in Hel's dark realm, ripped apart each day to be tossed into a giant iron kettle, to be gnawed at by dreaded Garm and his fellow witch dogs, which is the fate of all oath breakers in the next life. An official statement of resignation, including an explanation of the reason behind it, was required from each of us."

"Well, truth be told, I more alluded to the reason behind my sudden resignation and disappearance, rather than state it openly."

"I suspect you managed to communicate the gist of it." All the while that they were talking, Bo was busy carving at the largest pumpkin, with one of her many sharp knives. In time she'd cut a wide circle clear around the pumpkin's fat stem, and with a great heave, she lifted the heavy orange plug free from the rest of it.

"Help me scoop this out," she said.

"As soon as you finish explaining your cunning plan," he said.

"Simple enough. Once we've got this nicely hollowed out, I'm going to hide inside of it, while you take us through the military checkpoint."

"Why?"

"Because, I'm smaller than you are, silly man, and more limber. As big as this thing is, you'd never fit."

"I meant why does one of us have to do it at all?"

"Really?" she said. "You haven't figured it out yet?"

"What can I say?" he said. "I'm tired from too many days with too little sleep, and from the constant stress of being on the run. And, as you've so often pointed out — but always in a loving way — I can be dense at times."

"It's simple. With me hiding in here, and the plug pressed down just right, so the cut doesn't show, you will then be a single man on his own, bringing his goods to market. They aren't looking for a single man on his own. But, even if you could be the one to fit inside this grandfather of all gourds, a single woman bringing her goods to market, though she may not fit the description of the particular fugitives they may be seeking — well, a woman alone attracts a different kind of unwanted attention."

"Yes, I confess, that is rather clever."

"Now that we've only one last obstacle remaining between us and the ship that can carry us away to this new world of sanctuary, I don't want to take any chances. So help me get down inside this pumpkin, Peter, my love, and then put the plug back in. And be sure to pile other vegetables all over the top, just to be safe."

"Very well," he said, "but cut yourself a small air hole down low in the thing, and be sure to call out if you get a cramp or become claustrophobic."

"I don't get claustrophobic, and why should I bother calling out?" she said, with a wicked grin. "You'd likely not recognize my voice anyway."

"Are we going to discuss *that* again?" His smile matched hers. "I hadn't seen you in ten years. It was dark. There was a bloody damned stone wall between us — an exceptionally thick one at that. You were whispering. And your mouth, along with your whole face, was swaddled in that long black scarf you like to wrap around your head as a mask."

"I have white-blonde hair and perfect alabaster skin that shows up like a lit candle, in even the darkest room. I need a mask in order to skulk about in the night. But granting all of those fine excuses you constructed, you'd still think a man would know the voice of his own true love."

"Please, oh eternal light of my life, get into the damned pumpkin. We really need to be on our way, before anyone else comes along."

"Yes, dear. Thump once on the outside of it, when you need me to be completely silent inside, twice when we're clear of the tower, and then thrice once it's safe to come out."

It turned out they needed to hollow out two of the largest pumpkins. One was required to conceal Bo, as planned, and the other to hide their remaining treasure, and all of their baggage that couldn't be explained as belonging to a poor young farm boy. Working together, they accomplished this in little time. Then, throwing the wet, stringy pumpkin innards over the hedge, Peter took the donkey's guide rope in hand and led the cart back on its interrupted way.

THE ROAD MEANDERED past fields and farms, then its winding character increased, as it began to turn more sharply back and forth on itself, beginning its ascent into the hills. Peter led the cart up gentle grades and steep ones. Sometimes the donkey resisted, digging all four of its surprisingly strong hooves into the dirt, and braying its protests loudly. Peter tugged on its rope, while he cursed and bargained and pleaded with it.

"Come on, Gertraud," he'd complain. "Once we get to the top, it's downhill all the rest of the way. I promise!"

When this happened, sooner or later, he'd find the right combination of applied force and spoken imprecations to get the stubborn beast started again, and they'd press on.

Still going uphill, they quickly left the fields behind and passed through scattered woods of maple, ash and hawthorn, their leaves already dressed for the fall. Gradually these gave way to holly and then scrub pine, that sometimes clung to the sheer sides of the granite cliffs with impossible daring and determination. In the late afternoon, after a series of grueling switchbacks, they finally turned the corner and saw up close the dark tower Bo and Peter had only scouted from a distance the day before. The tower sat just off the road, which had grown quite narrow in the pass, threading a slim notch between steep scarps. A high wall and portcullis gate reached out from either side of the tower, sealing off the scant space between impassable rock cliffs.

Any traveler would have to pass by the tower, through the barred gate, or turn back. There was no other option.

Peter spotted one fat, squat goblin soldier at the open gateway, stationed so that he could release a single rope and thereby send the iron bars crashing down to close off the passageway. Another two gob troops, armed with curved horn bows, paced the tower top, three stories above them.

Peter paused the cart while still out a ways from the tower and walked once around it, as if inspecting how its contents might have shifted during the ascent. As he did so, he gave a single offhand thump against the largest pumpkin, nestled deepest into the cart's bed. Then he took Gertraud's guide rope once more in hand and proceeded the remaining thirty feet towards the checkpoint.

All the way up the hill, Peter had silently practiced all of the possible answers he'd give to as many questions as he could anticipate. He also made a few grim decisions on how he'd conduct himself if the guards got too curious about the cart and its contents. In his years of thieving, he'd practiced often with various weapons, until he was familiar with all of them and an expert with some. He could place a thrown dagger within an inch-wide circle, from nearly twenty paces. But he'd never once had to use a weapon in earnest. However, when Bo's life is at stake, he'd decided, I'll kill anyone I need to and not shed a tear of remorse afterwards.

All of this he had in his mind when he approached the gate, but the bored goblin guard simply waved him through, without making him stop, or asking him a single question. Fifty yards further down the twisting road, they'd circled three quarters round a giant pillar of rock and were well out of sight of the guard tower. Peter thumped three times on the big pumpkin and then helped Bo climb out of it, and rub life back into her cramped limbs.

"That feels grand," she said, as Peter massaged her legs. "Don't stop."

"You smell like pumpkin pie," Peter said. "I dearly love pumpkin pie, especially the way Queen Gisela used to make it for me, back in the Brotherhood. You're making me hungry."

"We'll have a proper supper in town," she said, "including as much pie as you like. We deserve a small celebration, before looking for the Tenacious and her captain." According to the information they'd purchased, at a dear price, the three-masted trading ship Tenacious should be anchored at SonnenSee until the end of October, at which time it would make sail in its last voyage of the year, bound for its winter port. But along the way, or so they were told, the captain could be bribed into making a brief side-trip, crossing a patch of magic-impregnated sea that connected to the seas of a much different world — the world of sanctuary they'd heard so much about, over the years. Anchoring off a nearby shore that was sometimes an island and sometimes part of a vast continent, they'd be put ashore to find their new lives in a new world, while the Tenacious sailed off to complete its appointments back in the Hesse.

"Well isn't this a fine picture," someone said, startling the couple. "I set off looking for one old score to settle and find two.

Fortune is indeed my sweetheart."

Both Peter and Bo came instantly alert, as a tall, slim figure appeared from around another bend in the road ahead of them. The newcomer was dressed in tunic, hose and a long coat, all of many discordant colors. He had long brown hair and a beard of the same shade. Both were so wild and tangled that they looked as if they'd never known the touch of a comb. The man carried a flute of deep red wood, and he had a mad and predatory look in his dark eyes.

Despite the years and wealth of changes in the fellow, Peter recognized him instantly.

"Max!" he cried, relaxing his hand away from the dagger he'd instinctively sought out, inside the open lapel of his jacket.

Bo hadn't made the connection as fast as Peter had, not realizing this was her husband's long lost brother, until Peter had named him aloud. But she'd known in the first moment that the man intended to kill them both. The evidence of it was written there in his eyes for anyone to read it.

"Careful, Peter," she warned. "He has blood in his heart."

"Your little bitch has the right of it," Max said. "I am going to kill the both of you, slowly and quite painfully in point of fact. But that doesn't preclude a friendly chat first. It's been so long. How've you been, brother? Have you had many adventures since we were separated, oh so long ago? The witch mentioned you'd had quite a few of note, when she finally put me on your trail last month."

But Bo hadn't waited for Max to finish his grotesque pretense at a friendly conversation. She sprang into deadly action immediately. Quick as a thought, two daggers flew towards Max, striking within an immeasurable moment of each other. But it wasn't flesh the daggers hit, but the air in front of him, as if an invisible shield of tempered adamant had been raised to protect him. The twin knives hung suspended in that solid wall of air for a moment, until one of them transformed into a red robin and flew away, while the other turned into a cluster of golden maple leaves that drifted merrily to the earth.

Max gave no sign that he even noticed these miraculous occurrences, or the violent acts that preceded them. He simply finished his questions to Peter, as if they were having an enjoyable reunion in fact, as well as pretense.

Peter was stunned, and for a long time had no idea what to do. Frost in its dull, worn and scuffed leather case was strung across his back, as always, but suddenly it seemed much heavier than normal. Peter could actually feel his brother's desire for it as a physical manifestation, as if his naked coveting was adding actual weight to it.

Following the failure of her knives, Bo unstoppered a tiny blue glass bottle and spilled its contents towards Max's face. But the heavy amber liquid, which began to pop and sizzle once it met the air, turned into a fine mist before it could touch the man. The mist corkscrewed and whirled for a while above Max's head, dipping and twisting into a dozen remarkable formations before fading away into nothing.

For the first time Max turned to regard her directly.

"Must you persist," he asked, "while I'm trying to catch up with my baby brother? You can't harm me. Over the years, as I traversed many a dark and blasted land, I played a hundred impenetrable armors and protections about myself. Neither you nor any of your child's toys can touch me, save that I wish it so."

Bo answered him by closing the distance between them and delivering a kick that would have exploded his kneecap, had it landed. But it simply slipped aside, without contact. Undeterred, she kicked again, and punched and slashed at him, with the edges of her hand, and with a third blade that she produced seemingly from nowhere. True to his boast, nothing she tried could touch him.

"You weary me, Bo Peep," Max said. Then turning to his brother, he said, "Peter, I'm going to do you one last favor, before I kill you today. First I'll give you an executioner's divorce from this annoying harlot. At least you'll have a few minutes of joy back in your life, before the end."

Max raised his flute to his lips and played a single loud note, which caused Bo to be lifted, as if by a giant's unseen hand, and then tossed far away from him. The road, which wound around a massive pillar of rock on one side, dropped off in a sheer cliff on the other side. Bo flew helpless towards the dropoff, tumbling through the air like a jester's comic pantomime of a circus acrobat. At first it looked as if she might strike the last few feet of solid, horizontal road surface before reaching the edge, but instead she flew past it. Then, at the last second, with a scream of agony, as her arm was nearly wrenched out of its socket, she managed to reach out and grab a branch of one of the scrub pines that clung like a spider to the vertical rock face. The tree was anchored just below the lip of the road. Too far away to be of any help to her, Peter gasped in incandescent horror, waiting a terrible second to see if Bo would manage to hang on, or if the small tree would give way. She did and it didn't. Slowly and painfully she was able to grab the tree with her other hand, improve her grip with the first hand, and pull herself up and over the lip of the precipice.

"That was a bit closer than I liked," she said, attempting a rakish smile.

Peter couldn't say anything over the violence of his own heart pounding in his chest.

Then Max blew another single half note on his pipe and Bo flew back again, this time disappearing entirely over the ledge, with no lucky branch within reach to help her.

"No!" Peter screamed, rushing towards the cliff's edge.

"You're well rid of her," Max said. "She always was a brat and a pest."

Peter looked down over the ledge and spied Bo lying perhaps as much as twenty feet below him, in the middle of the road, the same one he was on, which had obviously turned back on itself again, somewhere around the bend, to continue its descent down the cliff face. She seemed unconscious, but he could see that at least she was still breathing. There was some blood on her scalp and one of her arms lay twisted at an unnatural angle.

Max was standing well back from the ledge. He couldn't know that Bo was still alive, and Peter decided to keep it that way. This should have been a fight solely between the two of us anyway, he thought. With a cry of rage, he turned on his brother, hurling his own favorite throwing knife as he did so. It splashed against Max's invisible shield like water, which then fell to the ground in a miniature rainfall of a thousand cooling iron shards.

"I can't believe you tried that," Max said, "after seeing your late wife fail so miserably at the same thing."

"I wanted to see if your magic shield worked differently, under different conditions," Peter said, "such as if you weren't expecting an attack from your own brother."

"Aren't you clever? Father always pegged you as the smart one. You should have sworn off the musical life and entered the philosophic world instead, where you could have experimented with worldly phenomena, investigated the true nature of nature, and charted the stars in their courses. But, your theory in this case was — what's the word real philosophers use? Invalid? In any case, let me assure you, my protections aren't all that conditional and can't be fooled or distracted."

"So what do we do now?" Peter said, all the while wishing with every fiber of his being that Bo should stay safely unconscious below, making no sound, until he figured a way out of this.

"Now I kill you. But before that, I'll have my rightful inheritance — the flute that you stole from me. And though I could play a tune that would have you dancing on the end of my strings, forcing you to hand it over, I'd much rather have Frost from your hand, freely given. We both know I should've gotten it in the first place, and I expect you to acknowledge that much, without coercion."

"But you have another flute," Peter said, "much more powerful with darkest magic, from what I can see. Isn't that enough?"

"Fire is so much more powerful than Frost that they can hardly be compared, one with the other. But, no, to answer your question direct, it's not enough. Fire is mine by right of conquest. I found it and tamed it to my will. But Frost is also mine, because it's my birthright. I'll have both."

"And after I give Frost to you, you'll let me live, each of us free to go on our way?"

"No, not at all. Weren't you listening? After that I'm going to kill you."

"What happened, Max? We used to love each other. You couldn't have simply pretended at affection for all those years. I know it."

"So what? We also both used to shit our pants with reliable frequency. We grow older and learn better."

"Very well then." Peter slipped Frost's case from around his neck and shoulder. Then he opened the case and slid Frost out of it, white and gleaming, like an icicle. But instead of handing it over to Max, who reached out for it with one hand, Peter brought it to his lips and began to play. *Danger pass me by*, he silently implored, as he played.

"Are you serious?" Max smiled. "It's a battle of flutes you want? Very well. Let's see what we shall see." He raised Fire once again and began to play. This time it wasn't just a single note he played, but a mad and intricate melody that seemed to speak of monstrous things coursing through the night on their wild hunt. It was the sound of ancient bindings snapping, letting great and terrible old powers loose again in the world, to enact their vengeances of untold ages. Max played the anthems of every dark thing that lurked and growled in the back of pitch-black caves.

In response, Peter played a song of bright hope and escape. Danger pass me by, he chanted over and over in his mind. Go away from here, Max. Go far away!

But Fire was truly more powerful than Frost. Almost as soon as Max had begun playing, a burning sensation began in Peter's feet and started working its slow but steady way up his legs. Peter could feel his flesh begin to pucker and boil. The pain was incredible, but still Peter played on.

Danger pass me by. Go far away, Max. Run back up the hill, through the tower gate, and never stop until you're a thousand leagues away.

The burning in his legs continued, growing higher up his limbs and ever more painful. Through an impossible force of will, Peter managed to keep playing, but he began missing notes. Then he faltered for full measures. It was no use. His song couldn't be heard and understood against the more commanding tune his brother played. Peter's effort was a gentle prayer of deliverance, which was lost in the maelstrom of Max's thundering tale of gods and monsters in desperate battle.

Then, just as he was about to surrender, unable to stand for much longer on legs that had twisted out of true, and had begun to smell of burnt and rotting flesh, a final, desperate idea occurred to him.

He began playing again. But this time he didn't try to counter Max's tune. Instead he joined it. At first he merely played along – the same wild song Max did, trying to anticipate his composition and match him, note for note. Then, slowly and tentatively at first, but with more confidence every second, Peter began to strike out on his own, still following Max's central melody, but weaving a manic counterpoint to it, creating diabolic harmonies on the spot, dancing his notes between each one of Max's.

Danger pass me by! Peter no longer implored or pleaded his request, he demanded it. Danger pass me by! Go far away, Max! Run up the hill, through the tower gate, and never stop until you're a thousand leagues away!

He saw Max, just a few feet removed from him. As Max played, a worried look crept into his eyes. What was Peter doing to his song? Peter was guiding it, taking it over, and leading it off in directions Max didn't want it to go.

Peter continued to play, feeling a dozen trickles of blood coursing down his chin and neck, pooling and soaking into the rough weave of his shirt. Frost was exacting its accustomed price for its magic. Peter played Max's song, and note by note took it away from him. In his mind Peter felt turbulent sensations he'd never known before. Lunatic angers he'd never believed he could possess flared within him, with a frenzied and malign passion.

But at the same time, little by little, he felt the pain recede from his deformed hips, traversing its way back down his groin and upper legs. He felt flesh knit back into place.

Now it was Max who began to miss notes.

I'm a thief, Max, and you always knew the truth of that. And now I'm stealing your song away from you, turning it down my own pathways, taking it to places you dare not follow. And all the while Peter continued to think, danger pass me by! Go far away, Max! Run up the hill, through the tower gate, and never stop until you're a thousand leagues away!

The pain began to recede farther and faster down Peter's legs. His twisted bones strained to find their original shape again.

Danger pass me by! Go far away, Max! Run up the hill, through the tower gate, and never stop until you're a thousand leagues away!

Somewhere far away, barely making itself known, through the dual distractions of the maniacal song he played, and his internal litany of commands that Frost make danger pass him by for the third and last time, Peter heard a distant moaning, that grew into screams of pain.

That's Bo, Peter thought. She's finally woken up to discover her broken arm. Nothing I can do about it. Not yet.

Peter continued to play, leading the song in every respect, turning it incrementally into something better — something less openly malignant. The pain had almost entirely left Peter's legs and feet now. In a moment, he knew, they'd be whole and unscarred again, as if they'd never been harmed at all.

He heard more screaming from over the ledge, even more insistent, but still he played on.

Then, all of a sudden, a great and racking sob of profound anguish escaped Max's lips. He abruptly stopped playing, dropped Fire from his lips, and nearly dropped it, from his frantically clutching hands, which opened and closed in violent, spastic twitches, obeying no thought or design. Without further utterances, save an almost inaudible whimper, tears streaming copiously from his eyes, Max turned and started running. He ran uphill, away from the seaside town, back up the road, towards the guard tower and the endless lands beyond.

Winning the duel with Max had left Peter exhausted and nearly insensible. But the pull of his obligation towards Bo wouldn't let him rest. Leaving the donkey and cart where it was, Peter ran down the road, taking the switchback at a mad dash that nearly spilled him off the edge. He wiped blood away from his face as he ran, not wanting to frighten Bo with his wounds that were dramatic, but only superficial. Later he'd count at least thirty new small cuts on his lips, on his tongue, and at the corners of his mouth.

Bo was still conscious when he reached her. But instead of favoring her broken arm, as he'd pictured, she was writhing and clutching at her legs, crying and screaming in a pain too intense to be accounted for by a mere twisted limb – or even a broken one. Bo's too strong for that, he thought.

And then a horrifying realization came to him, just as he noticed the rotting-flesh smell. He cut away the dark brown hose covering her legs, using his last remaining knife. But even as he did so, he knew what he'd find underneath.

Bo's legs were a burned and twisted ruin. In some places, bits of charred flesh were sloughing off, leaving open slashes of bloodied and withered muscle underneath.

"I did this!" Peter cried, though Bo was in no condition to understand him. "I did this to you! I wished the danger to pass me by, which is exactly what it did! It didn't disappear, but it bypassed me only to go somewhere else!"

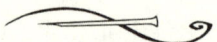

LATER, PETER WALKED BACK UP THE ROAD to retrieve the donkey and its cart. He led it down to Bo, where he emptied it of enough of its contents to allow Bo to lie in it. The pain she suffered as he lifted her into its bed made her pass out. He led the cart down the road, winding its way out of the high cliffs, which gradually became hills and then seaside lowlands. He'd take her into town, and use all of his remaining treasure to find the magicians and physicians she needed to save her. She woke only once during the journey, and then only for a moment.

"Where's Max?" she asked, in a voice drained of most of its former power.

"He's gone far away," Peter said. And he knew that it was true. Some lingering effect of the spent magic let him know for a certainty that everything he'd demanded of the duel had come to pass. Max wouldn't stop running, until he was at least a thousand leagues distant. If only he'd thought to demand just a little bit more from Frost's last service to him.

Bo's breathing was weak, broken and hesitant for the rest of the trip into town. For most of the way he wondered if she'd still be alive when they arrived.

Chapter Nineteen
Coming to America

*In which Max plays
his deadliest tune so far,
and then finds his way
to Fabletown, to reunite with
an old acquaintance.*

Max Piper visited America for the first time in the fall of 1918, in the wake of the Spanish Influenza pandemic's second wave, the one medical authorities would later name the killer wave, once the total cost in human lives had been added up.

He disembarked from his Argentinean passenger liner at Manhattan's Pier 61, within just a few dozen feet of where the heavy cruiser U.S.S. Seattle was moored, undergoing its refitting from a convoy escort into a troop transport, in anticipation of soon being able to bring the country's beloved doughboys home from the Great War. The four-stacked Seattle was a looming presence over the pier, its massive hull painted with "dazzle paint," angry, knife-edged slashes of dark and light colors, designed to hide its true outline from the deadly German U-boats, which still prowled the Atlantic, even though America's top generals and war experts insisted, almost daily now, that the Huns' collapse was imminent. Max paused on the wharf to admire the warship's giant gun batteries, wishing he could see them fire. Guns were one of the things he liked most about the mundy world, and the reason it had taken him an entire year to make it to New York, after arriving in the world. First, he'd traveled the battlefields and devastated cities of the war like a giddy tourist, glorying in the continentwide abattoir that Europe was making of itself.

But Max had finally, almost reluctantly, turned himself towards his true destination, coming to New York City's drab and mournful streets dressed to party. He wore a red and white, candy-striped silk suit jacket, over purple slacks, with golden pinstripes. Yellow spats topped his glistening, patent leather shoes, and a jaunty straw boater topped his head, worn at just the perfect angle, to properly convey his rakish charm to the new world. He carried no luggage, not requiring any, since he could magically conjure money, new clothes and personal sundries into existence as he needed them, with only the most minimal effort, and often without any of the wearying aftereffects that plagued him following a greater expenditure of power. He did bring one thing though. He carried the flute called Fire, openly, without covering or case, because he liked to have it always in hand, ready to play at any instant, should the need arise.

Max ignored the lines of black and green taxicabs clustered along the wharf, waiting to pick up arriving passengers, and instead set off into the city on foot. He wanted to explore among these amazing towers of steel and concrete, and walk the famous avenues that sliced their ways between them. More important, he wanted to be among the people he was killing by the hundreds and sometimes the thousands every day.

He'd wanted so much to be a part of the mundy world's great time of destruction that he simply had to find a way to participate. No, he didn't create the nasty strain of Swine Flu virus that gave birth to the Spanish Influenza. It had existed already in the mundy world, lurking dormant, occasionally mutating, husbanding its deadly potential and biding its time. But what he had done was to compose a powerful and compelling anthem of death, which had inspired the long-slumbering bug to wake and respond to Max's call, eager to be his agent in the grim and mortal undertaking.

For a while, Max let whim and caprice lead him on his journey into the heart of the city, going wherever the mood took him, having no specific plan or destination in mind for the day. Owing perhaps to the population's diminishment by disease and the staggering number of men and boys who'd gone off to the war, but more likely to the strict bans against public gatherings, the sidewalks were much less crowded than he'd expected.

In Europe and in Argentina, he'd seen photographs and moving pictures that depicted New York City's residents packed together, elbow-to-elbow. But here and now there were pedestrians out and about, to be sure, but they kept a wary distance from each other, having been thoroughly indoctrinated that the influenza spread more easily in crowds.

But, just as in the photographs, the city's streets were still packed with every possible sort of car and truck and other exotic motorized vehicle, constantly honking, growling and scolding each other in some indecipherable and arcane machine language. Perhaps their foolish drivers thought the glass and steel of their beloved automobiles protected them?

Almost to a man, folks were dressed drably, in blacks, browns and grays. Elegant clothes were viewed as an unjustified extravagance in these dark times, when everything not absolutely essential should be reserved for "our boys" overseas. The only exception to this dull and conservative trend was the surprising new direction in women's hemlines, which were tending decidedly upwards, but only because every inch of cloth saved from a civilian's skirt translated into a little more material that could go to support the war effort. Max spotted one woman after another who was actually out in public with a scandalous three or four inches showing above her ankles.

Of course, everyone was wearing white cloth masks.

"They won't help," Max said to a random passerby. "My executioner is much too small to be filtered out by even the tightest weave of your ridiculous gauze and butter-cloth constructions."

"Excuse me?" the startled woman said, but Max had already gone on his way.

Even in the daytime, much of the city was closed down. There were "Closed by order of the New York City Board of Health" signs on the doors of every school, church, theatre, moving picture house, dance hall and saloon that he passed. A man on one corner was standing on an apple box, brandishing an open and unloaded shotgun above his head.

"There's no medicine known to doctors that can stop the Influenza," he cried, quite truthfully (whether he knew it or not), "but placing a shotgun under your bed will save you! The gun's fine steel will draw out the fever! It's been proven!" Coincidentally perhaps, the fellow was ready with pamphlets to hand out, directing customers to a nearby gunsmith's shop. Other impromptu street-side proselytizers broadcast their own ideas to fight the pestilence, with proposed cures ranging from hours of deep sweating, to standing outside stark naked, to inhaling the vapors from one woman's proprietary pepper stew recipe – copies of which were also available, for a modest price. Each orator had a small crowd of spectators gathered around him, at least until roving police officers, or civic-minded busybodies shooed them away, citing the ordinances against public gatherings.

Max journeyed on, with a cockeyed smile on his lips and a jaunty kick to his stride. He ignored the rude stares he received from many passersby, perhaps incited by his outlandish dress in these funereal times, or his blatant lack of a cloth mask. He couldn't say, nor did he care. The prettier ones among them received a tip of his boater in reply, which only seemed to increase the knife-edged looks of disapproval brandished at him.

The street-level shop windows, whether on businesses open or closed, were plastered with all manner of bills and signs. Some exhorted citizens towards desired behavior, such as, "Open-faced sneezing is against the law! Report all open-faced sneezers!" Another admonished him to "Give to the Our Boys in France Tobacco Fund!" And still another, apparently willing to leave the specific details up to each reader, simply demanded, "Do your share!"

A green grocer, serving as an ad hoc satellite office of the Bureau of Labor, posted a huge outdoor banner that advertised for city-dwelling coloreds who were willing to relocate out to the country's farm belt states, to replace field hands who had gone to war or died of the flu. A boy selling newspapers shouted, "Extra! Extra! Tahiti builds pyres of influenza dead!" He waved a copy of the special edition over his head, like a Jack Ketch swinging his deadly ax. In the street immediately adjacent, four masked and gowned women, Red Cross volunteers, were struggling to load a blanket-draped body into a city ambulance.

"Have heart," Max said, *sotto voce*. "This time it's only the end of the world for some of you. I haven't yet learned to play Fire well enough to usher in a full worldwide apocalypse, but trust that I will, dear people. I'm dedicated and I practice daily, so someday I will."

Max took his supper at the elegant (but unpopular in these days of understandable rage against all things German) Kaiserhof restaurant, just across Broadway from the Metropolitan Opera House. Nearly alone in the large dining room, he ate a leisurely meal of assorted wursts and Bavarian-style potato salad, while reading the paper. He noted that the Billy Sunday Crusade was headed into town and, true to the afternoon paperboy's promise, things were indeed very bad in Tahiti. A full seventh of its major city Papeete's entire population had succumbed to the disease, food and medicine were scarce, and the massive piles of the burning dead were everywhere. A country-by-country list of death totals was published on page three, and the numbers were breathtaking. "Well done," he congratulated himself.

When the check arrived, he paid the exorbitant $1.25 fee with two glistening silver dollars, inviting the mildly astonished waiter to keep the change. Then he added, "But spend those quickly. They'll fade in a day or two." The waiter dismissed the strange admonition, thinking the confusion was entirely his fault, due to some defect in his admittedly shaky command of English, which was not his cradle tongue.

Afterwards, Max emerged onto a still-bustling Broadway, enjoying the cool of the evening. "Don't Try to Steal the Sweetheart of a Soldier" was playing softly from the broadcast speaker mounted outside of the Rexall Drug Store a few doors down. With a full belly and content that he'd seen at least some of the effect his work had done in this greatest of all mundy cities, he decided to head uptown, to be about the real reason for his visit to these shores.

With a short dash he was able to scramble aboard one of Broadway's electric trolleys, headed uptown, at full acceleration between two stops. Immediately he was greeted with curses and catcalls, as well as actual blows from some of the other passengers standing closest to him.

"Where's your mask?" one of them yelled.

Even the uniformed trolley operator shouted at him, when he tried to pay the six cent fee, saying, "Don't you know it's against the law to board a New York trolley unmasked?"

"But I have a mask," Max said, and suddenly it was true. A white, butter-cloth mask covered his mouth and nose, just like those worn by the astonished operator and his passengers. Every morning Max played a tune of general conjuration, which he could make use of throughout the day, drawing on it incrementally as a businessman draws upon his expense account. His skill with the magic flute had grown so acute over the ages that he no longer needed to play a separate tune for each small thing he desired.

No one bothered him for the remainder of the ride. In fact they backed as far away from him as the crowded coach would allow, leaving him a truly comfortable amount of room all to his own.

Carrying Fire with him, as always, he rode the merrily

clanging Broadway trolley all the way to Columbus Avenue, transferring there to one of the city's last horse-drawn omnibuses — most of the horses having been taken away to the New Jersey countryside, to help plow open mass trench graves for disposal of the influenza dead. The omnibus brought him due north, paralleling Central Park, deep into the neighborhood called the Upper West Side, where he finally disembarked at 104th Street. Max walked from there, following Fire's gentle pull, leading him to where he would stay the night. He walked east, along 104th, coming at last to Central Park and an impressive four-story stone castle that overlooked it. The building was bordered on its three remaining sides by luxury apartment towers, but not so close as to intrude on its wide lawns and gardens. It was a single-family mansion called Twilight Castle, and J. Randolph Coppersmith, the infamous oil and steel tycoon, owned it.

Max pondered the modern castle for a time, decided that it was fit to host him, and raised Fire to his lips. The cloth mask that had covered his mouth dutifully disappeared back into the nothingness it once was. He played a simple tune, and in no time at all, liveried servants, stout butlers, row upon row of maids and cooks, and two uniformed chauffeurs marched off the grounds, all in single file, and disappeared into the park. Just a few moments later, J. Randolph Coppersmith himself followed suit, marching at the lead of his pleasantly plump wife and two rotund children. Soon enough, they also vanished into the park.

Max entered his new home and settled in for the night.

HE ROSE EARLY THE NEXT MORNING, bathed, and fixed himself a hearty breakfast from the castle's well-stocked kitchen. Then he conjured a new set of clothes that were as gaudy as the previous day's ensemble. Leaving his old clothes behind, to fade when they would, he set out on foot for Fabletown. He strolled south until he was in the nineties, and then west towards the Hudson River until he came to a small cross street – hardly more than an alley – called Bullfinch. Actually he passed it several times at first, going back and forth along Andersen Street, being drawn one way and then the other by Fire's insistent pull, until at last he noticed the tiny Bullfinch Street, and the tall, gray Woodland Building which sat brooding like an ancient watchtower in its center.

"My name is Max Piper," he said to the uniformed security guard, who was quietly dozing behind a desk just inside of the Woodland's lobby. "I'm a lost Fable, newly arrived in the mundy world, and I'm here to join your community in exile." This was enough to startle the guard out of his slumbers.

"Excuse me?" the guard said, snorting and coughing himself into full wakefulness. He was short and slim. His uniform was gray and black, and he wore a revolver in a holster on his black patent-leather gun belt.

"Watch out," Max said. "Coughs and sneezes spread diseases. As dangerous as poison gas shells, or so the ubiquitous public notices claim." He smiled his most charming smile, and doffed his hat with a flourish.

"What did you say you wanted?" the guard said. Looking deeper now, Max could see that this fellow wasn't human after all. Peering beyond the powerful illusion, which surrounded the man like a cloak, he could dimly make out that the guard was in truth a large and fearsome bridge troll, with rough, pinkish skin and deadly yellow fighting tusks.

"Call your superiors, my good creature. I'm here to sign up."

In scant time, two actual human Fables, in fact as well as appearance, were summoned to the lobby. They were a lovely woman and an older gentleman. She introduced herself as Snow White, first assistant to the other fellow whom she identified as Ichabod Crane, the deputy mayor of Fabletown. After the introductions were settled, they invited Max up to one of the building's guest suites, where they could all be more comfortable while they worked things out.

"You don't have an office?" Max said as they rode the modern caged elevator skyward.

"We do," Ichabod explained, "but it's off limits to all but our own people."

"Of which I'm the latest," Max said.

"Perhaps," Snow said, "but that remains to be determined."

Once they were settled into the promised suite, Snow White immediately got down to business, even though the gangly and bespectacled Ichabod seemed content to hem and haw for a goodly while longer.

"Will you tell us more about who you are and how you escaped the Homelands?" Snow said. She had pale skin and night-dark hair, which she wore pulled back into a severe bun that allowed not the slightest strand free to dangle and play in any stray breezes the day might bring. She was dressed in dull brown, and though her skirt hem was as high as the current style demanded, her long laced canvas and leather "spectators" prevented any chance of the slightest hint of bare leg showing.

In response to her request, Max narrated a truncated and mostly fictional account of his history, up until his arrival in the mundy world. He omitted any mention of his conflict with Peter, nor his dealings with the Hamelin of the Hesse.

"He's lying," a voice said from behind him, once Max had concluded his story. Max turned to see that an old woman sat behind him, in a rocking chair that occupied one corner of the room that he would have sworn was empty when they'd first arrived. She had steel gray hair, and her face and hands were a symphony of wrinkles and wrines. She wore a faded print dress of small white flowers against a green field. She knitted from a straw basket in her lap as she rocked gently back and forth.

"Frau Totenkinder, I didn't know you'd be joining us," a flustered Ichabod said. He scrubbed frantically at his glasses with the end of his black necktie.

"I hadn't planned to," Totenkinder said, "but dear old Max got my attention when he arrived. I've past history with the man that I thought you should be made aware of before you do anything rash, like invite him to sign our compact."

"I've never seen this person in my life," Max said.

"Not like this," Totenkinder said. "I was younger and prettier when you borrowed that flute from me."

"Oh, it's you," Max said, and his eyes narrowed, perhaps to conceal the dangerous look that steeled their way into them. "Once again I have to remind you that Fire isn't yours, it's mine."

"Only in the sense that you've managed to prevent me from taking it back so far," she said.

"Yes," Max said, "I could feel you tugging at it over the years, but it's happy in my possession and not likely to abandon me for more centuries spent sitting ignored on a shelf. Fire likes to play and create among the myriad worlds. It has no love of rest and idleness."

"I don't understand what's going on between the two of you," Snow interrupted, "but one thing's for certain. If we accept you into our community, you wouldn't be allowed to keep any dangerous magic implements you bring with you. I assume this 'Fire' the two of you refer to is that flute you carry?"

"It is, but — "

"Then you will have to surrender it for storage in our Business Office," Snow continued. "One of the non-negotiable conditions of Fabletown citizenship is that all magic items spirited out of the Homelands are held communally, for the use and benefit of all of us."

"A sensible ordinance," Max said, with a crafty smile, "and one which I'll gladly obey. Of course, among its many virtues, Fire is indeed, as you've surmised, a dangerous weapon. More than once it's saved me from a tough scrape with the Empire's forces. But, since no imperial troops rule here, in this cozy island of peace and refuge, I don't need a dangerous weapon anymore, do I? However, in the interests of public safety, I'd need to train someone in the proper means of handling and storing it, which might take some time."

"There's no end to this reptile's deception," Totenkinder said. "If the two of you can't see he's lying, then I fear for our future under your administration. Max Piper has no intention of surrendering his flute. I believe his sole purpose in attempting to join Fabletown is so that he can learn the whereabouts of his brother, Peter — one of the few secrets that are beyond Fire's powers to reveal."

"Oh? Is my brother here?" Max said. "I had no idea. But yes, if that's the case, of course I want a reunion with him. Families should be together, but we've been kept apart from each other for too long."

"He tried to kill Peter in the past and plans to try again," Totenkinder said.

"My understanding is that all sins of the past are washed away, once I sign the Fabletown Compact. Is that not the case? If not, then there are many past deeds this witch has perpetrated that you should be made aware of."

"Past crimes are forgiven and forgotten," Ichabod said.

"But any new ones, after signing the Compact, are dealt with harshly," Snow leapt in to add.

"I promise you'll find my repentance is deep and sincere," Max said.

"Then we'll adjourn this matter until we've had a chance to discuss it," Ichabod said. "Max, you can stay here for the night, as our guest, and we'll let you know of our decision in the morning."

"Lovely!" Max said. "Wonderful! But there's no need to put me up like some freeloader off the streets. I've secured my own lodgings while in town. Just tell me when you want to see me in the morning and I'll be here."

THAT EVENING, AND LATE INTO THE NIGHT, the witch and the two Fabletown officers discussed Max's application for citizenship. They held the debate in the mayor's penthouse residence, high on top of the Woodland Building, with King Cole, the mayor, joining in the discussion. The arguments went round and round, as arguments will. Totenkinder was steadfastly against it, Snow expressed a wary need of caution, while Ichabod Crane and King Cole questioned, dithered and dissembled, as they often did, when hard decisions were in the offing. But finally King Cole resolved himself and said, "I believe I understand all of the reasons why we shouldn't trust this Mr. Piper, but the universal amnesty is the single foundation on which all of Fabletown rests. If we deny membership to one man, based upon what he's done in the past and what we fear he may do in the future, then the house of cards we've built may come tumbling down around us.

"Fabletown is a fragile experiment in a new way of living, where a pauper and a king enjoy equal freedoms and responsibilities. One misstep could end it. I believe, in the final analysis, we have to treat Max Piper just like we did Bigby, and you, Frau Totenkinder, and even me. Each of us committed terrible crimes and shameful deeds in the old worlds. We all came damaged and sinful into this new world, and only prospered as much as we have together, through borrowed grace. None of us deserved our place in Fabletown. Instead it was a gift we gave to each other. Barring unimpeachable evidence that he plans to further harm Peter, or his poor wife, or any other of us, I can't see any way we can avoid giving this man the same chance to start over that each of us has been granted. When he returns tomorrow, we have to let him sign the Compact and receive the general amnesty."

And so it was decided.

But later that same night, while Max slept peacefully in his stolen castle, a visitor appeared quietly in his bedroom. She made no sound, but nevertheless Max awoke before she could cross the room and remove Fire from where it lay next to him on the large bed that seemed to cover acres of floor.

"I thought you might try a midnight visit," Max said, coming fully awake in an instant. He lifted Fire, sat up in the bed and regarded her in the night-shrouded chamber.

"I can't let you sign the Compact tomorrow," the witch said. She still looked as old as she'd seemed the afternoon before, but now there wasn't a hint of frailty about her. She stood thin and small in the center of the floor, but this time there was a sense of weight and solidity attached to her, radiating invisibly but substantially from her.

"And I can't let you stop me," he said. "Unless you're ready to tell me where my brother and his miserable, broken little wife have hidden themselves. In that case I'd be willing to settle old matters with them alone and be on my way, like the proverbial happy wanderer, never to darken the Woodland's door again."

"I don't think I'll do that," she said. "Instead I think I'll do what I should have done ages ago and rid the world of you – rid all the worlds of you. At long last, I've finally learned that one can't bargain with monsters. They simply need to be destroyed when discovered."

Max stood up.

"You can't beat me," he said. "Fire's too strong and I'm its master."

"And you've wandered into my place of power," Totenkinder said. "I've had centuries here to prepare the ground." Tendrils of long dormant enchantments yawned into life and began to tickle the air around her, invisible to anyone but these two. "I can read the protections layered around you as if I'd written them myself. And I know what you've done and continue to do in this world – the plague you've unleashed. That was power ill spent, Max Piper, because, though it's killed and continues to kill many a mundy, it's had no effect on Fables."

"You think so?" he said. "Yes, my gift to the world kills many of the weak dullards who people this world, but that was just a side effect of its true purpose. They weren't its real target. I trained my influenza to affect Fables in a different way, and it's already done its work among you. Don't you know me by now, witch? I don't kill outright when I can attack you through your offspring. My bug has wormed its way in and taken all of your children away from you – not those you've already had, but those you might have had from now on. Fabletown is barren, old woman, from this day forward. Call it the most oft-repeating motif in the never-ending concerto of my life. I steal children.

That's what I do. That's what you created me to do."

"Then that's what I'll undo when I take Fire back from you." The witch spread her thin arms and gathered all of her fell powers around her. Max raised Fire to his lips, but he was too late.

Outside, over the past hour, black storm clouds had piled up over the city, building in fury. Now they released it. Ten thousand windows shattered from the thunderblasts, and hard rain pounded down from the heavens. The fevered and infirm thrashed in their sickbeds, crying out from nightmares, and then died in greater numbers that night than ever before. A dozen fires were started by lightning strikes throughout the five boroughs. Murders and suicides increased by a factor of ten, and a hundred other deaths were attributed to inexplicable acts of God. But no god played any part in them. Every calamity in the city was caused by the overflow of dark energies emanating from a gray stone castle on Central Park.

The battle lasted for hours, and the forces it unleashed spilled over into other worlds as well. Great strongholds shuddered and cracked, releasing ancient and fearsome beasts, things long bound and imprisoned, to wander again through dark lands, feeding and destroying wheresoever they went. Ripples of terrible possibility spread out from the battle's epicenter, birthing new horrors that had never existed before.

By dawn, long after the spent storms had dissipated, city firemen found that the castle named Twilight had been razed while its former occupants, masters and servants alike, were discovered more than a mile away, huddled together, dead in the park. The firemen uncovered evidence that a fire had blazed so hot through the night that the mansion's stones themselves had begun to burn. And, most bizarrely, at the center of the destruction they found a little old lady in a green print dress, unconscious but unharmed.

It was more than a year before she woke up. In that time she'd been identified by relatives, with impeccable credentials, who quietly had her transferred to a private clinic in town. Her first words upon waking were, "I couldn't beat him." Later, among those most trusted in Fabletown, she'd had the opportunity to elaborate. "He was too strong, so ultimately, the best I could do was to open a door that sent him tumbling into the deepest abyss and then away through the farthest netherworlds. He'll likely be a long time finding his way back, but he will return, for I fear nothing in any realm can harm him now."

Then she remarked, "And know now that it'll be much worse the next time, because he's sampled all that I could bring against him. Even as I kept his own attacks at bay, I could perceive him studying mine, learning from them."

The last dreg of the influenza had played itself out in the meantime. Armistice was signed in Europe, the boys came home, and all of the nations of the world vowed to make war no more, because at last it had grown too terrible to contemplate. In Fabletown few children were conceived, and those that were, were delivered stillborn in horrifying shapes of deformation. Frau Totenkinder, the Black Forest Witch, along with her sorcerous colleagues on the Woodland's thirteenth floor, worked for decades to undo the curse. In time, nearly a century later, she developed a potion, which she contrived to place in the hands of a scoundrel, knowing he'd use it (not entirely understanding it) against his perceived enemies, the Great Wolf and his one true love. Nine months later seven live children were born to them.

"That's a good start," she said to her associates. "But both of them were among the most highly magical of our community. The Wolf is the offspring of one of the most powerful of the gods, while his woman occupies the center of countless fateful crossings in the primordial magic flow. I suspect their own enchanted natures strove to help the remedy along. So, though we can consider ourselves on the right track, we've still much work to do to perfect a lasting and universal cure."

And up at the Farm, Peter and Bo lived their lonely lives together in their remote home, always waiting, without always realizing it, for word that his brother had returned.

Chapter Twenty
CELEBRATION

In which, at long last, Max finally gets his wish.

In mundy Germany's Hamelin Town, in the waning days of October, Max Piper appeared before his brother, for the first time in ages, and for the very first time in this world. "My oh my, brother, how you've changed!" Max cried. "This world has beaten you down, Peter, for in truth I've seen you grim before, angry, and even desperate, but always with a healthy resolve behind it. I've never seen you so miserable though, as if you've let yourself become bent, weighed down, veritably encrusted with a heavy mail coat of gloom and failure."

"Max," was all Peter could manage in reply. He tried to rise from his seat on the edge of the fountain, but discovered he was unable to do so.

"Oh no, Peter. You don't get to move, until I let you. I've already attached my strings to you, and now I decide when you can rise up and dance for me." Max was dressed identically to the other costumed Pipers, in his colorful tights and cape and pheasant feathered cap. As far as any tourists could tell, he was just another one of the musicians hired by the town to help celebrate the annual Pied Piper festival.

"If you imagined this was going to be some sort of confrontation between us," Max said, "a heroic duel, or in any way a repeat of our last encounter, then I must sadly lay your childish hopes to rest. I didn't send for you in order to let you make some courageous last gesture of defiance before your demise. Oh yes, Peter, I sent for you. Did you actually believe it was some sort of detective skill on your part that led you to deduce where I'd be in the wide world? You were never that clever, baby brother. After centuries of failing to find you, due to Frost's misguided loyalties, it finally occurred to me to call out to you instead — to invite you to come to me. You followed my magical trail of breadcrumbs perfectly. And now, on this most glorious day of the year, this day devoted to me and my great works, we meet for the final time. I have one last bit of unfinished business to conclude with you, after which I'll enjoy the rest of the day and then be on my way. You, on the other hand, will not be on your way.

This meeting ends with your death, Peter. But I suspect you already know that much."

"Yes, I know that," Peter said. He attempted to reach out and take Frost's case from the edge of the fountain, and was mildly surprised to find that he could.

"Go ahead," Max said. "Hold Frost close to you. Embrace it one last time. But it can't help you anymore. Its three magical protections are long spent, isn't that so? You can't send me scampering off in sorcery-induced fear this time, can you?"

"How far did you run?" Peter said.

"Oh, quite far indeed," Max said. "You should be proud of how well your musical spell worked. For years I ran, and cowered, and hid, and then ran again, always fearful that you might be too near. And even though I could never divine where you were, I was ever paranoid that you might be closing in. I put worlds between us, and traveled in distant lands where men should never go. I hope you enjoyed your victory over me, because even though it spanned many lifetimes of normal men, it was still only a temporary one. Eventually it wore off, and now it can't be repeated."

As they talked, tourists would stroll by, from time to time snapping pictures of Max in his bright costume. On each occasion he would break off his conversation long enough to strike a pose for the crowds. And sometimes he'd dash off a few notes on his red flute. At those times the tourists would lose their happy smiles and quickly move along. Fire never played any but the most drear and mournful notes in Max's hands.

"Isn't this lovely?" Max said. He turned and threw one arm out, in a gesture that took in the entire town. "Isn't it incredible, Peter? These mundys had their own tiny version of Hamelin Town, and it turns out they lost children from it as well. My capturing spell was so powerful, my song so enticing, that the evil deed was mirrored here. And in some rudimentary way, they knew I was the cause of it, even though I was never here. To be sure, they got some of the details wrong, but look how much they got right! My legend seeped through along with Fire's magic. I wonder now if there were other versions of Hamelin, in other unknown worlds, and if each one of them lost their precious little darlings on the same night? Do you think so? How many children did I end up taking, all told?"

"What happened to them, Max?"

"The children?"

Peter nodded.

"I had debts to pay. Some of those worlds I traveled were dangerous places, and I had to strike many bargains in order to survive them. The little brats didn't die happy, I'll tell you that much. But that's all blood under the bridge. Where were we?" A bright smile returned to Max's face.

"Oh yes, I remember," he said. "We were discussing this version of Hamelin. How bizarre is it that, not only do they know of me here, but they celebrate me? I stole away a hundred and thirty of their kids, the most horrifying deed in the city's history, and they love me for it! I almost wish you could stay long enough to see every moment of the great party they're throwing in my honor."

"So do I," Peter said.

"Yes, I imagine so. But that's not to be. This is my day, and I can't let you remain to spoil it for me. You're just too gloomy."

"So what are we going to do?"

"It's simple enough. First, you're going to stand up — Yes, you can do that now — and divest yourself of all those nasty toys your wife made you bring along."

Peter stood up and started removing the knives and other killing things. One by one he dropped each deadly implement into the fountain's lower pool. Each object made a satisfying plop as it sank into the water.

"How is the lovely Bo Peep by the way?" Max said. "Are her

kisses still as sweet, now that they're the only marital joys you can ever receive from her? Or have you actually tried to poke around down among her scars, desperate for a husband's rightful privilege?"

"Are you going to kill her too, once you've disposed of me?" Peter asked. He twisted a bright copper ring off and dropped it into the pool, where it sparkled next to the miniature blowgun, and its darts, and the other discarded weapons. And though it wasn't among his weapons, and posed no possible threat, Peter was also compelled to twist his wedding ring off his finger and add that to his dropped possessions in the water.

"I don't think so. I'm enjoying her suffering too much. Why end it for her? Besides, she'll no doubt pass away on her own, once she learns what became of her loving husband. You two seem to enjoy that rare storybook sort of love, where one can't live without the other."

"You seem to know a lot about us."

"Absolutely everything, except where you were," Max said. "That was the one little detail Fire could never uncover for me. You have no idea how frustrating that was."

Peter was finished depositing all of his weapons in the fountain. He stood there, holding Frost's case in one hand, waiting for Max to command him in some new way.

"Now strip," Max said. "Just in case you missed anything." Peter did so, and the tourists looked on, snapping pictures all the while. Perhaps they thought this was some sort of hypnotism show, to demonstrate the powers the legendary

Piper was supposed to possess over people. Peter set Frost down again, on the edge of the fountain, worried that Max might rush forward to take it. But Max stayed away, reveling in the things he was forcing his brother to do. Peter removed his jacket and let it drop at his feet. Then he unbuckled his pants and let them fall beside it. He stepped out of his shoes, pulled off his socks and began unbuttoning his shirt.

Some of the impromptu audience members began to gasp and *tsk tsk* at this crude public display. "They go too far," one of them said. "We have children here."

"Don't fret, my darlings," Max turned to them. "I won't be taking any of them today." Then, after thinking a moment, "Well, I probably won't. We'll see how the evening goes."

Peter stood naked in the street, in front of the Piper's Fountain. He realized he was able to pick up Frost again, and did so. Some of the tourists began to huff away from them, looking for someone to complain to.

"And now," Max said, "we come to the final part. Long ago you refused to hand Frost over to me, even though we both knew it was my rightful inheritance. That's what you're going to do now. And then, once Frost is mine, I have a final promise to fulfill to an old and treasured companion." A long sword appeared in Max's hand — the one that wasn't already holding Fire.

"This is Frost Taker, and long ago I promised him he would be the one to taste your life's blood on his blade. Take Frost out of its case, step forward and hand it to me. And then steel yourself for my gift in return."

Peter did as he was commanded. In fact he found himself eager to do it. After all, despite his promises to Bo and to the authorities in Fabletown, this is what he'd planned to do all along, wasn't it? He opened Frost's case and let it fall away from the thin bone-white flute. Then, grasping Frost by its slightly belled end, he boldly walked forward and shoved its razor-sharp mouthpiece deep into Max's chest.

As in the past, Max was cloaked in every sort of protective spell. Nothing could get through his invisible, magical armor save what Max wanted to get through. But Max wanted Frost more than he'd ever wanted anything else. Frost's sharp end sliced through Max's spells as though they weren't there. It pierced his jacket and the flesh beneath it. It cut through bone and muscle, and finally penetrated Max's coal-black heart. He was dead before he realized it. His legs crumpled beneath him. Dropping Fire and Frost Taker, Max's lifeless body followed them in a tardy spray of blood.

Someone in the diminished crowd of onlookers screamed. Another shouted for the police to be called.

Peter ignored them. He placed a foot against Max's still chest and pulled Frost out from it with both hands. Then he grabbed up Fire, followed by as many of his clothes as he could scoop up on the run, making sure at least that he took his pants, with its car keys, wallet and identification inside.

Holding his bundle of flutes and clothes tightly to his chest, Peter ran off, down Market Street, towards the old town's south gate. In the distance he could hear the wa-wee, wa-wee of German police sirens. Closer behind him he heard a shouted "Halt!" followed by two sharp blasts on a whistle.

He ran faster, recalling the old days in a different, bigger version of Hamelin, when he was the boldest thief in the city.

Epilogue

In which our story concludes.

F OLLOWING THE LONG HARSH WINTER OF THE new year, Beast, the sheriff of Fabletown, kissed his Beauty goodbye and drove the rusted red delivery truck north out of Manhattan, up past Albany, and into the wider expanses of Upstate New York, until he came to the Farm. The mixed human and animal Fables of the Farm helped him unload the supplies he'd brought up from the city, after which he shared a late dinner with Rose Red. He retired that night in the main house's single VIP guest room and slept fitfully, which he always did when his wife Beauty wasn't beside him.

The next morning Beast and Rose Red took her Range Rover out to Peter and Bo's house, where they found the two of them sitting out on one of their many porches. Bo was sitting down on the deck, a tartan blanket covering her legs. Her wheelchair stood empty nearby. Peter sat close to her and played a low, haunting tune on the red wooden flute named Fire.

"Good morning," Bo said cheerfully, when Beast and Rose Red climbed out of the truck.

"Good morning," Beast said. "I see you two managed to get through the winter okay." There were still many patches of snow here and there, on hill and meadow. The morning breeze was chilly, but not oppressively so.

"We had plenty to keep us busy," Peter said. He'd stopped playing with Fire when their guests had arrived. "I've still got a lot to learn with this thing." He held the flute up for all to see.

"That's what I came up here to talk to you about," Beast said. "The Witch tells me that's a very dangerous weapon — perhaps the deadliest magic thing in existence. I can't let you keep it, Peter. It needs to be locked away in the Business Office."

"And it will be," Peter said. "I promise. But only after I've mastered one specific tune on it. I'm determined to undo what my brother did to Bo."

"We've already made progress," Bo said. Her smile contained

none of the sadness that it had borne for so many years. "There are actual patches of pink flesh on my legs — you'll understand if I don't show you. And yesterday my toes itched something awful for hours on end! Isn't that marvelous?"

"It is!" Rose Red said.

"How much longer will this take?" Beast said.

"Who can say?" Peter said. "But the moment it's accomplished, you can bet your bottom dollar that I'll turn Fire over to you, without hesitation. It's a foul and sullen thing, and I dearly wish I didn't have to have anything to do with it. Unlike Frost, there are no joyful songs that can be wrung from it."

"Hurry then," Beast said. "And, in the meantime, every two weeks you're to report down to the city, for as long as Fire's in your possession. This is nonnegotiable. The Witch is going to examine you, on a regular basis, to make sure you don't succumb to Fire's corruption the way Max did."

"That seems fair," Peter said. "But, as awful as this is to say about my own brother, I suspect Fire succumbed more to Max's corruption, rather than the other way around. Makes no difference now though. The damage is long done. If anyone can restore goodness to this flute, it'll take centuries, and it won't be me. Once Bo is made well, I plan to play nothing but Frost, until the end of my days."

In the months that followed, Peter and Bo showed up more often to the Farm's many dances and firelight celebrations. Peter played with the band, marrying Frost's wild and joyful tunes to Boy Blue's trumpet, Seamus's harp, Joe Sheppard's

drums and Puss's mad, screaming fiddle. Bo would surprise them all then by enthusiastically clapping along, and sometimes even singing off key, which everyone enjoyed, even though it was generally agreed that she couldn't carry a tune, even if she made extra trips.

Then, one evening, almost a year later, Bo appeared at the dance standing (albeit not too steadily) on her own two feet, needing only the help of two matched wooden canes.

"My wheelchair?" she said. "Oh, I threw that horrid old thing away ages ago."

HERE ARE SOME CLOSELY GUARDED MILITARY SECRETS YOU CAN *NEVER* REPEAT.

THE ENTIRETY OF THE ASSAULT IS GOING TO BE LAUNCHED AGAINST THE IMPERIAL HOMEWORLD ON THREE FRONTS...

...BUT WE WANT TO CREATE THE ILLUSION THAT ATTACKS ARE COMING ON MANY MORE FRONTS, AGAINST MORE THAN JUST THE ONE WORLD.

THAT'S *MY* PART OF THE WAR. I'M IN THE DISCRETE OPERATIONS COMMAND.

ACTUALLY, TO BE ACCURATE, I'M THE *ENTIRE* COMMAND, SO FAR. AN ARMY OF ONE.

BUT I'M HOPING YOU TWO WILL COME ON BOARD TO MAKE IT *THREE* OF US.

I THINK I'M CATCHING ON. YOU WANT PETER AND ME TO DO SOME DIRTY BUSINESS BEHIND ENEMY LINES.

A SERIES OF STRATEGIC ASSASSINATIONS IN VARIOUS WORLDS. YOU TWO HAVE THE PARTICULAR *SKILLS* TO CARRY OUT SUCH MISSIONS.

THE COURAGE OF THE FEW AGAINST THE MANY.

HERE THEY COME AGAIN!

HOLD THEM!

BUT SOME STORIES HAVE NEVER BEEN TOLD BEFORE.

OF HOW PETER AND BO AND CLARA SOWED FEAR, DISRUPTION AND CONFUSION OVER MANY WORLDS.

Acknowledgments
And a few (non musical) notes of interest

I am indebted to many people whose generous help was essential to the completion of this story, so many in fact that I apologize in advance to those I'm about to inadvertently leave out.

At DC/Vertigo, Shelly Bond, my editor, caught and corrected a host of sins on my part, after which copy editor Arlene Lo (Robin to Shelly's Batman) weighed in, and like any good alchemist, found a way to transform my rough gibberish into something resembling actual language. Any mistakes still in the text are there at my barbaric insistence and not the fault of these two stalwarts of proper syntax and clarity of prose. Also at DC, Karen, Paul, Bob, John, and so many others helped to make this novel a reality. Thank you all for your great efforts, above and beyond, and of course for your patience.

My friend and colleague Mark Buckingham, along with the fine gentlemen of Clockwork Storybook, the second greatest writing group in the history of English letters (coming in close, right behind The Inklings), read the chapters as they were completed, and provided many helpful suggestions. They are: Mark Finn, Chris Roberson, Matthew Sturges, and Bill Williams. Mike Sinner, the fellow in the dedication, was always on hand, at the end of the phone, to help me recall details of our shared days in Germany, on those all too frequent occasions when my poor memory wasn't quite up to the task. Thanks, Mike.

Dr. Radu Florescu's scholarly work *In Search of the Pied Piper* was enormously helpful in finding the character Max, and in constructing both versions of Hamelin Town found in this story. I would also like to thank the good people of Germany, who were fine and generous hosts during my years living there, and specifically the citizens of Hamelin. Let me apologize now for the gross liberties I took with your country and your town. My sole excuse is that the changes I made were never for capricious reasons, but were always for the good of the story. Some readers will have caught that I had Peter pay in Deutschmarks, rather than in Euros, in this story, and that was intentional. My version of Germany steadfastly exists sans Euro, for reasons too complex, or petty, to explain here. Certain things, like the robotic missile silo car park, the ice cream rats, and many of the more extraordinary details of modern Hamelin and its environs actually exist as described. I couldn't make such things up. But some of them have been moved a bit, here and there, to better suit my needs.

The first half of this book was written in Vermont, in the house once owned by Rudyard Kipling, painstakingly restored by the Heritage Foundation, using Kipling's original books, furniture and fixtures, which they were happily surprised to discover stored in an old barn on the property. Peter and Max were created in the same room, on the same desk in fact, that Kipling created Mowgli, the rest of the *Jungle Book* characters, Kim, the Captains Courageous, and many others. To say that it was an inspirational setting in which to begin a fantasy adventure story is to be guilty of criminal understatement. Thank you to the kind men and women of the Heritage Foundation, for opening the property to me and for your hard work in making my stay so comfortable, restful, and productive. Thank you, too, to the good ghost in that home for the use of your writing room and library, which always seemed to have just the right text on some obscure subject of medieval history, technology or nature, within arm's reach, whenever I needed it.

Finally I must single out Steve Leialoha, artist extraordinaire, who provided the illustrations for this tale. Steve has been one of the insiders, illustrating FABLES stories for as long as they've been published (eight years now, and counting). With PETER AND MAX he not only interpreted these characters and settings wonderfully, but offered many helpful suggestions on how to make the story stronger.

Some of you readers know that this novel is set in the same fictional world as my long-running comic book series called FABLES, also published by DC/Vertigo. For those who've yet to encounter the FABLES comics but who might now be inspired to seek them out after reading this novel, you can find some helpful information on how to do just that in the pages that immediately follow. I hope you'll decide to linger a while longer in our enchanted woods, and that you find your extended stay rewarding and enjoyable.

BILL WILLINGHAM

I'd like to thank Bill and Shelly for giving me this opportunity to indulge my love of fantasy and music in illustrating this wonderful tale. And to Trina for her patience with the long hours it took getting there...

Steve Leialoha

Follow the monthly adventures of the multiple Eisner Award-winning FABLES *series:*

Vol. 1: LEGENDS IN EXILE
The immortal characters of popular fairy tales have been driven from their homelands and now live hidden among us, trying to cope with life in 21st-century Manhattan.

Vol. 2: ANIMAL FARM
Non-human Fable characters have found refuge in upstate New York on The Farm, miles from mankind. But a conspiracy to free them from their perceived imprisonment may lead to a war that could wrest control of the Fables community away from Snow White.

Vol. 3: STORYBOOK LOVE
Love may be blooming between two of the most hard-bitten, no-nonsense Fables around. But are Snow White and Bigby Wolf destined for happiness — or a quick and untimely death?

Vol. 4: MARCH OF THE WOODEN SOLDIERS
When Little Red Riding Hood suddenly walks through the gate between this world and the lost Fable Homelands, she's welcomed as a miraculous survivor by nearly everyone — except for her old nemesis, Bigby Wolf, who smells spying and subversion more than survival.

Vol. 5: THE MEAN SEASONS
This trade paperback features two tales of Bigby's exploits during World War II as well as "The Year After," which follows the aftermath of the Adversary's attempt to conquer Fabletown — including the birth of Snow White and Bigby's cubs!

Vol. 6: HOMELANDS
Boy Blue is on a mission of revenge as he uncovers the Adversary's true identity! Plus, the two-part story of Jack's adventures in Hollywood, and the tale of Mowgli's return to Fabletown.

Vol. 7: ARABIAN NIGHTS AND DAYS
Opening a new front in the struggle between the Fables and the Adversary, the worlds of the Arabian Fables are invaded — leading to an unprecedented diplomatic mission to Manhattan and a nasty case of culture shock.

Vol. 8: WOLVES
The community of Fables living undercover in our midst has endured plenty of suffering at the hands of the Adversary. Now it's time to return the favor, but the one Fable who can accomplish this mission has hidden himself away in the wild and will take some convincing if he can even be found.

Vol. 9: SONS OF EMPIRE
Pinocchio suffers seriously divided loyalties between his father and his fellow Fable refugees in New York City. Plus, Bigby Wolf reluctantly decides it's finally time to square accounts with his long-estranged father, the North Wind, and makes a journey with Snow White and their cubs to find him.

Vol. 10: THE GOOD PRINCE
Flycatcher is drawn into the spotlight as he discovers the startling truth about his own past as The Frog Prince. At the same time, he learns that the Adversary plans to destroy his enemies once and for all. Can the meek Flycatcher actually stop this deadly foe?

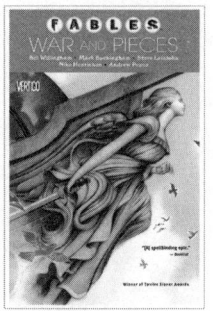

Vol. 11: WAR AND PIECES
The war against Fabletown heats up! Cinderella heads out on a cloak-and-dagger mission to bring a mysterious package back into town. But when the Empire goes after the same prize, there's no telling who will be left standing when the smoke clears.